Face

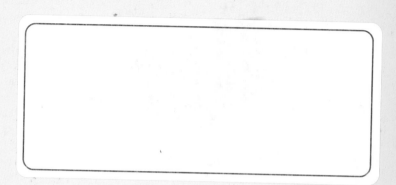

Books by Ray Harrison

French ordinary murder (1983)
Death of an Honourable Member (1984)
Deathwatch (1985)
Death of a dancing lady (1985)
Counterfeit of murder (1986)
A season for death (1987)
Harvest of death (1988)
Tincture of death (1989)
Sphere of death (1990)
Patently murder (1991)
Akin to murder (1992)
Murder in Petticoat Square (1993)
Hallmark of murder (1995)
Murder by design (1996)

FACETS OF MURDER

Ray Harrison

Constable · London

First published in Great Britain 1997
by Constable & Company Ltd
3 The Lanchesters, 162 Fulham Palace Road
London W6 9ER
Copyright © 1997 by Ray Harrison
ISBN 0 09 477180 4
The right of Ray Harrison to be
identified as the author of this work
has been asserted by him in accordance
with the Copyright, Designs and Patents Act 1988
Set in Linotron Palatino 10pt by
CentraCet, Cambridge
Printed and bound in Great Britain by
Hartnolls Ltd, Bodmin, Cornwall

A CIP catalogue record for this book
is available from the British Library

To our Grandchildren
Past Present and Future.

1

Catherine Marsden drew a line under her article for the next Saturday's edition, then began to read it critically. As a newspaper, the *City Press* was predominantly concerned with happenings in the City of London; with price movements in commodities, and investment opportunities in the empire. Five years ago she had been engaged to write on less esoteric subjects. She could not judge how many extra copies had been sold because the paper now contained articles of interest to women. Probably not many. The female part of the City's workforce was predominantly young typewriters and clerks; with no ambition beyond marriage and domestic bliss. And she doubted if many men would buy a copy, just to take it home to their wives. She sometimes had the uncomfortable feeling that her appointment was solely due to her father's influence. He had been painting a portrait of the major shareholder's wife at the time; a very pleasing – not to say flattering – portrait. And there were endless opportunities for inconsequential chat during the sittings. But even if the initial appointment had been due to favour, she told herself, her employment would not have been maintained for four-and-a-half years without real merit. Indeed, the editor had occasionally told her of congratulatory messages he had received on her work. And Mr Tranter was not free with his praise.

Of course, from May to midsummer the subjects of the articles almost suggested themselves. During the Season there were operas, concerts, receptions, balls. As Catherine had been presented at court, she could write about these happenings with more insight than a male reporter. Her current article was an account of Queen Victoria's visit to the private viewing at the Royal Academy. Catherine had been gratified to see Her Majesty sit and scrutinise one of her father's paintings, before strolling on. When she told him, he had passed off the incident lightly. The old dear had probably needed an excuse for a rest, he said. But it had been genuine interest and appreciation, she was sure of it.

Even in Catherine's head that sounded smug. Indeed, smugness had been her besetting sin since she turned sixteen – or so she had frequently been told. But now she was not smug. That was much too passive a term. So was contentment. Rather she felt a constant excitement bubbling in her, a feeling of widening horizons, of limitless possibilities. 'Mrs James Morton,' she murmured to herself. In time it would be Lady Morton ... She mentally shook herself from this reverie. There was time enough for day-dreaming, and she had fences to mend. She went to the editor's office, and was relieved to find that he had already gone to lunch. She scribbled a pencilled note at the top of her article, and left it on his desk. Then she took a hansom cab to Lanesborough House.

She went up the great curving staircase, past the large portrait which had established the reputation of the young William Marsden, and went into Lady Lanesborough's boudoir. She was reclining on a *chaise-longue*, with pads of cotton wool over her eyes.

'How much longer must I submit to this, Joan?' she asked irritably. 'Both of us know perfectly well that it will not make a jot of difference to my wrinkles!'

'It is not Joan but Catherine, your dutiful god-daughter!'

Lady Lanesborough swept the pads from her eyes and sat up. 'Dutiful is hardly the word I would use,' she said crossly.

'But surely you received my letter?'

'Yes, I received it. But only hours before the announcement appeared in *The Times* ... And I have to say that Thursday is a distinctly unfashionable day to announce one's engagement!'

Catherine smiled. 'I am sorry,' she said contritely. 'But I have become caught up in the Morton family's problems, before I have even joined it!'

Lady Lanesborough sniffed. 'And I have been scheming to introduce you to young Lord Prescott,' she said. 'He has a thousand acres in Wiltshire, and a fortune made by his grandfather in the West Indies. He is personable and not very bright. Ideal in a society husband. You could capture him easily enough.'

Catherine laughed. 'He hardly sounds worth the effort,' she said.

'Nonsense, child! You know perfectly well that most married couples end up merely tolerating each other. The important thing is to do so in comfort and security.'

'I want love, esteem and respect from my husband, as well as security, ma'am. And I could not bear to be merely tolerated!'

'Ah, well. I see that your mind is made up ... And the Morton baronetcy was earned, not bought. I suppose it could be worse.'

Catherine crossed over to the *chaise-longue* and hugged her godmother. 'I assure you that my parents are delighted,' she said.

'I know. Your mother, at least, wrote to me. I suspect that she felt relief and joy in equal measure. No doubt you manipulated them as much as me.'

Catherine laughed. 'I have never manipulated anyone in my life!' she protested.

'Then it is time you learned. You cannot go through life at the mercy of events ... Tell me about the Mortons. They seem to hide themselves away in the depths of Kent.'

'What do you wish to know?' Catherine asked.

'Why, Lady Morton. What is she like? It is always the women-folk who set the tone of a family.'

'She is a very warm-natured person.'

'American, is she not?'

'Yes. Her father was, for a time, the American ambassador in London. She met her husband here, when he was a major in the Life Guards.'

'Hmm ... He became a general, I seem to remember.'

'Yes.'

'Well, I suppose the American idea of society is rather different from ours. They prefer wide-open spaces, I believe ... But there was money there?'

Catherine smiled. 'Enough to keep us out of the poorhouse!'

'You are a vexing child!' Lady Lanesborough exclaimed. 'How am I to keep my reputation in society, without the odd morsel of gossip to trade?'

'I believe that James's maternal grandfather set up a trust for each of his grandchildren.'

Lady Lanesborough frowned. 'That is something, I suppose. But you have to live in the real world. Expectations can be but thin gruel.'

'Well, I think that even you would be satisfied. At present he is entitled only to the income. But I understand that, on marriage, the capital of the trust will vest in him. I gather from his sister that he will become a millionaire at the stroke of a pen.'

Lady Lanesborough smiled warmly. 'In that case, my responsibility for you would be satisfactorily resolved, child. I am delighted for you!'

'I shall be much more than delighted to have a husband who is considerate and charming and loving,' Catherine retorted.

'Yes, yes. These things are all very well; but husbands can be irksome ... It would be a great mistake to bury yourself in the country; embrace a rough bucolic bliss, and lose touch with society.'

Catherine laughed. 'I do not think there is any immediate danger of that,' she said. 'Sir Henry Morton is still hale and hearty. He will enjoy running the estates for years yet. He must have found it very irksome to stand back and watch Edwin trying to run them from his sick-bed.'

Lady Lanesborough frowned. 'Edwin was James's elder brother, was he not? Does his death mean that his American trust monies will pass to James?'

'I doubt it! But there will be more than enough for us and our children.'

'Hmm ... It may be providential that the brother died before you were actually married,' Lady Lanesborough said musingly. 'You will be able to start with a clean sheet, as it were.'

'Perhaps. Anyway, we have no intention of marooning ourselves in the country, as you seem to think. We shall find a house or an apartment in London, and continue our careers.'

Lady Lanesborough's face fell. 'But what is the point of that?' she asked. 'James Morton is a mere police constable – though heaven knows why! And your journalising is hardly a preparation for taking a prominent place in society.'

'We both feel that they are useful occupations,' Catherine said. 'And we see no reason to change. We shall, of course, have servants to look after us.'

Lady Lanesborough snorted. 'Is that not somewhat absurd?' she asked. 'You would be paying the servants more than you earn together!'

Catherine smiled. 'Perhaps a little absurdity would not come amiss in this remorselessly logical world,' she said.

'And how was your engagement received by the Morton family?' Lady Lanesborough asked, raising an eyebrow.

A shadow crossed Catherine's face. 'Not well, I fear. Edwin's parents have spent the last ten years in willing him to recover from the ghastly wound he received in the Sudan. Probably they feel responsible, in that they encouraged him to follow in the family's military tradition. To have James bounding about in rude health, playing cricket for Kent, and going on overseas tours for England, must have been a constant reproach for them.'

'But surely they like you?'

'I am sure that they do, deep down,' Catherine said. 'Indeed, I regard Emily, the daughter of the family, as my best friend. Of course, since she married she has lived in London; so we meet frequently.'

Lady Lanesborough frowned, then her face cleared. 'Ah, yes. The Smith boy; the heir to the banking family.'

'She is expecting a child,' Catherine said. 'That may help Lady Morton to get over Edwin's death.'

'So Charlotte is the bugbear, not Sir Henry?'

'I fear so. Indeed, quite unintentionally, I may have made matters worse between us. When it was realised that Edwin was sinking, Sir Henry sent a telegram to James summoning him to the Priory. Three days later, I received one from James saying that Edwin had died, and that the funeral was to be on Tuesday the thirtieth of April.'

'A little more than a week ago.'

'Yes. I took it that he wanted me to attend the funeral, and went down on Tuesday morning ... I can only say that when Lady Morton saw me, she seemed indignant, almost hostile.'

'She has been through a decade of anguish, my dear,' Lady Lanesborough said gently. 'The contrast between Edwin's fate and your future with James must have seemed an unbearable injustice ... But tell me about the funeral ceremony. I suppose it was in the village church.'

'Yes. Ashwell has a delightful little Saxon church.' Catherine smiled. 'For some reason I expected that the Morton family would always have been buried in the floor of the nave. I even imagined myself ending there, some day! But no. The grave was in a sunny corner of the churchyard, beneath an old elm tree ... Of course, since Edwin and Sir Henry had both been officers in the Life Guards there was a guard of honour from the regiment. Serving officers bore the coffin, there was a regimental firing-party, the Last Post was sounded. It was all very solemn and dignified.'

11

'And then?' Lady Lanesborough prompted.

'Why, everyone had a cup of tea; then James and I came back to London.'

'And had he expected you to go to the funeral?'

Catherine frowned. 'I cannot say. He made no comment either way. But at least he was pleased to see me.'

'Hmm . . . Well, I am sure that the Morton family will come to your wedding! Though, obviously, it will have to be delayed.'

Catherine looked up irritably. 'I can hardly accept that,' she said. 'I would go far to accommodate my future parents-in-law. But some things are more important than their long-expected mourning.'

Lady Lanesborough cocked her head. 'Are you saying that there is an overriding reason for flying in the face of society's usage?' she asked. 'Have you anticipated the delights of the marriage bed?'

Catherine blushed. 'Of course not, godmother! I am happy to say that I am still a virgin.'

'Good, good! Then perhaps you should come to see me when I have more time, so that I can explain what you should expect on your wedding night.'

Catherine laughed. 'You forget that I went to Cheltenham Ladies College!' she said. 'I know all about procreation.'

'Put like that, it scarcely sounds like a recommendation for the school . . . Now, let me see . . . You have been presented at court, so you will be entitled to wear a court train. Do you think white silk for your dress? . . . In the old days, to wear white was an affirmation of virginity. There would be precious few white weddings nowadays, if society gossip is to be believed! I put it all down to that wretched Colonel Condom . . . And no doubt you got to know about that at Cheltenham also.'

'Indeed!'

'Huh! . . . Have your parents given any thought to the wedding arrangements?'

'Since our house overlooks Hyde Park, and the ceremony would be in St Mark's church, my father suggests that we could hold the reception in a marquee, erected on the edge of the park.'

Lady Lanesborough pursed her lips in thought. 'Yes,' she said finally. 'Though the weather might not be good enough then.'

'I do not understand,' Catherine said, frowning. 'We have all the summer before us.'

'Come, child! You have said you are not pregnant. There can be no valid reason to disregard the usages of society. It would be an unimaginable solecism for Lady Morton and Emily to come to your wedding in deep mourning! Or, indeed, any ladies connected with the Morton family.'

'But . . .'

'There can be no buts!' Lady Lanesborough said firmly. 'You could not possibly be married for nine months. So you might just as well wait a year . . . May is quite the best month for a wedding.'

'I do not know what James will say,' Catherine said doubtfully.

'It matters not a jot! What do men know about social etiquette? His only function is to be there, and to say "I do" in the right places!'

'And if he demurs?'

'Then tell him to discuss the matter with his sister and his mother.'

'Oh, dear,' Catherine said, crestfallen. 'And I intended to have a party, at home, to celebrate our engagement. I suppose that would be unacceptable also.'

Lady Lanesborough smiled. 'Not a bit of it, my dear; so long as it is informal. And I myself will be present, to ensure that society does not disapprove!'

Detective Sergeant Joseph Bragg struck a match, and sucked the flame into his battered briar pipe. Ugh! This new blend of tobacco tasted like the flea-ridden bedding of an incontinent tom-cat. 'No call for it nowadays,' they had said when he asked for his usual twist. Well, if this was the best they could do they had lost a customer . . . Not that they would care about his threepence-worth. Their trade depended on the thousands of people flocking daily into the City of London, from every point of the compass. He doubted he would live here himself, if the regulations did not require it. But he was right enough, lodging with Mrs Jenks. He tossed the spent match into the ashtray on his desk. On the twelfth of June he would be forty-five. He had only a few more years to serve. Then he could retire – would have to retire. That

13

would be a facer. Now he could fill what spare time he had in the garden; though he usually succeeded in uprooting some special plant Mrs Jenks was trying to bring on, and getting the rough edge of her tongue. But how would he manage with no job?

Life was odd, he thought. He had come to live here in 1875; soon after his wife had died in childbirth. He had had to get out of the married quarter, of course. He was a single man again – no responsibilities in the world, except to stay sober and keep out of debt . . . It was odd how things worked out. Tommy Jenks had been a dustman, with his own horse and cart. Well set up; a man of consequence in the area bordering on Whitechapel. He had not been best pleased when his wife advertised for a lodger. But the house was far too big for the two of them. And when did a bit of extra money come amiss? Tommy had been a bit short with Bragg, when he first moved in. But he had come round. They had got to wandering up to the pub on a Saturday night, all three of them, for a pint of stout and some oysters. It was like belonging to a family again . . . Then Tommy cut his hand on a tin can. He shrugged it off. He had cut himself scores of times, he said; it would heal. But instead it took bad ways. His arm swelled up like a sausage. Septicaemia, they said. While he lingered, Bragg had taken to spending time with Mrs Jenks in the basement kitchen, so that she would not be on her own. And he had kept it up after Tommy died . . . for nigh on twenty years. She fed him, washed his clothes, allowed him the run of the house – all for twelve shillings a week. In return he did the rough work in the garden, and kept the place tidy. He supposed it was much like being a married couple – except for the obvious disadvantages. She had made it clear she was having none of that nonsense! Time and again he had thought his luck was in. They would be strolling back from the music hall; her all excited, saying how shameless Marie Lloyd had been – running her pearls across her tongue like that! He would unlock the door, step back . . . and she would be up the stairs like a whippet, locking her door against him. Worst of all, next morning she would be chattering about the show, as she bustled about the kitchen. It was against nature for a woman in her mid-forties to turn into a cock-teaser, he thought . . . But he was comfortable in Tan House Lane, and there was always Bertha at the pub . . .

He picked up the file on the robbery at the fur warehouse. For

14

once the judge had ignored the pleas of the defence lawyers. Three years' hard labour, and sod their families! If more courts took that line, criminals would pack it up – or move north. But the pickings weren't so good up there ... Bragg mused on the prospect of a City free of crime. Not that it would ever come to pass. He reckoned that there was more crime among the money people than would ever be discovered. Fraud was more often hushed up than reported to the police, he reckoned; because the top people had been negligent in ever allowing it to happen ... But suppose he were left with an empty desk, and that gloating bugger Inspector Cotton told him he was being pensioned off, what would he do? He tugged thoughtfully at his ragged moustache. He could hardly carry on living with Mrs Jenks. They only got on because he was out most of the time. Neither of them would want to be lumbered with the other, day in day out. No, he would go back to the country again, back to his roots in Dorset. He still had a share in his cousin's carter's business. He could move back to Bere Regis, do the odd trip for him. That way he would renew his acquaintance with the elegant Miss Hildred. She had seemed keen on him a couple of years ago. And her mother had badly wanted him to take over the running of the family brewery. He sighed. That was the trouble with getting older. You lost your optimism, your confidence. Instead of being in control of events, it was the other way round ...

Rubbish! He mentally shook himself. It was always the same when he was left on his own. He had come to rely on Constable Morton, that was the truth of it ... Yet it was more complicated than that. He was a real toff, with a Cambridge degree and a pedigree stretching back to William the Conqueror. Yet because of some quirk in his nature, he chose to spend his young manhood playing at policemen ... No, that was unfair. He was as committed as anyone else in the City force, and more effective than most. In a way he had the toffs of the City at a disadvantage, because he was one of them. And, since he had a pile of money of his own, he had an instinct for what the fraudsters were up to ... The fact of it was that they complemented one another, relied on each other as a team. So where the hell was he? His brother's funeral had taken place over a week ago. Most officers would have been given half a day, to go to the ceremony – a day, at most, if they had to travel. Bragg got to his feet, rammed his bowler hat on his head, and marched into the street to walk off his ill temper.

He lunched on cheese and pickle and a pint of beer, in Leadenhall market. Then he strolled down to St Paul's Cathedral. The weather seemed to be on the turn, he thought. Not before time either. The year was half gone already. But the solid banks of grey cloud were at last giving way. The sky was a dark blue, speckled with puff-balls of white. The wind had shifted to the south, too, and it was at last getting warm. He loosened his tie and took off his jacket. Mrs Jenks had been telling him for days that its heavy serge was more like winter than spring. She was right, as usual. Funny how women were more sensitive to temperature than men. And yet society women could happily go to a ball in deep midwinter, with bare arms and a low-cut dress ... He had never been able to fathom women. Well, it was too late to bother now. He crossed to the shady side of the street and made his way back to Old Jewry.

On entering his room he found Morton gazing out of the window. He took in the fine Savile Row clothes on his athletic frame. 'Ah, you are back,' he said gruffly.

Morton smiled. 'Yet technically still on leave,' he said. 'I called in to see what is afoot.'

'I expected you on Monday, lad. Did they have to postpone the funeral, or something?'

'No, I was delayed in Ashwell. As the heir apparent, my late brother had been owner of some properties and concerns in the Priory estates. It was an inscrutable lawyer's device, to enable effective control to continue in the event of my father's death.'

'Except that, as I understand it, Edwin would not have been capable of exercising it.'

Morton shrugged. 'Indeed. However, as I have now stepped into his shoes, the arrangement will work in practice as well as in theory.'

'And are you going to be popping down and back all the time?' Bragg asked gruffly.

'By no means! My father is still in vigorous health. He will enjoy running the estates, untrammelled by the masquerade that Edwin was in charge.'

'Right. Well, sit yourself down and I will tell you what little is afoot.'

16

Morton glanced at the clock. 'Perhaps it should be left until tomorrow,' he said. 'I shall be devoting the remaining afternoon of my leave to a far more pleasurable pursuit. Miss Marsden will call shortly, and I intend to take her to choose her engagement ring!'

Bragg raised his eyebrows. 'I see. She will know about your brother's death, I take it.'

'Yes, indeed. She came to the funeral of her own volition; quietly showing that she is one of the family. I was proud of her. She will make a worthy chatelaine in due course.'

'If she wants to, I assume.'

Morton laughed. 'If she wants to.'

'I suppose all this will have taken the shine off your engagement, for her,' Bragg said thoughtfully.

'Yes. I regret that most of all . . . However, I will try to make it up to her. Do you remember the raid at Furlonger & Searle, last year?'

'The jewellers in Poultry?'

'Yes. You will recollect that the sale of silver plate and jewellery is only a sideline. Their main activity is that of diamond broking. When I returned the silver that had been stolen, Searle – the proprietor – made me promise that, if ever I got engaged to be married, I would give him the opportunity of making my fiancée's engagement ring.'

'And that appeals to you, does it?'

Morton smiled. 'Yes. I have to confess that it does. It will be much more personal. It will have been made with her in mind; indeed, with our marriage in mind. In a sense it will be more than a token. Its creation will be an active element in the joining of our two lives in one.'

'Huh! You talk more like a bloody parson every day!' Bragg said sourly. 'There was something odd about that case, wasn't there, lad?'

'In that Searle did not press charges, you mean?'

'That's it! Seemed queer at the time.'

'Well, we could not actually pin the crime on Billy Larkins, although all the signs pointed in his direction.'

'I remember. He had some sort of cooked-up alibi . . . But why did we not have a crack at the fence?'

'As I remember it, Searle thought that the problematic prosecution of a registered pawnbroker, on a charge of knowingly receiving stolen goods, would have done his business more damage than not proceeding.'

Bragg shrugged. 'Well, it is one way of looking at it. But, to my mind, it shouldn't be an option. We should not need to have a formal . . .'

There was a tap on the door, and Catherine Marsden came in. Bragg jumped to his feet and strode across to her. 'Let me wish you all the happiness you could desire, miss,' he said, hugging her. 'I don't know what you see in this great oaf; but you may make something of him in time.'

Catherine kissed his cheek lightly. 'Then take care of him, sergeant, while I consider my other options!'

Morton grinned. 'I am sorry if I have inconvenienced you, Miss Marsden,' he said. 'Mr Searle originally arranged that we should go to his premises at four o'clock. But his assistant sent me a message this morning, suggesting that we should be there at half-past three.'

Catherine smiled. 'It is no trouble whatever. And Mr Tranter is so concerned I might embrace domesticity that he raised not the slightest objection.'

'Get something special, miss,' Bragg interposed. 'He can afford it!'

'As I was leaving the house this morning,' Catherine said, 'I was given an invaluable piece of advice by Cook. "Get the biggest diamond out of him you can, Miss Catherine," she said. "They can't take your engagement ring off you!" It almost put me off the whole proceeding!'

'Then it shall be the most special ring that craftsmanship can devise!' Morton said buoyantly. He proffered his arm. 'Come along, my dear,' he said. 'Does it sound right? "My dear". Perhaps that should wait until we are old and grey. How about "my sweet", "my precious one" . . .?'

'I think that "Catherine" would be perfect,' she said, smiling. 'It has the merit of being my name. And it is quite enough of an advance, for the moment, on the rather frosty "Miss Marsden" I have experienced for the last four and three-quarter years!'

Catherine took his arm possessively as they strolled down Old Jewry towards Poultry. She smiled inwardly at the thought of finding an engagement ring where once a thriving poultry market had been held ... Perhaps she could do a series of articles comparing the medieval character of various parts of the City with their modern function. Fish Street might serve; Pudding Lane ... But her thoughts flitted back to the present, to the excitement welling up inside her, to the sheer elation of strolling along a sunlit street with the man she was going to marry.

When they reached Poultry there was the usual tangle of two-horse omnibuses, brewers' drays, covered vans, stretching as far as the Bank crossing. Bowler-hatted clerks were dodging between them, seemingly taking their lives in their hands. Even James would not be able to impose order on this chaos, she thought. But there was no need for them to cross. He turned left and they stopped outside a building that seemed unable to decide whether it was a shop or not. The door, on the left of the frontage, had a heavy iron grille over the glass. To the right of it was a barred window. She peered through it. A crystal gaselier was burning in the room. She could see a counter, where a man was bending over a ledger. Beyond was a second window, also barred, where jewellery and articles of silver were displayed. It was hardly welcoming, she thought. In her day-dreams she had fancied herself being cosseted, surrounded with deep pile carpets and sumptuous furnishings as she made her choice. This was too ... well, too workaday for such a momentous transaction.

There was a momentary look of surprise in the man's face when they entered. 'Ah, Mr Morton, you are in good time,' he said effusively. 'And have I the honour to meet the future Mrs Morton?'

'Yes, indeed!' Morton said proudly. 'Miss Catherine Marsden. Catherine, this is Mr John Searle, one of the foremost authorities on jewels in England.'

Searle was in his mid-forties, Catherine decided. His smile seemed rather challenging, as he held out his hand. 'I am delighted to make your acquaintance,' he said.

The pressure of his hand-clasp was greater than was called for, Catherine thought; the warm tone of his voice fractionally insinuating.

James appeared to have noticed nothing. 'We are hoping that you will be able to provide something rather special by way of an engagement ring,' he said.

Searle smiled at Catherine. 'I am sure that we can meet that challenge. When you wrote to say that you would bring your fiancée to see me, Mr Morton, I gave the matter some thought . . . But first, the wishes of the most important person in all this must be ascertained.'

Catherine had thought that she might repeat Cook's quip about getting the biggest diamond she could; it was too amusing to be allowed to expire after the one telling. But she was loath to encourage the slightest informality, lest it be taken as an invitation to intimacy.

'Both James and I think that it should be a diamond ring,' she said, trying to inject some excitement into her voice for James's sake.

'Excellent! And I am sure that a young lady of your sophistication has a very clear idea of the kind of ring you require.'

Catherine was momentarily nonplussed. She turned to Morton. 'I think a solitaire diamond. Do you?'

Morton smiled broadly. 'That should at least satisfy Sergeant Bragg's aspirations for you,' he said.

Searle raised a questioning eyebrow, but Morton did not elaborate.

'Good, good!' he said, and walked to the back of the shop. A glazed screen had been installed, to create an office running the whole width of the premises. Through an open door in the left-hand corner of the screen, Catherine could see the railings at the head of a spiral staircase. Searle peered down it.

'Ibbs!' he called. 'Would you bring from the strong-room the packet I brought from Amsterdam?'

There was a muffled answer and Searle came back to them, an ingratiating smile on his face. 'It often happens', he said, 'that because of circumstances – inevitable circumstances – the least valuable piece of a society lady's jewellery is her engagement ring.'

'But not the least precious,' Catherine said sharply.

He gave her a calculating look, then smiled. 'Just so . . . But, because of your fiancé's position, I made an assumption that he would wish your engagement ring to be not only an exquisite token of your affection for each other, but something that would fittingly adorn you, whatever station in life you may achieve.'

'I agree,' Morton said firmly. 'Certainly cost is of no importance whatever. This will be the most significant gift I shall ever be able to give you.'

Catherine mentally shook herself. She was allowing her dislike of Searle to spoil what should be one of the most momentous days of their lives – short only of the wedding day itself. She saw a slight middle-aged man, with a mournful moustache, coming up the spiral staircase. He crossed over to them, placed a small packet in Searle's hand and retired downstairs again.

'This has been in the strong-room since I brought it back two days ago,' Searle said fulsomely. He gestured to a low table near the door. 'If you will take a seat, I will explain what I propose.'

There was such a look of excitement and pride on Morton's face that Catherine could not demur. They sat round the table and, with great solemnity, Searle broke open the package. Out tumbled a small, irregular, dull piece of what seemed like glass.

'That', Searle said portentously, 'is one of the finest rough diamonds I have ever seen.' He glanced at the clock on the wall. 'Diamonds have held a lifelong fascination for me,' he went on with a smile. 'Do you know, the crystal you see there is made of pure carbon. It is the hardest substance in the world. Indeed, the only material that will cut a diamond is another diamond! Amazing, is it not? The scientists tell us that it was formed by unimaginable pressure and temperature, two hundred miles below the surface of the earth.'

Catherine gave a polite murmur.

'This particular diamond has come from Kimberley, in South Africa. In that area the diamonds are found in vertical pipes of clay, which was presumably forced up with them. The value of that crystal, in its present state, is five thousand pounds . . .' He looked sideways to judge Morton's reaction, and received a nod of assent.

'Of course,' he went on, 'this is a white diamond – that is to say virtually colourless. There are also diamonds which do have a distinct colour – red, blue, pink, purple; even yellow or green. If such is your desire, Miss Marsden, I can obtain a selection for you.'

'No. Coloured diamonds seem too frivolous for an engagement ring,' Catherine said, regretting that she had to endorse his judgement.

Searle smiled. 'May I commend your discernment?' he said. 'As to the cut, there is a fashion, at the moment, for emerald-cut stones – that is oblong, with a large facet at the top, and . . .'

'I would want my engagement ring to be round and brilliant-cut,' Catherine said firmly.

'Yes . . . Yes. And I would place the cutting of it in the hands of the finest craftsman in the world . . . Now, if we consider this particular rough diamond, it would be entirely possible for him to so cleave the stone that you could have a matching pair of ear-rings! Not many ladies have ear-rings and engagement ring from the same gemstone. Moeller & Kreiber, who supplied the stone, will be able to achieve it. Of that I am sure.'

Catherine frowned. 'We seem to be somewhat at odds,' she said. 'Our concern is to buy an engagement ring. To James and me it will have great symbolic importance; but that will in no way depend on the size of the stone in it. For me, my engagement ring has to be a working ring; a symbol of a lifelong compact, not a piece to display. I must be able to wear it as part of me, not be always afraid of pulling it off with my glove.'

Searle gave a superior smile. 'Indeed,' he said. 'But you must also consider that, one day soon, you will be a great lady, a leader of fashion. You would not wish . . .'

The door crashed open. A burly man rushed in, revolver in hand. Searle's head jerked round, a mixture of puzzlement and irritation on his face. The man strode up to Searle, raised his gun and shot him through the head. Catherine stifled a scream as the jeweller's body toppled to the floor. The man seized her arm and put the gun to her head.

'You,' he cried roughly, nodding his head in Morton's direction. 'Handcuff yourself to the railings back there! Then throw the key over here.'

Morton hesitated, then ran to the top of the staircase. He took out his handcuffs, closed one end round his left wrist and the other round the stair-rail.

'The key!'

Catherine felt panic in her throat; there was a click as the revolver was cocked. Then Morton fumbled in his pocket.

'No tricks!' the man cried menacingly.

Slowly Morton withdrew his hand, and held up a key in his

fingers. Then he tossed it awkwardly towards the front of the shop. It hit the counter and bounced behind it.

The man dragged Catherine to her feet. 'You are coming with me,' he said harshly. 'And no messing!' He picked up the rough diamond from the table and slipped it into his pocket. 'You will walk arm-in-arm with me. If you try to attract attention, you are dead!'

'Do as he says!' Morton called. He saw the man seize Catherine's arm and drag her towards the door. Then they had vanished.

He pulled at the handcuff, but he could not get his hand out of it. Stupid idiot that he was! He should have merely pretended to put it on – the gunman had not come to check. But had he done so . . . He had already killed once. Morton remembered that Ibbs was down in the strong-room, and shouted for him. There was no response. In the dead silence Morton thought through everything that had happened. The whole thing was bizarre. Yet Searle's body, slumped by the table, was real enough. The rough diamond had gone – reason enough for the raid. Though it seemed unlikely that the gunman would have known about its presence. Gratefully accepted as a bonus then . . . But, in truth, it did not at all look like the public's conception of a valuable gemstone. And why take Catherine? To prevent her from raising the alarm, he supposed. He narrowed his eyes to see if there was a key in the door-lock. Had there been, she could have been locked inside, while the killer got away. But he could see none . . . At all events, there would be little point in keeping Catherine, once the thief was well away from the scene. Morton hoped fervently that she would not try to do anything foolish or heroic. She was sensible, he told himself. She had far too much to lose; she would never imperil their future together for the sake of a sensational story. But even as the words formed in his mind, he knew that he was deluding himself. Neither engagement nor marriage would turn her into a timid, compliant woman. Her instincts would always prompt her to fight against injustice; and crime was the most extreme embodiment of injustice . . . And it would all be his fault; insisting that her engagement ring must be special, unique. As if it mattered . . . A fly was now buzzing around Searle's corpse. At any moment it would alight on the head and begin to feed . . . He wrenched his mind away.

'Ibbs!' he shouted ... Perhaps there was another door to the premises. He could have slipped out. No! He was being stupid. There could be no other way out of the basement than the stairs he was handcuffed to ... Anyway, why was no one else coming into the shop? He glanced at the clock. A quarter past four. By this time most diamond buyers would regard their working day as over. Their thoughts would be on cigars and brandy in St John's Wood or Surbiton. There would be cleaners, but they would not ... The door crashed open; a man rushed in. He checked.

'Christ all-bloody-mighty!' he cried hoarsely, seeing Searle's corpse. He spun on his heel and rushed out again.

There was silence for a space, then Morton heard the sound of a footfall at the bottom of the staircase. Ibbs's head appeared, looking cautiously upwards.

'Where in God's name have you been?' Morton shouted angrily.

'I heard what sounded like a shot,' Ibbs said timidly. His voice had a distinct South London accent. 'Mr Searle says that if ever there is a raid, and one of us is in the strong-room, we are to lock the door from the inside and stay there till danger is past.'

'Look behind the counter, and see if you can find the key to these handcuffs,' Morton said irritably.

Ibbs stepped past him and saw the body of Searle. 'Dear God!' he exclaimed.

'The key!'

He sidled white-faced past the body of his employer, then ducked down behind the counter. Moments later he emerged with the key. His hand was trembling as he released Morton's wrist. 'Where is your young lady?' he asked.

'She has been abducted by Searle's killer. He has stolen the rough diamond.'

'Oh dear! How dreadful!'

Morton stood up and stretched his cramped limbs. 'Where is Searle's residence?' he demanded.

'In Blomfield Street – number three.'

'Will anyone be there?'

'He has a manservant. Thompson, I believe.'

'Right. I will see that a van comes to collect the body. Keep the street door locked until it arrives ... And do not touch anything! When the body has been taken away, you may go home.'

'Very well.'

'Put your address on a piece of paper for me, and make sure that you are here tomorrow morning at nine o'clock.'

'Right.' Ibbs scribbled briefly, and handed the paper to Morton.

'Thank you. In the meantime I want no one else to have access . . . What about cleaners?'

'I will call at their premises, and tell them not to come until further notice.'

'Have you got a spare key that we can borrow?' Morton asked.

Ibbs frowned. 'Mr Searle would have a bunch of keys in his pocket,' he said.

Morton went over, noting exactly how the body lay. Then he unbuttoned Searle's morning coat and found the keys in an inside pocket. 'Is there a rear door to the premises?' he asked.

'There is a side door giving on to Chapel Place. But it has not been opened in years.'

'Right, Mr Ibbs. I suggest that you lock up now, and go home.'

Morton found himself sprinting back to Old Jewry, dodging round knots of pedestrians, running in the gutter. The full horror of it all seemed to grip him at last. He had stopped being a policeman, and become a panic-stricken victim of crime. He dashed into the headquarters building.

'Is Sergeant Bragg in?' he gasped.

The duty sergeant looked at him calmly. 'Something up?' he asked.

'A kidnapping and a murder!'

'Joe will be pleased. He was here not a minute ago, complaining there was nothing interesting going on.'

Morton dashed to Bragg's room and burst through the door. 'Catherine has been abducted and Searle murdered!' he blurted out.

Bragg's head jerked up. 'Where? How long ago?'

'Well over half an hour . . . We must do something!'

Bragg frowned. 'Sit down, lad, and tell me what happened,' he said quietly. He stared out of the window as Morton gave a disjointed account of what had occurred. There was a silence, then Bragg got to his feet.

'It was bad luck you happened to be there at the time,' he said

25

calmly. 'But one thing is certain, your young lady is only a pawn. Once they have got away, they will let her go.'

'I hope to God no one tried to hinder their escape!'

'You've kept your head, up to now,' Bragg said curtly. 'Don't start imagining things ... They cannot have walked far, at this time in the afternoon, without someone realising she was under duress. My guess is they would let her go as soon as they could leave her in a quiet street.'

'But I was handcuffed to the stair-rail for half an hour! It is almost an hour since it happened!'

'Hmm ...' Bragg chewed at his ragged moustache. 'I'll tell you what,' he said. 'You go to all the cab-ranks in the area around Poultry. Ask the drivers if a couple like Miss Marsden and the murderer has been picked up this afternoon. Give them her description, ask them to spread the word. And be sure of this ... We will get her back safe and sound!'

In sheer terror, Catherine had allowed herself to be dragged, unprotesting, out of the shop. The man was holding her in a fierce grip; she sensed that he would kill her if she resisted. He hurried her across the junction with Old Jewry, wrenching at her arm. She hoped one of James's colleagues might see her and realise that she was under duress. But the street was empty. As they approached Mercers' Hall, she could see a carriage standing by the kerb, its blinds drawn. At their approach, the driver got down and opened the door. Without a word passing, her captor bundled her inside, the door was closed and the carriage trotted off. Her mind was a-whirl; she set herself to remember the man's features. In the dimness she could make out cold grey eyes, long nose, thin sneering lips. A murderer ... One who would kill her, too, without compunction.

She tried to guess where the carriage was going. They seemed to be away from the congested streets now, for the horse's hooves had settled into an easy rhythm. Almost certainly they must be going north. She set herself to count the seconds. They had already been travelling for some time; nevertheless it might be useful. She dropped her head as if dejected, and sensed that her captor had relaxed. Out of the corner of her eye she could see the handle for opening the door. Given a moment's opportunity she could throw herself across, twist the handle and the door would open under the impetus. Once out, someone would protect her ... As if he had sensed her thoughts, the man took the revolver from his pocket. He was almost caressing it, gloating at the power it gave him, exulting that it had taken one life that day and could kill again ... Catherine forced her eyes closed; she must do nothing to provoke him. She began to count the seconds again, but she had forgotten the previous total. Was it nine minutes? But where had they been when she began counting? It was utterly useless ... Now they seemed to be in a quiet street, away from the clatter of traffic. The carriage was slowing. She heard the crackle of the wheels on gravel, then the carriage came to a halt. The man leaned forward, and seized her arm. He tapped her nose with the barrel of his gun.

'No lip from you,' he said truculently, 'or you are dead! Got it?'

Terrified, she nodded her head.

'We are getting out here. You are going to see some people. But you say nothing. Right?'

Again she nodded.

The man put his gun in his coat pocket, opened a door and pulled Catherine after him. She could see that she was in the driveway of a large brick house, surrounded by lawns and beds of daffodils. Strange, there were bars at the windows of all the upper floors; a blur of white faces at some of them. Her captor pulled her up a flight of stone steps leading to an imposing entrance. Beside it she could see a brass plate bearing the words GREENLANDS SANATORIUM. He jerked on a brass bell-pull. The door was opened by a uniformed porter and there was a brief exchange. Then she was marched along a corridor which smelled of carbolic, to an office at the back of the building. A raw-boned woman looked up from her desk.

'Yes?' she said.

Her captor seemed ill at ease. 'This is Miss Brown,' he said. 'You are expecting her. I am to tell you that she is violent, and screams a lot.'

The woman gazed at Catherine as if she were a specimen in a jar. 'I am sure that you will be very happy with us,' she said with a bleak smile. She rang a bell and two heavily built women came into the office.

27

'Number two, on the top floor,' she said.

Catherine felt her arms seized. She was hustled along a corridor, up several flights of stairs and down another corridor. One of the attendants took a key, which was dangling on a piece of ribbon from her belt, and opened a door. Catherine was pushed inside.

'There are some clothes in the cupboard,' one of them said harshly. 'Put them on.'

'But I want to keep my own,' Catherine protested.

The woman gave a sadistic leer. 'I can see that we are going to have trouble with you,' she said. She pushed her face forward until it almost touched Catherine's. 'But it don't pay, see? It don't pay! . . . Ten minutes, or we do it for you.'

The two nurses went out cackling and locked the door behind them.

Numbly Catherine took off her blouse and skirt, and put on the faded blue cotton dress. Then she looked about her. This was a bedroom in what had once been a handsome house. Even up here there were elaborate moulded cornices, now black with dirt. As well as a bed, there was a chest of drawers, a table and a couple of bentwood chairs. In one corner was a commode. Greenlands Sanatorium . . . Catherine shivered. She began to feel that she had really gone out of her mind. What had happened to her was the stuff of nightmares. A mere two hours ago she had been preparing to go, with James, to choose her engagement ring. Now she was being treated like a mad woman . . . By now, her parents would be expecting her to arrive home, full of excitement and happiness. When she did not come, they would think for a time that she had been detained – was perhaps working late, to make up for time lost . . . But surely, at some stage Searle's assistant must have emerged from the strong-room at the shop; released James from the handcuffs. Even now the City police would be looking for her . . . The City police . . . She must be several miles beyond the boundary of the City. It would be up to the Metropolitan police to find her. And, from what James had said, there was little love lost between the two forces . . . She could be here for ever! Tears were pricking at her eyes. It should have been such a happy day . . .

The key rattled in the door, and one of the nurses came in.

'I have brought you a cup of tea,' she said, with a hint of kindness in her voice. 'Nice sweet tea.'

Catherine looked at the cup. 'I do not take milk in tea,' she said.

'You will here,' the nurse said brusquely. 'This isn't the Ritz!' She put the cup down on the chest of drawers. 'I will get these out of the way for you.' She scooped up the clothes that Catherine had taken off and went out.

Catherine picked up the cup, and sipped at the sickly brew. She was very thirsty, and the water in the dusty carafe did not look very appealing. But sipping the tea was merely prolonging her disgust. She took a deep breath, and gulped it all down. Then she crossed to the window. This room must be at the back of the house. Below was a lawn, fringed with trees. Beyond them were the gardens of the houses in the next road. Houses built for prosperous merchants, in the days before it became fashionable to live in the country. She flattened her face against the glass. She could not catch even a glimpse of a street. Overcome by despair, Catherine lay down on the bed and wept.

Sergeant Bragg hurried along Fleet Street and turned down Inner Temple Lane. A group of schoolboys stood by the Temple church, while a master gestured towards the various buildings around them. Would-be barristers, Bragg thought. Somebody should tell them that more starved than made a pile in that game. The solicitors were the winners; nice steady fees from property conveyancing and wills; they would even get their spoonful out of a bankruptcy. But the barristers were the romantic figures, jousting in court over the ruins of other people's lives. Bragg turned into Pump Court, and climbed the staircase to where Sir Rufus Stone had his chambers.

He had been the coroner for the City of London for four years now. His predecessor's background had been in medicine. And he had been less than rigorous in probing the death of one of the City's Members of Parliament. Once Bragg had demonstrated that the man had been murdered, and arrested the killer, there had been accusations of political jobbery. As a result, Dr Primrose had been compelled to resign. So the members of the Common

29

Council had been determined to appoint, as their new coroner, someone whose reputation and stature would place him beyond reproach. It was said that Sir Rufus had set two years as the limit of his tenure of the post. He used to proclaim that he had been appointed to cleanse the Augean stables; and, by God, cleanse them he would! It was not as if he needed the stipend. He had built up a lucrative practice at the Chancery bar. And his knighthood was evidence of the esteem in which he was held. So he must actually enjoy being coroner, Bragg thought. Certainly the two years had come and gone without even a whisper that he might resign. But even a vicarious involvement in blood and guts must be welcome, in a life otherwise spent in dry-as-dust Chancery work.

Bragg went into the clerk's room. 'Is his eminence in, then?' he asked.

The clerk smiled. 'He has a client with him. But the consultation should not take much longer.'

'Then I will wait.' Bragg sat in the draughty corridor which served as a waiting-room for the chambers. He wondered how Morton was getting on. It was likely to be a wild-goose chase. Nobody would rob a jeweller's shop, abduct a young woman, then stand with her at a cab-rank like a loony. They must have had a carriage waiting nearby ... But it was something for him to be doing. He had to be involved in the case, certainly. But whether he could be relied upon was another matter.

The door to Sir Rufus's room was thrown open. The coroner came billowing down the corridor, a florid-faced man in tow. He momentarily checked as he saw Bragg, but ignored him. It was a full ten minutes before he came striding back alone. Shortly afterwards, the clerk told Bragg he could go in.

Sir Rufus had shed his gown, and was sitting at his desk leafing through a file.

'A profitable day, sir? Bragg asked innocently.

Sir Rufus snorted. 'For my clients certainly,' he said. 'But for me a pittance! Well? I take it that you have not come here merely for the exercise.'

'No, sir. There has been a shooting at the premises of a diamond broker. The proprietor has been murdered.'

'Name?'

'John Searle, of Furlonger & Searle, in Poultry. My constable, James Morton, had taken his young lady there to buy her an engagement ring. Miss Marsden was abducted by the killer.'

Sir Rufus frowned. 'Are you saying that this miscreant entered the premises and shot the proprietor, merely to obtain possession of this young woman?' he asked. 'She must be uncommonly attractive.'

'No, sir. A valuable rough diamond was taken as well. Apparently a rough diamond is . . .'

'I am well aware of the import of the term, Bragg. So, she was taken incidentally to the robbery; perhaps as a kind of protection . . . But what on earth was your constable doing meantime?'

'He had been compelled to handcuff himself to some railings, sir.'

The coroner raised his eyebrows. 'Compelled?'

'Under threat that his fiancée would be murdered too.'

'I see . . . So you are investigating both a murder and a robbery.'

'And the kidnapping as well.'

'Yes, of course . . . This diamond. I assume that it was of considerable value.'

'Five thousand pounds, I gather.'

'Great heavens! However, my concern is with the murder, which was presumably incidental to the robbery.'

'Well . . . Constable Morton said that it did not seem like that. Almost the other way round. And he was there.'

'Huh! His perception of the events must be coloured by the abduction of his young lady . . . Miss Marsden, of the *City Press*, is she not?'

'Yes, sir.'

'Hmm . . . I would be sorry if she were placed in peril. She has won for herself a well-deserved reputation for fairness and objectivity in her reporting. Particularly in relation to the area in which we both operate. She would be a great loss to her profession.'

'Not if I can stop it!' Bragg said firmly.

'So, is it your wish to be appointed as my officer for the murder?' Sir Rufus asked.

'I am already down for it, sir, under the usual procedure.'

31

'Ah, yes ... finders keepers. All rather childish, I have thought. But are you not too close to the young lady? Would you have the necessary objectivity to properly handle the case?'

'I would not let it influence me,' Bragg said earnestly.

Sir Rufus pondered. 'Well,' he said at length, 'the murder and the robbery are inextricably linked. As to the abduction, it is outside my sphere. But it would seem logical to investigate it at the same time. My only interest is that it should not diminish the effort applied to identifying and arresting the murderer.'

'So you confirm my appointment as your officer?' Bragg said.

The coroner frowned. 'You do not normally come here, request-ing my personal ratification,' he said. 'However, I can see that with you as my officer, I shall also benefit from the knowledge of your constable; the only person – apart from Miss Marsden – who actually saw the murder. Very well ... But I require you to maintain the necessary objectivity.'

'Oh, I will,' Bragg said earnestly. 'You can rely on that.'

Sir Rufus got up from his desk, and took a copy of *Who's Who* from the book-case. He flicked rapidly through the pages. 'John Searle?' he asked.

'Yes, sir.'

'Ah, I have him! ... Principal of Furlonger & Searle ... Wellington College ... He was in the army at one time. A major ... Only son of Alfred Searle ... Member of the Goldsmiths' Company ... Clubs: Naval & Military, and Gresham's. Appar-ently unmarried ... Strange. I have a vague notion that he was something of a womaniser ... I will try to find out about that. Now, be off with you, Bragg. I have my living to earn!'

It was almost eight o'clock when Morton rang the door bell of Catherine's parents' house in Park Lane. He was ushered into the sitting-room overlooking Hyde Park. William Marsden got up and held out his hand.

'Good evening, James,' he said warmly. 'I am afraid that our perversely working daughter is still perversely working!'

'Then she has not ...' Morton began.

Alarm was growing in Harriet Marsden's face. 'Did you expect to find her here?' she asked. 'Certainly any well-brought-up young lady ought to be back home by this time!'

'I . . . I hoped that I might find her here,' Morton said dejectedly.

'But surely you must know of her whereabouts!' William said irritably. 'You were together this afternoon, choosing her engagement ring! Or are you saying that she has had second thoughts?' He forced a smile. 'I tell you, James; if you have daughters, never educate them! They get completely out of control. They managed things better in Jane Austen's time.'

'Hush, William!' Harriet broke in. 'May we get this clear, James? Did you see her this afternoon, or not?'

Morton slumped into a chair. 'Yes. We went together to Furlonger & Searle's, to choose the stone for her ring. We were there for, I suppose, half an hour. Searle, the principal of the firm, had brought a rather special rough diamond from Amsterdam. As I remember it, we were discussing whether a pair of ear-rings could be cut from the stone, in addition to the diamond for her ring . . .'

'Go on!' William said anxiously.

'Then the door burst open. A man with a revolver rushed in. He shot Searle dead. Then he grabbed Catherine and held the gun to her head. I was forced to handcuff myself to a stair-rail, otherwise he would have killed her too. Then he made off with the diamond, compelling Catherine to go with him . . . I had hoped that, once he had made his escape, he would have let her go.'

'But this is intolerable!' her father burst out. 'We are at the end of the nineteenth century! In the heart of the British Empire, not some wild-west American frontier town!'

'I know, sir!' Morton said defeatedly.

'Well, man! What is being done to find her?'

'For the past three hours I have been going the rounds of every cab-stand in the area ... Asking drivers if they have seen Catherine, with a man, about four o'clock. Describing her over and over again; stressing that she would be under duress, that there would be something odd about the couple. Begging them to tell other drivers . . . But, so far, to no avail.'

Mrs Marsden looked stunned. 'But why?' she asked. 'Why abduct Catherine?'

Morton sighed. 'It makes no kind of sense. If anything it would impede the robber's escape. Once I was immobilised, there was no point in abducting her, unless . . .'

'Unless what?' Mr Marsden demanded.

'Unless he intends to hold her for ransom.'

'But that is absurd!'

'Not totally, sir. Any young woman sitting in Furlonger & Searle's shop, examining a large rough diamond, could be assumed to come from a wealthy background.'

'So, are you saying that at any moment we may receive a demand for money in exchange for her release?'

'It is a possibility.'

'And if we do?'

'It is clearly a police matter.'

Mr Marsden snorted. 'It is no use leaving it to the Metropolitan police. They are more concerned with keeping the traffic moving than chasing missing daughters!'

'Then we can proceed on the footing that the abduction took place in the area of the City police, and therefore demands for ransom should be dealt with by us.'

'Good!'

Mrs Marsden was blinking away tears. 'She had no need of a career,' she said. 'Why could she not be like the other girls of her class? . . . You will find her, won't you, James?'

Morton dropped on his knees and took her hand. 'I will do nothing else until I find her,' he said. 'I promise you that.'

2

Morton arrived at Old Jewry next morning, red-eyed from lack of sleep.

Bragg looked at him speculatively. 'I see Fleet Street is quick off the mark,' he said. 'There is a paragraph in the *Chronicle* about the murder. But no mention about your fiancée's abduction . . . Strange, that.'

Morton slumped into his chair. 'As you can imagine,' he said, 'I have been thinking about it all night; going over and over it, until the details became a senseless tangle in my mind.'

'I reckon you could wangle some compassionate leave, if you wanted, lad. In any case, I am not at all sure you should be involved in the investigation.'

'But why?' Morton said forcefully. 'She is my future wife!'

Bragg picked up his pipe, and poked in the bowl with a match. 'Exactly because of that,' he said quietly. 'Mind you, I am coroner's officer for the murder.'

'That is one thing in our favour,' Morton said.

'Yes. And the coroner does accept that it is part and parcel with the robbery . . . Yet he is not so sure about the abduction. But I expect we could work them all together, if . . .'

The door opened, and the Commissioner wandered in.

'Ah, Bragg,' he said. 'And Constable Morton . . . I am sorry to hear about the kidnapping of your young lady. Has she been released yet?'

'No, sir,' Morton said bleakly.

'Hmm . . . I expect that she will be. Not a lot of point in keeping her.' He went over to the window and stared out. Lieutenant-Colonel Sir William Sumner had finished his army career as officer commanding an infantry regiment. Left to his own devices, he would happily have retired to tend roses in a country garden. But, at a social occasion, it had been suggested that he might be interested in becoming the next Commissioner of the City of London police. Foolishly, he had told his wife of the conversation, and Hilda had got the bit between her teeth. Relentlessly ambitious for him, she had lobbied the wives of City figures; dragged him from function to function . . . Now she was Lady Sumner, and obviously enjoying it.

He turned from the window. 'I understand that you are coroner's officer for the Searle murder, Bragg,' he said.

'Yes, sir. As Constable Morton was present when it happened, the coroner insisted, sir.'

'And no doubt you would make the same point in connection with the abduction and the robbery,' Sir William said pensively.

'Sir Rufus seemed to think they were all of a piece, sir; that they should all be worked together.'

The Commissioner cleared his throat. 'This seems exactly the kind of complicated case which Inspector Cotton agreed you should work under my direction,' he said. 'Yes, please report to me.' He hovered uncertainly for a moment, then wandered out of the room.

Morton raised a smile. 'I am not sure that Inspector Cotton had cases such as this in mind when he agreed to satisfy Sir William's penchant for meddling,' he said.

'But we could not have asked for more. Now, lad, go over that bit about Tommy Potts again.'

Morton thought for a moment. 'I was handcuffed to the rails, with the key yards away. Catherine had been taken, I suppose, fifteen minutes before. Ibbs was still in the basement, hiding in the strong-room ... It was very still and quiet. I cannot even remember the noise of traffic ... Then the door burst open again and there was Tommy Potts, wild and threatening.'

'Did you see a gun in his hand?'

'I ... Let me think ... No. His right hand was in his coat pocket. I inferred that it was holding a gun, because of the previous incident. It could have been a black-jack.'

'And what happened then?'

'He rushed into the shop, saw the body of Searle, uttered an oath, and ran off.'

'Hmm ... It does seem odd that a diamond broker's shop should be the target of two raids inside half an hour. And nobody in their right mind would trust Tommy with a gun. Did you see any others of the Blackwall gang?'

'No.'

'Doing a bit of moonlighting on his own, was he?'

'Perhaps.'

Bragg pondered. 'I don't see that,' he said. 'Warehouse breaking is more their mark. Still, it would do no harm to have a chat ...'

The door banged open and Inspector Cotton strode in, his face puce with anger.

'What the bloody hell are you up to, Bragg?' he demanded.

'I don't understand, sir,' Bragg said innocently.

'This shooting in Poultry! You have got the Commissioner to front for you, so you can do as you bloody please!'

'I would never do that, sir,' Bragg said piously. 'I value your advice too much for that.'

'Don't give me that shit! You would piss in my pocket, given half a chance ... What is this about an abduction?'

'Constable Morton's fiancée was there, choosing her engagement ring. The murderer compelled her to go with him.'

Cotton stared at Morton, his lip curling in distaste. 'A journalist, isn't she? On the *City Press*?'

'Yes, sir,' Morton said.

'I knew I was right...' His face became thoughtful. 'Well, you are out of that one, lad,' he said. 'Much too close to home ... Yes, I will take on the abduction. She will be well out of the City area by now. I have a good relationship with the Met. We shall need their help to find her.' He turned to Bragg. 'So keep out of my bloody way on that!' He swung round and strode out of the room.

Bragg put down his pipe. 'It can do no harm, lad,' he said reassuringly. 'Even though he is only doing it to get his name in the papers. But as for keeping out of his way, I fancy we can still poke about a bit on our own account. Now, then, we will go down to the scene of the murder, and you can tell me exactly what happened.'

They arrived at Furlonger & Searle's shop, to find the door unlocked. Ibbs was behind the counter, wrapping a trinket for a young man in frock coat and topper. Ibbs looked sombre, as he gave the man his change, but well in control of himself. The customer gave them an excited grin as he departed.

'Business is brisk, then,' Bragg remarked, showing his warrant-card.

'It is ghoulish, officer,' Ibbs said sombrely.

'Well, you do not have to open.'

'It is what Mr Searle would have wanted.' He turned to Morton. 'I hope your young lady is safe, sir,' he remarked.

'She has not yet been found,' Morton said curtly.

'I am sorry.'

Bragg examined the shop. A towel lay on the floor, near to the table. He pushed it to one side with the toe of his boot, to reveal a patch of dried blood.

'Just a few strides from the door,' Bragg remarked. 'You were all sitting round this table?'

'Searle, Catherine and I,' Morton said. 'Mr Ibbs was down in the strong-room.'

'Did the intruder make any attempt to go down there?'

'No, sir. He did not move from the table. His concern, after the murder, was to make his escape with Catherine. The theft of the diamond seemed almost an afterthought.'

Bragg turned to Ibbs. 'Some valuable stuff down there, I expect,' he said.

'Into the hundreds of thousands of pounds.'

'Hmm ... You would have thought he would do the job properly, while he was at it ... So the only thing taken was the rough diamond?'

Ibbs nodded. 'Worth five thousand pounds.'

'But which looks more like a lump of glass than a gem.'

'Yes, sergeant.'

Bragg prowled about the shop. Behind the counter was a row of display cases, filled with silver cups and salvers, trinkets of gold and silver. The whole lot would not be worth swinging for. But the rough diamond was worth a small fortune. Was it just luck? Maybe, if Morton was right. On the wall between the windows was a portrait of a man. It was painted with the head half-turned to one side. He had a jutting chin, and a bigger nose than the Duke of Wellington's.

'Who is he?' he asked. 'The man with the conk!'

'That is Mr Thomas Furlonger,' Ibbs said deprecatingly. 'A former principal of the firm.'

'With a nose like that, I wonder he didn't frighten off the customers! Where does he fit in?'

Ibbs gazed at the portrait. 'He was the third generation of Furlongers in the business. He was really quite distinguished. His father sent him into the army, to get him from under his feet. He had a commission bought for him, in the 77th East Middlesex Regiment of Foot. He served in the Napoleonic wars, and fought at Waterloo. Then, in 1818, he resigned his commission and came into the firm.'

'Why keep his picture up there?'

Ibbs shrugged. 'I think it is a kind of talisman. When he was in the firm it prospered; though that must have been attributable as much to the long years of peace as to his abilities.'

'I see. And are there any Furlongers left in the business?'

'No. He was the last.'

'So, where do the Searles come in?'

'Thomas Furlonger had a daughter, who married a man called Alfred Searle. The Searles had a much smaller diamond broking business in Hatton Garden. On Thomas's death, Alfred combined the two businesses here, in the City.'

'Hmm ... And would you say that John Searle had any enemies?' Bragg asked.

Ibbs wrinkled his brow. 'Obviously he had competitors in the trade . . . I would say rivals, not enemies.'

'Right.' Bragg pondered for a moment, then: 'John Searle went into the army, as well. Was that to keep him from under his father's feet too?'

'Perhaps.'

'And you have never heard of any enemies from his army days?'

'No, sergeant.'

'How long have you been working here, Mr Ibbs?' Bragg asked.

'Eighteen years. My family are retail jewellers in Clapham. I worked there for four years, but it was hardly exciting. I fancied a change; something to get my teeth into. And I fell on my feet. Alfred Searle took me on as an assistant.'

'That was exciting, was it?'

Ibbs gave a rueful smile. 'Is any job as interesting as you hope it will be?' he asked. 'People must think that being a police detective is exciting. I expect you know better . . . I make a good living here. Though what will happen now, goodness only knows.'

'Hmm . . . You say that Searle had rivals, but not enemies. Yet it seems to me that a rival would be the very person who would recognise the value of a rough diamond; something that anyone else would think was a chunk of glass.'

Ibbs raised his eyebrows. 'I had not thought of it in those terms,' he said.

Bragg pondered. 'And you were down in the strong-room when your employer was shot.'

'Yes, sergeant. The first intimation I had of the raid was the sound of the gun going off.'

'You didn't think to rush up and scare them off? You know, shout and bang about a bit?'

'I might well have done, were it not for Mr Searle's express instructions.'

'So, what precisely did you do?'

'When I heard the sound of the shot, I picked up the articles I was checking, and took them back into the strong-room again. Then I locked the door after me.'

'How did you know when to come out?'

'I waited for quite some minutes, then I unlocked the door and listened. All seemed quiet. But I waited for a little longer; then I locked the strong-room, crept up the stairs and found your constable handcuffed to the railing.'

'I see ... Tell me, Mr Ibbs, what kind of a man was John Searle?'

Ibbs looked up in surprise. 'He was a fine man!'

'Yes. But that means nothing. And don't tell me he was a gentleman, either.'

Ibbs frowned in thought. 'I suppose one would say he was a man's man,' he said finally. 'He was in the army for twelve years.'

'What regiment?' Morton asked.

'The Second Dragoon Guards.'

'Ah! The Queen's Bays.'

Ibbs nodded. 'He had got to the rank of major, when he resigned his commission and came into the firm.'

'And when would that be?'

'Let me think ... He was here six years before Mr Alfred died ... I suppose it would be in the summer of 1879.'

'We have heard he was a bit of a ladies' man,' Bragg said.

Ibbs raised his eyebrows. 'I know nothing about that,' he said. 'But he kept his personal affairs to himself.'

'I bet he did!' Bragg paused, then: 'It seems the object of the raid was to steal the rough diamond,' he said. 'Even if we are wrong there, that was what happened. Now, how would the thief set about turning it into money?'

Ibbs pursed his lips. 'It would only be of value to the trade,' he said. 'Though the thief might keep it, against a rainy day.'

'Suppose he wanted to be rid of it?'

'To get full value out of it, he would have to get it to a cutter – back into the trade again ... But, after this morning's newspaper report, the London brokers would be chary of touching anything that did not come from a reputable source.'

'Where, then?'

'The Continent. The trade there is split between Antwerp and Amsterdam. Mr Searle brought the diamond back from Amsterdam. I could telegraph Moeller & Kreiber, if you like; tell them to keep an eye open for it.'

'Yes. Do that, will you? ... What date did he bring it back?'

'The sixth of May. That was a Monday. He went over on the Sunday for it.'

'A nice little jaunt. But you mentioned Antwerp.'

'Yes ... I know that Mr Searle had a good connection with Moeller's, in Amsterdam. But, if it were left to me, I would have the cleavage of a stone like that carried out in Antwerp. The real experts are there, in my opinion.'

Bragg raised an eyebrow. 'But your opinion counted for nothing, eh?'

'Not exactly. And Mr Searle was the principal of the firm. He carried the ultimate responsibility.'

'If the lecture that we were treated to is any guide,' Morton said, 'Mr Searle regarded himself as a considerable expert in his own right.'

'Oh, indeed he was!' Ibbs replied. 'And, as I said, these things are matters of opinion.'

'What sort of mood had Mr Searle been in of late?' Bragg asked.

'Why, he had been in good spirits; particularly after he had seen the announcement of Mr Morton's engagement in *The Times*. He loved a special project, did Mr Searle. To be honest, he was not cut out for the humdrum side of commerce. I imagine the excitements of army life had not prepared him for the routine of shopkeeping. I suppose that explains a lot of things.'

Bragg frowned. 'Such as?' he asked.

'Well, in Mr Furlonger's time we dominated the wholesale market. We were bigger than anyone in Hatton Garden, in terms of both volume and value. Now we are of only moderate importance. We have not handled a stone comparable to the one stolen for years.'

'Are you saying Searle was taking a chance on Miss Marsden's wanting it?'

'Not exactly. The rough diamond was obtained on a sale or return basis. If Miss Marsden had not approved, it would have been taken back to Moeller's.'

Bragg turned to Morton. 'There you are, lad,' he said. 'Someone else thinks your young lady is special. All the same, it seems a bit risky. Two long journeys possibly; Searle known to be a diamond broker. Did he never think he might be tapped on the head, and the diamond stolen?'

Ibbs smiled. 'You forget that Mr Searle had been in the army,

41

and was still full of vigour! As to the value of the stone, we took out a special all-risks insurance policy with Lloyd's, through Burbank & Co., the brokers.'

'Do you usually do that?'

'For a particularly fine stone . . . Just a moment, I will get the certificate.' He disappeared into the room behind the glass partition, and they could see him searching in a box-file. In a few moments he was back.

'There you are.' He handed a flimsy cover-note to Bragg. 'It was for a period of one week, from the sixth of May.'

Bragg examined the document. 'This covers a stone up to a value of four thousand two hundred and fifty pounds,' he said.

'Yes. That would retail at five thousand pounds.'

'That is a hell of a profit,' Bragg exclaimed, 'for something that looks like a rough bit of glass! No wonder he pestered you, lad!' He turned to Ibbs. 'So, the business will recover the cost of the stone,' he said.

Ibbs nodded. 'Once we demonstrate that we have paid for it – which we shall have to do.'

'Hmm . . . What happens to the business now?' Bragg asked.

'It will be up to Mr Searle's executors, I suppose.'

'He would have made a will, then?'

'I am certain he would. He was a prudent man. No doubt his solicitors would be able to give you details.'

'I see. And who are his solicitors?'

'Gribble & Oddie, of Bedford Row – that is west of Gray's Inn.'

'I know it,' Bragg said curtly. 'Which partner did Searle deal with?'

'I believe it was Mr Vernon . . . Yes, I am sure it was he who drew up the will.'

Bragg and Morton made their way past Liverpool Street railway station, and into the area behind Spitalfields market. This was a district of mean houses and narrow streets; Jack the Ripper country. They walked down Hanbury Street. In the yard of number twenty-nine, the hideously mutilated body of Annie Chapman had been found. That was barely seven years ago. And no one had been charged with the Ripper murders. He could be walking along the street in front of them, Morton thought; hugging his guilty secret to himself.

They turned into Spelman Street, and made for the pawn-broker's shop kept by Foxy Jock McGregor. Three balls hung drunkenly from the corner of the building. They were so encrusted with dirt that no trace of brass gleamed through. The paint was peeling from the windows, and the panes were almost opaque with grime. Bragg pushed inside. At the jangle of the bell, a face peered out from a curtained alcove behind the counter. A fringe of yellowish-white hair surrounded a grimy bald head. The flaccid face was a mottled pink, threaded with purple veins converging on the nose. A pair of rheumy eyes regarded them.

'Ah, Sergeant Bragg,' he said in a hoarse Scottish voice. 'And Constable Morton . . . How nice to see you.'

'Cut out the shit, Jock,' Bragg said harshly. 'We are after a man who has abducted the newspaper reporter, Catherine Marsden.'

Jock looked at them warily and said nothing.

'He had already murdered John Searle, the diamond broker. So he is dangerous.'

'I read about that in the newspaper,' Jock said defensively.

'Are you sure it was only the newspaper? Or were you in it with him?'

'I'm an honest man, trying to scrape a living,' Jock said in an injured tone. 'Why would I have anything to do with murders, and young women?'

· 'Because you are the biggest bloody fence in the area. And because, after he'd killed Searle, he stole a valuable diamond from the shop.'

A flicker of interest crossed Jock's raddled features. 'A diamond?' he asked.

'Yes, but it was a rough diamond.'

'Uncut?'

'Yes.'

'Valuable, was it?'

'Five thousand pounds retail. Or so I'm told.'

Jock pursed his lips. 'No one is going to pledge that kind of diamond in Whitechapel,' he said. 'You would get a loan from a bank on it more cheaply.'

'Not if you have just thieved it, you wouldn't! If it comes your way, Jock, I want to know.'

Jock spread his hands deprecatingly. 'I have not got that kind of money to lend, even against such security. A hundred pounds is my limit.'

'Cut out the bullshit, Jock,' Bragg said angrily. 'All I want is to save the young woman. I don't care who ends up with the diamond.'

Jock sniffed. 'Well, Mr Bragg, if I hear anything, you can be sure I will let you know.'

'Right. And listen out for Miss Marsden's whereabouts too.'

Catherine was being dragged along a path; above her were dark menacing trees. Her heels were bouncing over the rough stones; her wrists were held in a fierce grip. She screamed, but knew that no one would hear her. The two women were implacable, demonic. She knew they were nearing a dreadful chasm, where they would hurl her into the blackness. She gave a last despairing shout . . . and woke up. Daylight. A strange room, an iron bedstead, bars at the window. For a moment it was reassuring; then the dire reality came to her. She was imprisoned; they were saying she was mad . . . She consciously emptied her mind of conjecture. Mechanically she got out of bed, and went to the wash-stand. There was a jug of cold water. She poured some of it into the basin and washed herself. She was Catherine Marsden, she told herself; a newspaper reporter; engaged to be married. She was as sane as anyone . . . It was all because of James's stupid whim to have a ring made especially for her . . . No, that was unfair. It was a delightful idea. It was something she would have enjoyed relating to her daughters and granddaughters. But it had gone horrifically wrong. She set herself to the routine of dressing. Her hair was tangled, and there was neither brush nor comb in the room. She must have left her handbag in the office . . . Or had she taken it to Furlonger's? Her mind shied away from the happenings there.

She went to the mirror over the wash-stand. Her familiar reflection peered out at her. It even managed a wry smile. She combed her hair as best she could with her fingers. If only her head were clearer, she would know what to do.

There was a rattle of keys at the door, and two nurses came in.

44

One of them placed a tray on the table. The other set about making the bed. Both of them ignored her.

'I should not be here,' Catherine said.

One of the nurses glanced briefly in her direction. 'Some nice breakfast there,' she said mechanically. 'Drink your tea, while it is hot.'

'But I do not take milk in tea!'

'We will remember next time.' She picked up the cup and brought it over to Catherine. 'Come on! Drink it.'

She pushed the cup against her mouth, trapping her lip against her teeth.

'There is no need to be so rough!' Catherine exclaimed.

'Not if you do as you are told . . . Drink it!'

Catherine sipped the tea, revolted by its sickly sweetness.

'Get it down you!'

Catherine took a deep breath and gulped it down.

'That's a good girl!' Apparently satisfied, the two nurses departed.

Catherine spread some jam on a piece of bread and butter, and took it to the window. There was no sun today. The houses beyond their gardens seemed grim and unappealing. She tried to work out what day it was . . . A man had been killed, because she wanted a stone for her engagement ring . . . No, that was not right, for she did not want it . . . And the man had been insistent and objectionable. James had been there. But another man had taken her from him . . . and brought her here. But why? She was feeling sleepy . . . No, not quite sleepy. Just fuzzy in her mind. Then she knew it was a dream, a nightmare she could not break out of. Any moment she would wake up in her own room at home; the maid would bring in tea, she would . . .

There was the rattle of a key in the lock, and a man came into the room. He was dressed in a white coat, and a stethoscope dangled from his neck. He locked the door behind him, then glanced at the clip-board he was carrying.

'I am the medical director, Miss Brown,' he said in a soothing tone. 'It is my duty to examine you, to ensure that any condition you may have is properly addressed.'

'I am perfectly well!' Catherine cried. 'I should not be here at all!'

'Indeed?' He placed his fingers on her wrist and took out his watch. After a pause he grunted. 'Your pulse is a trifle rapid,' he observed.

'Are you surprised, when I have been abducted and brought here against my will?'

'It is for your own good, Miss Brown.'

'I am not Miss Brown! My name is Catherine Marsden. I am a reporter on the *City Press* newspaper. Ask the editor!'

He raised his eyebrows. 'I see. And who is the editor?'

'He is Mr . . .' Suddenly Catherine's mind was a blank. Yet she knew it as well as her own. 'Mr . . .'

The doctor was looking at her with cool detachment.

'Anyway, my father is William Marsden, the painter. And we live in Park Lane . . . I can look out over Hyde Park from my bedroom . . . and I am engaged to be married to James Morton.'

'The cricketer?' he asked with a smile.

'Yes. We were choosing my engagement ring when all this happened.'

'I see.'

'A man came into the shop and shot the proprietor . . . and then he brought me here . . .'

'You have a very colourful imagination, Miss Brown,' he said. 'But that often serves as a refuge. There is no need to fight against it. I will see you again soon . . . And be sure to drink plenty of tea.'

Morton followed Bragg into the City mortuary in Golden Lane. It was a big windowless building, with a ridged glass roof. From the walls jutted grey slate slabs. Several of them bore white-swathed forms. Noaks, the mortuary attendant, jerked his thumb towards a door in the corner.

'Dr Burney is doing your man in the examination room,' he said.

They went into a room which was furnished as a laboratory. Under the window was a long bench, with instruments and specimen jars on it. In one corner was a glazed white sink and, next to it, a cabinet containing books and bottles. In the middle of the room was a slab; on it was the eviscerated body of John Searle.

46

Burney looked up as they entered, and his slack mouth grinned a ghoulish welcome. 'Ah, Sergeant Bragg, and young Morton too!' He held out a bloodstained hand, which the policemen ignored.

'Constable Morton was a witness of the murder,' Bragg said.

'So we know what happened.'

Burney's smile became sheepish. 'Then you remove a considerable element of my professional satisfaction, sergeant. Conjecture – informed conjecture – as to the events which caused death, is one of the few gratifications of the autoptic art.'

'I am sure you will have plenty to tell us, sir,' Bragg said contritely.

'I will do my best, sergeant.' He gestured towards the corpse. 'The bullet entered the left eye, shattering the ethnoid bone and lodging in the brain. I have the bullet somewhere ... Ah! Here it is.' He picked it out of an enamel kidney-dish and dropped it in Morton's palm. 'Death was virtually instantaneous, with little bleeding.'

'We were relying on you to tell us something we did not already know,' Bragg said peevishly.

Burney's smile sagged in reproach. 'I can only read what is in the book, sergeant,' he said. 'As to generalities, the subject has good muscular development. He obviously lived an athletic life. I would say that his general health was good; though there is some deterioration of the liver, which might have given him trouble later on.'

'He was an army officer for most of his life, sir.'

Burney beamed in satisfaction. 'That explains it,' he said. 'Do you see the scar above the left eyebrow? I was wondering where I had seen something similar. Now I remember. That is, beyond peradventure, a duelling scar – sabre, I shouldn't wonder. A cutting, not a thrusting weapon. Having said that, it will hardly assist your enquiries; it must be fifteen to twenty years old.'

Number three, Blomfield Street was a substantial three-storeyed house in a Georgian terrace. It was a stone's throw from the gardens in Finsbury Circus; an oasis of green at this time of year. Bragg hammered on the front door.

'Not a bad place to have, for a single man,' Bragg remarked darkly. 'You could bring up fifteen kids here!'

'It would certainly be convenient for the City,' Morton said. 'And it is entirely possible that it had been his family home. We have only the sketchy information given to us by Ibbs. Perhaps I ought to construct a family tree of the Furlongers and Searles.'

'If you must,' Bragg said ungraciously. 'I can see that you won't settle to anything till we get your young lady back.'

'I admit that my brain is thoroughly addled,' Morton said. 'Half the time I am hoping that Inspector Cotton will find her; the other half wishing that he would give the case back to us.'

'Well, the worst is past, if that is any comfort to you,' Bragg said cheerfully. 'If they were going to kill her, we would have found her body by now.'

Morton sighed. 'I wish I could think so,' he said.

'Of course you bloody can! Wake up! A keep off the grass notice would be no good when we had already trampled all over everywhere. To kill her now would only make doubly sure they would swing.' Bragg banged again on the knocker.

'You say "they",' Morton remarked.

'Well, there is the killer: and following him, Tommy Potts. There has to be a connection. In my book, there is no way two completely separate raids could be made, on one diamond broker out of a score, within half an hour of each other.'

There came the squeak of a hinge, and the door was opened a crack. An eye peered out.

'Police!' Bragg shouted. 'Open up!'

There was the rattle of a chain, and the door swung open.

'What do you want?' He was burly and middle-aged. He had a green apron over his shirt. A fragment of paper stuck to his chin, where he had cut himself while shaving.

'Mr Thompson?' Bragg asked.

'Yes,' he said gruffly.

'We are investigating the murder of your employer. May we come in?'

The man blinked, then turned without speaking. He led them up to a parlour on the first floor. To Morton the furnishings were of the last century. There was a large mahogany book-case, a buttoned leather settee, armchairs scattered around the red-patterned carpet.

48

'Did Mr Searle have family?' Bragg asked.

Thompson shook his head. 'Not that I know of,' he said. 'No one close.'

'Who will be making the arrangements?'

'For the funeral, you mean? I don't know. Maybe I should get on to the regiment.'

'We are told that his solicitors are Gribble & Oddie,' Bragg said. 'Perhaps they would know what he intended.'

A frown crossed Thompson's face. 'No,' he said irritably. 'He was a soldier, first and last. I've been with the major for twenty-five years. I know better than any solicitor what he would have wanted!'

Morton intervened to cool his rising anger. 'I come from a military family myself,' he said. 'My father is General Morton ... Life Guards ... In fact, we have just buried my brother; wounded in the Sudan.'

Thompson stared uncertainly at him.

'I had forgotten', Morton went on, 'that the Dragoon Guards had ordinary army ranks.'

'Yes, sir,' Thompson said. 'I was with Major Searle from the start. We joined the same month, in 1867 ... Real gentleman he was. I was his batman.'

'What kind of a man was he?' Morton asked.

'Very generous, I'll say that for him. If his luck was in at cards, he would think nothing of giving me a sovereign. "Blue that, Tommers," he would say. "I shall only lose it again." A real gentleman he was.'

'Soldiering in peacetime must seem rather unreal,' Morton remarked. 'You are training for war, with not an enemy in sight.'

Thompson shrugged and said nothing.

'Was he a good officer?' Morton asked.

'It depends what you mean, I suppose ... A bit of a daredevil, he was. The men would follow him anywhere ... But some of the other officers looked down on him.'

'How could that be?' Morton asked. 'He had been to Wellington College. One could not wish for a better pedigree as an army officer.'

Thompson sniffed. 'Most of them were from the landed gentry. I reckon it was because his father was a shopkeeper.'

'I imagine he could have bought and sold most of them,' Bragg said gruffly. 'Why do you think he resigned his commission when he did?'

'I dunno,' Thompson said guardedly. 'I expect he was let know that he'd got as far as he was going to.'

'Ambitious, was he?'

'Well, he couldn't bear to be beaten at anything . . . But I reckon his old man brought him back. The family business needed him – or so it was said.'

'Hmm . . .' Bragg pondered, then: 'Tell me about the scar,' he said.

'Which one are you talking about?'

'The one over his left eye . . . The pathologist reckoned it was a duelling scar.'

'Then he knows what he is about! . . . Over a woman, it was. Hell of a row . . . The other bloke had to be invalided out! The barmy thing was, she didn't give a toss about either of them!'

'So he liked the ladies? I wonder why he never married . . . Was he not concerned that there would be no one to follow him?'

Thompson pursed his lips. 'He used to say that he didn't care what happened, once he had cashed in his chips . . . But a bit ago he seemed to be taking things a bit more seriously. He said he would see I had enough to buy a nice little pub, to last me my days.'

'Why did he get to thinking like that?' Bragg asked in surprise. 'After all, you were much of an age.'

'I don't know. And I never asked him, in case he changed his mind.'

'Did he become ill, or anything?'

'No. Fit as a fiddle all his days.'

'Did he get across anyone?'

Thompson scratched his head. 'Not that I know of. He never said anything to me, that's for sure . . . Nah! He carried on as always, right to the end.'

'That sounds like a splendid epitaph,' Morton said. 'Are we to understand that he made a will recently?'

Thompson frowned. 'I dunno,' he said. 'I bloody hope so!'

Late that evening, Morton was shown into the drawing-room of Catherine's parents. Her mother was sitting by the empty grate, red-eyed; a handkerchief clutched in her hand. William Marsden was at the window, staring woodenly over Hyde Park. On hearing the door open, he turned.

'Have you any news, James?' he asked anxiously.

'Not precisely, sir,' Morton said. 'But Inspector Cotton has personally taken charge of the investigation into Catherine's abduction. There are advantages to that, since he has a good rapport with the Metropolitan police; and more resources himself than we have.'

'From my recollections of Catherine's chatter,' Mr Marsden said, 'I think that neither you nor Sergeant Bragg have much regard for Inspector Cotton's abilities.'

Morton managed a grin. 'Nothing more than professional jealousy, sir, I assure you.'

'Then I will leave you to decide whether to pass this over to him, or not.' He took a fold of paper from the mantelpiece and passed it over. Morton read it with a surge of alarm.

WE HAVE YOUR DAUGHTER
DO NOT LOOK FOR HER
ON PAIN OF DEATH

'Thank goodness you have heard something at last!' he said, trying to inject relief into his voice. 'It is all very theatrical. The writer has seen too many melodramas!'

'But she is in mortal danger!' Mrs Marsden broke in, her voice trembling.

'In no more danger than before you received this,' Morton said quietly. 'In fact, I regard it as a favourable sign. Catherine is clearly still alive. I cannot see any circumstance arising hereafter which would cause them to harm her.'

William Marsden frowned. 'I would have thought that they were making the circumstance very explicit,' he said.

'Yes . . . And yet I would have expected a demand for ransom. But there is none.'

'Does that improve matters?'

'In a sense it does. One has to wonder why she was taken at all. If it was merely to cover the thief's retreat, then that purpose has surely been served by now.'

He folded the message and slipped it into his pocket-book. 'Be

51

cheerful,' he said. 'I am sure that she will be back home before long.'

3

Bragg pushed away the ledger, and began to fill his pipe. In front of the desk he had commandeered were the railings to which Morton had handcuffed himself. The thought came back in his mind that the raider had known he was a policeman. Yet Morton had not recognised the killer – and he had had plenty of time to have a good look at him. Had the murderer known that Morton was a policeman because he already knew he would be there? The way Morton told it, the gunman was clear about his purpose. Yet surely, any raider would avoid making his move while a copper was on the premises ... But, then, the rough diamond would only be out of the strong-room for the few minutes that Morton and Miss Marsden were in the shop.

Somebody in the know, then. Had Searle been indiscreet? Put it about that he was creating an engagement ring on behalf of England's batsman hero of the moment? Supplying jewellery was no different from any other trade, despite their bowing and scraping, their toffee-nosed accents ... A stone worth four-and-a-quarter thousand pounds to the trade. Nick it, then sell it as if it were your normal stock. No entries in the books; slip the lolly in your back pocket. Easy! Retire and put your feet up. Not that the word need have come from anybody connected with Searle. This was an international trade. But if the Amsterdam dealers were behind it, how could they have known when the rough diamond would emerge from Searle's strong-room?

Bragg sighed. He was beginning to over-complicate matters, he thought. If the Dutch were involved, it would have been far easier to bash Searle one while he was still in Amsterdam; tip his body into one of their canals. Once the stone had reached England, it was likely to be a home-grown villain ... or more than one! Tommy Potts hadn't been for asking the price of a diamond bracelet when he showed up. But he had been too late to swipe it ... Which brought Bragg round in a circle. Nobody aware of his reputation would trust Tommy with a job like this.

Bragg looked through the glass screen into the shop. Ibbs seemed to be haggling, in a decorous sort of way, with a customer. It was almost as if they were playing a board-game; moving glittering jewels about the baize square on the counter. And the portrait of old Thomas Furlonger looked down his great nose at the proceedings. Finally the deal was done, the customer signed a receipt, pocketed the jewels and strode out. Bragg saw a burly bodyguard join him as he walked briskly away. He got up from the desk and went into the shop.

'I would like you to close up for a bit,' he said. 'There are one or two things I want to ask you about.'

Ibbs glanced towards the front of the shop and, apparently having received permission from old Furlonger, nodded assent.

Bragg strolled into the back office and pulled out his pipe. It might help him concentrate. He was well out of his depth here . . . But he shoved it back in his pocket. This wasn't a place for a pipe – not even with this poncey shag . . . On one wall of the room was a wooden plaque in the shape of a shield, quartered with two golden covered cups and two lions' heads.

'What is that?' he asked as Ibbs came in.

'The arms of the Worshipful Company of Goldsmiths,' Ibbs said. 'Mr Searle was a member. But in his day, his father was on the Court of Assistants.'

'And Tommy the nose?'

Ibbs looked at him reproachfully. 'Mr Furlonger reached the office of Second Warden,' he said.

'That made him a big cheese, did it?'

'Indeed! He was second only to the Prime Warden.'

'I think I could have just about worked that out for myself, sir . . . And what did John Searle become?'

'He was just an ordinary liveryman.'

'I see . . . And that was good for trade, was it? I would have thought he should go for the jewellers' guild, or the diamond-mongers'!'

Ibbs frowned. 'There are no such companies – as I am sure you are well aware.'

'So the few bits of silverware and such, in the far window, made him a trader in gold and silver, did they?'

53

'They serve their purpose.' Ibbs seemed disinclined to elaborate.

'Right,' Bragg said. 'I have been going through the business books. So perhaps you can help me over one or two things.'

'I have never had anything to do with the books,' Ibbs protested. 'Mr Searle kept all that side to himself.'

Bragg raised his eyebrows. 'Then you are guilty of a grave dereliction of duty ... Or did you not know that you are down here as a one-eighth partner?'

'Of course I knew!' Ibbs said impatiently. 'But my place was in the shop. I never troubled myself about the books. That was Mr Searle's domain.'

'As well as all the big deals, and all the important clients ... But you were content to dogsbody around, were you?' Bragg said contemptuously. 'As long as you could tell your wife you had a partnership.'

'My wife is fully aware of my position here. Indeed, she has, on several occasions, acted as hostess at our Christmas receptions for clients.'

'And who was it made you a partner? Old Alfred Searle?'

'No. Mr John gave me my partnership in 1888.'

'Ah, yes. I remember ... Did you know that he insured your life for two thousand pounds recently?'

Ibbs frowned. 'I do not understand,' he said.

'Well, let's be more precise, shall we. The firm Furlonger & Searle entered into a policy with the Commercial Marine Insurance Company on the third of May. In the event of your death, the firm would receive the two thousand pounds.'

Ibbs gave a puzzled smile. 'I didn't know my services were appreciated to that extent,' he said. 'Perhaps he ought to have taken out a policy on his own life as well.'

'Oh, your services were appreciated, all right. You didn't have to pay anything for your little slice of the business either!'

'That is true. But Mr Searle said he could not manage without me. He referred to it as my golden shackle.'

'So you have done well here?'

'Well enough to move out of Clapham into a nice little house in Islington.'

Bragg sniffed. 'And that is progress, is it?'

'In my book it is.'

'Right . . .' Bragg made a brief jotting, then: 'Do you know anything about the history of the business?' he asked. 'I mean, it seems to have been here for generations.'

'Whatever I could tell you would hardly be reliable – at least for the years before I came here. I suggest that you ask Drewin & Co., our accountants. Mr Drewin was the senior partner then. He is long retired, but has all his faculties. He would enjoy talking to you about the old days, and how Mr Furlonger used to carry on!'

'You reckon he would have some notion as to why the business is going downhill?'

Ibbs looked up in astonishment. 'Downhill?' he exclaimed.

'In turnover and in net profit,' Bragg said. 'You are a partner. You ought to know.'

'I . . . I did not trouble myself about profitability. That was Mr Searle's province . . . And I did not feel my position was strong enough to sustain enquiries.'

'And what did you feel about the disparity in drawings?'

'Disparity? But of course there was disparity! I had only one eighth of the business; he had seven times more than I did.'

'Yes. He was taking his share of the profits, as you say. But if you look in the books, you will see there is an account there in Searle's name, which is headed "Capital Account". What is that all about?'

Ibbs frowned. 'I think I remember,' he said. 'The business was valued on the day before I was brought in. It seemed perfectly fair. All that value had to be ascribed to Mr Searle. I brought no money into the business whatsoever.'

'Maybe. But Searle has been drawing thousands of pounds against the capital account over the last few years. And money drawn out isn't going into stock. That is why the business is in decline . . . Have you any idea why he would draw out such sums?'

Ibbs shrugged. 'I have not the faintest idea,' he said.

Bragg leaned back in his chair. 'Well, that's over,' he said with a smile. 'Sorry to give you such a hard time, but it has to be done.'

'I understand that, sergeant.'

'Particularly as you have been a good friend of ours in the past. It was you who tipped us off about the raid on Saqui's shop in Bishopsgate, wasn't it?'

'That is true. We jewellers keep our ear to the ground; it is not only the police who have underworld informers.'

'But surely, if one business was cleaned out, the others could only benefit?'

Ibbs smiled. 'Perhaps. But we have to consider the reputation of the City as a whole. After all, the most vulnerable people are our customers; the men who actually walk through the street with gems in their pockets. If they did not feel safe on our streets, they could easily go elsewhere.'

'But you did not get even a whisper of this raid?'

'No, sergeant. And you can assume that no one else did, either.'

'Right . . .' Bragg pondered for a moment, then: 'This Hurford correspondence,' he said. 'Everybody seems to have been getting hot under the collar. I cannot see what the fuss is about.'

Ibbs frowned. 'I knew there was some dispute, of course. But that was Mr Searle's province.'

'Hmm . . . Let me get it straight. You are diamond brokers, the first link in the chain, as it were. Yet here you are, selling to Hurford, who runs a retail shop in Tunbridge Wells.'

Ibbs smiled. 'There is no rigid demarcation of function,' he said. 'Our main activity is to buy parcels of gemstones – generally from Dutch brokers – and make them available to smaller wholesalers throughout this country. In London the situation is more fluid. Small manufacturers can come direct to us, to select their stones. And, as you will all too well appreciate, occasionally a valued client, such as your Mr Morton, will come straight to us for a gem.'

'Yes,' Bragg said grimly. 'And all we do is go round in bloody circles.'

Morton pounded along Cheapside, and turned into St Martin's le Grand. He had been marching around the City for two days, as if the animal energy expended would somehow bring success of itself. Not that it had been aimless. He had divided the City into sections, and dealt with each in turn. He had reasoned that Catherine could not have been taken far on foot, without its being obvious to passers-by that she was under duress. So he had visited each cab-rank in turn. He must have recited his litany scores of times . . . early twenties, longish nose, hazel eyes, brown hair, taller than average ... The drivers had listened, world-weary. No, they had not seen her. Yes, they would pass the word. But the drivers did not operate from fixed points. When they set down a fare, they would go to the nearest cab-rank if no one waved them down on the street ... And young women went missing every day.

He went towards the cabbies' shelter opposite the post office. This was the last on his list, if he drew a blank here, his systematic search was at an end. All he could do then was to wander around the streets asking the same dreary questions. He wondered what Inspector Cotton was doing. He was afraid to ask at the station. Cotton was such an aggressive, petulant man that any questions might cause him to terminate the search out of hand ... That at least would set Bragg free to probe himself. Yet the sergeant seemed certain that Catherine would have been taken outside the City boundary – and Cotton was the liaison officer with the Met.

There were several hansoms pulled up by the shelter, their horses nuzzling in their nosebags. The air inside the shelter was thick with pipe-smoke.

'City police,' he said. 'We are looking for a young woman.'

'This the one kidnapped on Wednesday?' one of the men asked. 'Long nose, tall, brown hair?'

Morton's heart leapt. 'Yes, yes it is!' he cried. 'Where did you see her?'

The man sniffed. 'I didn't, mate. Only this is the third time I've 'eard you ask the same bleedin' question.'

'But it is vitally important!' Morton said angrily.

'Yer. And this is Friday afternoon. I seen scores of women, hundreds of 'em since Wednesday. You can spend all your bleedin' time looking for her – even if she don't want to be found. My job is to take people where they want to go, and not be nosy about who they are with.'

Morton felt all the hope, all the optimism drain out of him. The faces around were uninterested, even hostile. It was useless to press them, even plead with them. The relationship between cab drivers and the police was tenuous at best. Every day brought wrangles between the cabby and the constable on the beat trying to keep the traffic moving. They had co-operated for two days; now life had moved on.

'Well, if you do see her . . .' he said, then went dispiritedly out into the street.

'Mr Renfrew will see you now, sir.'

She was a pretty young thing, Bragg thought. Too good to be spending her time in the dusty office of Burbank & Co. She ought to be out in God's good air; bring a bloom to her cheeks . . . But she would have her sights set on marrying a City gent; who would keep her in comfort while he played around with a mistress. What a bloody world!

She showed him into a first-floor office, with a view down the river to Tower Bridge. A man in his late thirties rose as he entered. He was carefully dressed in black frock coat and checked grey waistcoat. A pearl pin nestled in his grey silk tie.

'Sergeant Bragg?' He held out his hand. 'I do not believe that I have had the privilege of meeting you.'

'No, you haven't, sir. And all I have come for is information.'

Renfrew smiled in simulated relief. 'Then we can both relax!'

Bragg sat down heavily. 'I am out of my depth in insurance matters, as you can well imagine,' he said.

'Most people are, sergeant. Which is the very reason for our existence. Is it a particular problem you wish to raise?'

'Yes . . . Not that I am saying you dealt with the matter. It was probably run-of-the-mill to your firm. I doubt if you even know about it . . . I am investigating the murder of John Searle, the diamond broker.'

Renfrew's face clouded. 'Ah, yes. A great loss to the City,' he said.

'He was one of your clients, I believe.'

'Yes indeed!'

'Now, he took out an all-risks policy recently.'

'Do I need to get our papers, sergeant? I cannot recall the transaction myself. It was probably dealt with by a clerk.'

'Not for the moment, sir. I would like to get the principle clear in my mind. The situation is this. Searle had a client that was in the market for something special in the way of engagement rings.'

'Ah! Jim Morton! I remember now, Searle mentioned it to me at the club. Presumably that was the diamond stolen in the raid.'

58

Bragg frowned. 'Yes. But let's not get ahead of ourselves. What happened was this. Morton had promised that Searle could find the stone for his fiancée's engagement ring. That was ages ago. But Morton, being a gentleman, had to keep his word ... Not that Searle waited for him to trot along to his shop. As soon as the engagement was announced in *The Times*, he sends a letter to Morton reminding him ... I am not faulting him for that. Business is business; and Morton has more money than is good for any man. Anyway, this letter from Searle was sent on the twenty-ninth of April. Now, because of a family funeral, Morton did not get it until the first of May. He wrote back, saying that he would bring his fiancée in a week later; Wednesday the eighth. Are you with me so far?'

'Yes.'

'Right. Now, Searle got this letter on Thursday, the second of May. He obviously had a clear intention in his mind – to talk Morton into buying the biggest rough diamond he could lay his hands on. He was going to fix Miss Marsden up not only with a stone for her engagement ring, but a couple of ear-rings as well ... Don't get me wrong, I am not complaining about that, Searle was a businessman, and I am not for a moment suggesting that anything he did was wrong.'

Renfrew smiled. 'I am relieved to hear it,' he said.

'Well, now, Searle came to your office on Thursday the second of May. At that point, he obviously had no clear idea of what he would be buying – or, indeed whether Morton would fall in with his plan. And he didn't want to be stuck with a very expensive rough diamond, if Miss Marsden took against it. So what he decided to do was bring back the gem on a sale or return basis. That way, he would only have lost the price of his fares to Amsterdam. Follow me?'

Renfrew gave a tolerant smile. 'Perfectly, sergeant,' he said.

'Right. And, because he was a prudent man, he took out a transit insurance policy, through your firm, with Lloyd's. If Miss Marsden gave it the thumbs down, the gem would be covered from the time it left Amsterdam to the time it got back again.'

Renfrew pressed an electric bell on his desk. 'That is something which would depend on the precise wording of the policy,' he said. 'Perhaps we ought to clarify the point before we go further.'

The door opened quietly, and the young typewriter came in.

'Miss Leighton, would you get me the Furlonger & Searle file – the current one?'

She smiled, lighting up the fussy office. 'Yes, Mr Renfrew.' She skipped out again.

'Nice to see young women in offices,' Bragg said genially.

'What? ... Ah, yes. Tell me ... They say Searle was shot through the head.'

'Indeed he was, sir.'

'A shocking thing to happen in the City, in all conscience. But in broad daylight, in one of the most prestigious streets of the capital ... it beggars belief!'

'Some would say it was a reckless enterprise, sir. But it paid off ... and Lloyd's will be the poorer by five thousand pounds.'

Renfrew shrugged. 'That is exactly the point that I seek to clarify.'

The door opened and the young woman came in again. She placed a folder on the desk before Renfrew, smiled and slipped out again.

Renfrew opened the file. 'Here we are,' he said. 'Ah, yes ... As you say, Mr Searle was by no means confident of disposing of the gem to Mr Morton. The insurance cover under this policy was for a specific period, from Monday the sixth of May to Monday the thirteenth, that would have covered a journey back to Amsterdam, if Mr Morton had not been disposed to buy.'

'I see. So it was not just for the train and boat journeys.'

'No, sergeant. If the jewel was lost or stolen, between noon on those dates, a claim would lie under the policy.'

'I see ... Well, Searle's executors will be pleased, anyway.'

'Of course,' Renfrew said, 'there will probably be an interaction with the main insurance policy on the premises. We do not handle that. I understand the landlord prescribed that such insurance should be placed with a nominated insurance company.'

Bragg looked up in surprise. 'Can they do that, sir?' he asked.

'Indeed! To an extent it is understandable. The owner is entitled to ensure that his premises are fully insured; and what better way? And I expect that he gets a commission as an inducement.'

Bragg sighed. 'This case seems to be about as tangled as it can be,' he said.

'Yet the principles are clear enough. Under the policies, the true owner of the diamond will be recompensed. If a risk is covered by more than one policy, then the various insurers will bear the loss proportionately.'

'So what will happen now?'

'I will take this interview as being a formal notification of the loss of the diamond. We will make a claim against the Lloyd's syndicates involved. Someone should explore the cover under the premises policy. If Ibbs will give me the details I will pursue it on behalf of the executors ... We will see that everyone is put in the position they were in prior to the robbery. Except the insurers, that is!'

Bragg snorted. 'And some murderous thug who has a diamond worth a fortune in his pocket.'

Having been rebuffed by the cab drivers, Morton wondered what avenues there were left to explore. Catherine could not have been forced to walk far, without someone's suspicions being aroused. It had been the middle of the afternoon. There had been people around ... So a hansom cab would not serve. The passengers were exposed to the elements; Catherine could have been recognised, have cried out for help. No. If there had been planning behind the raid, and if her abduction had been intended, there would have been a four-wheeler waiting nearby. There were plenty of growlers on the streets; though nothing like the number of hansoms. Yet his enquiries had been made of cab drivers in general, not of hansoms only. And the message he had received was that Catherine had not been seen, and they were tired of looking for her ... Then a thought struck him. How stupid he was! It was possible to hire a carriage. Wealthy families coming up for the Season would hire one by the month – complete with driver ... And discretion was of the essence in that trade. But surely it would not be maintained in the face of police enquiries.

He took a cab to Piccadilly, and soon found the office of John H. Sadler, in Swallow Street. He stood by the door, while a flustered clerk tried to satisfy the demands of a portly American. Instead of taking a carriage for a month, he was intent on arranging a series of daily hirings over the period. Eventually they reached stalemate.

'Is there anywhere else in this benighted city where a man may get what he wants, instead of what the tradesman wants?' the customer demanded.

'There is only Newman's, in Regent Street,' the clerk murmured.

'Right!' The man glared at the clerk, then at Morton, and stamped out of the office.

The clerk shrugged apologetically at Morton. 'These Americans,' he said. 'And what can I do for you, sir?'

'Police.' Morton showed him his warrant-card. 'A young lady has been abducted from premises in the City. She was taken, at gunpoint, by a man who had just committed a murder. He had also stolen a valuable diamond.'

'Goodness me!'

'We have interviewed all the cab drivers; but none of them picked up a fare answering to their description. So we begin to wonder if the vehicle was hired.'

'It could have been a private carriage,' the clerk said. 'There are still a few families that keep their own ... Not that they would be likely to go around abducting young ladies, and stealing diamonds.'

'Exactly. Which is why I have come to you.'

'When did this ... this incident take place?' the clerk asked.

'On the afternoon of Wednesday the eighth.'

'Two days ago?'

'Yes ... I suppose it must be. It seems longer.'

The clerk flipped back through his ledger, scrutinising the pages. He sucked in his breath through his teeth. 'No,' he said. 'It is the beginning of the Season, you see. And that was the day of Lady Campbell's garden party, in Richmond. All our carriages had been booked for weeks ... and to reputable customers. I am sorry.'

Morton looked at the man's earnest face, and his heart sank. 'Is there anyone else I could try?' he asked.

The man pursed his lips. 'If it is carriages you are looking for, there really is only Newman's ... But I expect they would be no different from us.'

*

Catherine picked up the bible from the top of her chest of drawers, and opened it at random. The print swayed before her eyes, now clear, now dim. She blinked rapidly ... it made little difference. Anyway, her brain was so befuddled she could not tell what it was about. She tried to concentrate ... 'And Gideon had three score and ten sons ...' the print faded into a grey haze again. Why was this happening to her? All she had done was to get engaged ... The thought formed in her mind that Lady Morton was behind it. She had not wanted her at the funeral. She did not want James to marry her ... But that would not make her brain fuzzy ... She did not feel ill; her brow was not hot. Was her mind going? She had seen a man shot; but it was not James ... James had gone to the back of the shop; had left her ... A man had taken her in a carriage. She remembered climbing flights of stairs to this room ... Pitiless faces mouthing at her; urging her to drink her tea. Why place so much stress on the tea? It was so milky and sweet she could not taste ... She tried to focus her mind. The sweetness was not to prevent her from tasting the tea, but something else ... Something they had put in the tea, which was making her feel giddy and fuddled. She went over to the wash-stand, and splashed some cold water on her face. They were doing this to her, and she must stop them ... She poured some water from the carafe into a glass and sipped. It tasted just as it would at home.

There was the rattle of a key in the lock. A nurse came in with a tray. She placed a plate of sandwiches on the table, and a cup of tea.

'I have told you I do not take milk in tea,' Catherine said peevishly.

The woman decided to humour her. 'All right, love,' she said. 'There's no reason in the world why you should.'

She took the cup out into the corridor, and Catherine heard the rattle of crockery. She dimly realised that the door had been left open. She ought to try to escape; get away from this dreadful place. She got to her feet ... But the nurse was already coming back.

'Drink it down while it is hot,' she admonished, placing the cup on the table.

Catherine picked it up in her two hands and put it to her lips. Satisfied, the nurse bustled out and locked the door behind her.

Catherine waited, listening, for a time. Then she got to her feet, picked up the cup and emptied it into the commode. From now on she would drink nothing but water.

Morton wasted another hour in confirming the prediction of Sadler's clerk. Lady Campbell's garden party must indeed be one of the high points of the Season. All Newman's carriages had been booked, in advance, for the afternoon of Catherine's abduction. No doubt there would be small concerns in the area around the City that might have a vehicle suitable for the kidnapper's purpose. But it would take an army of men to comb the whole area. And even a hint of a search would bring down Cotton's wrath upon them. They would have to rely on his vaunted rapport with the Met. Determined to achieve something, Morton walked to South Audley Street, and went into the showroom of Purdey & Sons, the gunsmiths. The immaculately dressed manager greeted him deferentially, then a smile of recognition lit up his face.

'Why, Mr Morton! What a pleasure it is to see you!' he said effusively. 'So you have changed your mind!'

Morton laughed. 'You are miles ahead of me in this conversation,' he said. 'I am hardly aware, at the moment, that I have a mind to make up!'

'Your father was going to present you with a pair of shotguns on your twenty-first birthday. We were straining at the leash to make them for you. But, for some inexplicable reason, you turned against the project.'

'I am sorry! The truth of it is that I get little or no pleasure from blasting driven birds out of the sky. A pair of your superlative guns would be wasted on me.'

The man laughed. 'We would happily put the matter to the test,' he said.

'No. Police detection and cricket give me all the excitement and satisfaction I need.'

'As a member of the Surrey club, I ought to do all in my power to induce you to give up cricket,' the manager said ruefully. 'That century for Kent, at the Oval last season, absolutely had us on the rack.'

Morton smiled. 'Ah, well. It is only a game . . . But I would like to pick your brains on a matter within your own sphere.' He took from his pocket the bullet that Burney had removed from Searle's body, and dropped it on the counter. 'This was fired in a raid on a jeweller's showroom,' he said. 'It was extracted from the head of the murdered man. I wonder if you can tell me anything about it.'

The manager took the bullet from Morton's palm and examined it. Then he beckoned Morton to follow him into a workshop at the rear. He went over to a microscope.

'Can you tell me anything about the incident?' he asked.

'I was in the shop at the time,' Morton said. 'As a customer, not as a policeman. The gunman burst into the shop and shot the proprietor at close range.'

'Ah! I seem to remember reading something about it.' He peered into the microscope. 'There is a certain amount of distortion,' he said.

'It struck the victim's eye, then passed through a bony structure with a distinctly unmemorable name, and came to rest in the brain. I was hoping that you could tell me something about the weapon it was fired from.'

'Hmm . . .' The man took another look, then straightened up. 'We are, of course, not manufacturers of revolvers. If it came to a question of expert evidence in court, you would have to go to someone like Webley, in Birmingham.'

'I appreciate that,' Morton said.

The man picked up a pair of calipers and took a measurement. 'You are looking for a gun of ·32 calibre,' he said. 'Possibly – even probably – a Webley revolver. From the clear impression left by the rifling of the barrel, the weapon is fairly new – or has been but little used. Certainly I can see nothing which one might contend was unique to this particular weapon. And they were produced by the thousand for the military.'

Morton had a snack in a pub, then hurried back to Old Jewry. He hoped against hope that the desk sergeant would wave him over, shout that Catherine was safe. But all he got was a sympathetic half-glance. Bragg was sitting in his shirt-sleeves when he entered the room, the air blue with pipe-smoke.

'Any luck, lad?' he asked, without looking up from his desk.

'No, sir. The carriage which we postulate must have taken Catherine away appears to have been obtained from outside the West End and the City.'

'So we have no leads, then?'

'None,' Morton said dispiritedly.

Bragg stood up. 'Right!' he said briskly. 'Then let us tug at another loose end, and see what happens.'

They took a cab to the Gresham Club. They were kept waiting in the marble entrance hall for a good twenty minutes before they were ushered down a corridor to the side of the building. Their guide opened a door, and they found themselves in a small shabby office. A balding man with an unhealthy pallor rose from his desk.

'Have a good lunch, did you, sir?' Bragg asked disagreeably.

The man looked nonplussed. 'I, er ... I understand that you wish to see me,' he said tentatively.

'Do I take it that you are Mr White, the secretary of this club?'

'Yes ... Yes, I am he.'

'And what do you have to do to become a member of this place? Just fork out a hundred quid, and stick up for the others?'

White looked bewildered. 'Well ... there is a membership fee, of course. We could not function otherwise. We aim to provide a civilised oasis, where people can meet to socialise, perhaps discuss a little business in a relaxed atmosphere ...'

'People being men, I suppose, not women.'

'Indeed, sergeant.' He gave a thin smile. 'Fortunately the feminists are only concerned to demand rights, not to demean themselves with commerce.'

Bragg paused, then: 'One of your members was John Searle; and he's dead,' he said abruptly.

'Indeed ... I read about his quite dreadful end. But I do not see why the supposed guardians of the City's peace should come to me.'

Bragg grunted. 'To be honest with you, sir,' he said in a reasonable tone, 'we are having a hard time finding anyone who knew him well.'

'I see ... I am afraid that I do not come into that category either.'

'Hmm ... What is your impression of him as a man?' Bragg asked.

'Well, he was not involved in City politics. So, in a sense, what you saw is what you got.'

'And that was?'

'Amiable, a man of his word, financially sound, honourable in all his dealings.'

Bragg snorted. 'You make him out to be a paragon,' he said.

White shrugged. '*De mortuis*,' he said.

'But somebody hated him enough to murder him.'

'As I understood from the newspapers, it was just a random underworld killing,' White said emphatically. 'Whatever occurred can have no possible connection with this club, or its members. Now I will bid you good-day. I have work to do!'

'A fiery little man,' Bragg observed, as they reached the street. 'Do you think he was holding something back?'

Morton shrugged. 'I doubt it,' he said.

'What was this *de mortuis* business?'

'It is the beginning of a Latin tag: *De mortuis nil nisi bonum*.'

'Meaning?'

'One ought to say nothing but good of the dead.'

'Then he was letting us know he was concealing something?'

'I cannot believe', Morton said, 'that anyone would withhold evidence bearing on a murder under that principle – if one can call it that. After all, if he were doing so, he would hardly proclaim the fact.'

'Hmm ... well, we drew a blank there, lad, and no mistake. And we would do the same, with knobs on, at the Naval & Military Club. So I reckon you should go home; get yourself a sleeping draught, or down a bottle of whisky. Try and knock yourself out for a night.'

Morton gave a weary smile. 'I will do something of the kind,' he said. 'But first I must write to my parents. As yet they are unaware of what has happened.'

Bragg took a hansom to the offices of Drewin & Co., and was shown into the room of the senior partner. He stood up as Bragg entered.

'My name is Templeton,' he said. 'I understand that you are making enquiries concerning Furlonger & Searle.'

'That's right, sir.' Bragg took the proffered chair.

'A terrible tragedy,' Templeton said. 'One is not safe from desperadoes, even in the City!'

'True, sir,' Bragg said evenly. 'But we will catch him.'

'That is not what is being said at large,' Templeton observed. 'It is rumoured that one of your men was actually on the premises at the time!'

'We don't concern ourselves with rumours, sir,' Bragg said stolidly. 'But my purpose in coming here is to clarify a few facts about the business.'

Templeton nodded. 'Of course, sergeant. But I have to say that I only took over that particular audit three years ago, when the previous senior partner retired.'

'That would be Mr Drewin, would it, sir?'

'Yes, sergeant.'

'I see . . . Tell me, sir; would you say that the business is sound?'

Templeton frowned. 'I have never had cause to doubt the solvency of Furlonger & Searle, if that is what you mean.'

'Not quite. You see, sir, I have been having a look at the books. Now, I know I am not an accountant or anything. It is as much as I can manage to get my pay to stretch to the end of the month. But from what I could make out, that business has been in decline for years now.'

The accountant shrugged. 'I have not done any analysis of the years before I took over, of course. But it would hardly surprise me if what you have just said is true.'

'Why is that, sir?'

'Well . . . The business is concerned in the supply of gems to the manufacturing side of the jewellery trade. I suppose, over the years, competition within Europe has increased; while markets overseas have dwindled. Even our colonies are acquiring the capacity to process jewellery themselves.'

'You mean places like Canada and Australia?'

'Exactly . . . And, at the same time, the jewellery market within Britain itself is in the doldrums.'

'Why is that, sir?' Bragg asked in surprise.

Templeton shrugged. 'We are in what one might call a transitional situation which resolutely refuses to move.'

'Sounds like a contradiction, sir.'

'Yes, sergeant . . . You must understand that no one actually needs jewels. Almost perversely, they have become a useful repository of value. And, when skilfully cut and polished, they have been accepted as the supreme adornment of beauty. The finest stones are inevitably acquired by the wealthiest men in society. And, almost as inevitably, they are desired by the most beautiful women. In normal times, both wealth and beauty are attracted to the royal court. There is constant competition to be distinctive, to outdo one's peers. So there is a continuing demand for new jewellery to assert one's ascendancy or confirm one's dominance.'

Bragg laughed. 'If you say so, sir!'

'Well, that is the general principle, anyway. But what has England as a focal point in its society? A court that has been in mourning since the death of Prince Albert in 1861. A Queen who has become a recluse . . . And the raffish set which surround the Prince of Wales are more concerned with pleasure than display. It is hardly surprising that the jewellery trade is in the doldrums!'

Bragg smiled. 'So, you are saying that every single jeweller is praying that the old Queen would die?'

'Put like that, it is nothing short of sedition,' Templeton said. 'Yet it is uncomfortably close to the truth.'

'Hmm . . . But I suppose Searle had plenty of money outside the business?'

'We do not deal with his personal affairs. Indeed, he has always completed his own return of income for tax purposes. However, it is safe to say that he had considerable personal resources. You will have seen his withdrawals from his capital account. It would require considerable dedication to get through that kind of money!'

'Yes . . . Mr Ibbs, the junior partner in Furlonger & Searle, said that your Mr Drewin would be happy to talk over old times with us.'

'What a good idea! And, since the suggestion came from the remaining principal in the firm, it must be unexceptionable. I will jot down his address for you.'

When Morton got back to Old Jewry, he went straight upstairs and knocked on the door of Inspector Cotton's room. The inspector looked up as he entered.

'Well?' he asked curtly.

'I would like to know what progress is being made in the search for Catherine Marsden, sir.'

Cotton's lip curled in dislike. 'Enquiries are proceeding, constable,' he said.

'But what is being done?' Morton exclaimed. 'It is now two days since she was abducted!'

'So?'

'So she must have been taken away in a carriage of some kind. That carriage must have been hired from outside the City. It should be possible to find out who hired it!'

Cotton leaned back in his chair. 'I doubt if I could persuade the Met to mount such a search,' he said complacently. 'They would say they had better uses for their manpower.'

'Then let me go to see them!'

'In what capacity, lad? As an England cricketer and part-time policeman?'

'I am engaged to be married to her!' Morton protested.

'That does not give you any status. Only her next-of-kin matter in this, as you well know. I have satisfied myself that she is unlikely to be within the City itself. So we are in the hands of the Met. All we are responsible for is investigating the murder and the robbery.'

'But the abduction took place within the City! We are entitled to make enquiries anywhere!'

'Use your bloody head, man! The Met know their own territory. They have their own squealers. The word will be out. If we go blundering in, we shall only cock things up. And we shall get bugger all co-operation from them in future. So just sod off, and leave me to get on with it!'

Morton banged out of the police headquarters in frustration and fury. He strode heedlessly along the streets, his mind in a turmoil. He had been betrayed by the very force to which his allegiance was bound. Inspector Cotton had taken a perverse delight in thwarting him . . . And it could not go on! He stopped on the corner of Gresham Street and tried to calm the turmoil of his thoughts. Whatever he felt, he must be circumspect. If he openly defied him, the inspector was quite capable of calling off the search for Catherine; telling the Met that the case was being closed. On the other hand, Sergeant Bragg would support him as far as he was able. And they were working under the aegis of the Commissioner, so far as the murder of Searle was concerned; the theft of the diamond also. If they succeeded in finding the diamond, they could well find Catherine. He was certainly not going to be cowed by Inspector Cotton into doing nothing.

He walked on. He knew that Sergeant Bragg would go to the limits of his authority, and beyond, to find Catherine. Yet, surely there was something that could be done outside the constraints of officialdom ... Something any citizen was entitled to do ... He came to the junction with Aldersgate Street. A little way along it, on the right, were the offices of the *City Press*. Catherine ought to be there at this very moment, finalising her copy for the Saturday edition ... It was remiss of him not to have called on Mr Tranter, the editor; he should not have been left dangling. At least, that was something he could put right.

He hurried to the newspaper's office, and asked to see the editor's secretary. He waited at the counter for some minutes; then a plump young woman approached. On seeing him she checked, putting her hand to her breast.

'Oh, Mr Morton!' she gasped, her eyes filling with tears. 'Whatever can have happened to Catherine?'

'I wish I knew,' he said quietly. 'Is Mr Tranter in?'

'Of course. He was so upset ... He got us all together – us girls, that is – the day after it happened. He told us it must be an isolated occurrence. That we should not go thinking it could happen to us ... But I tell you, every morning I go for the train I wonder if I shall be coming back again.'

'I do not think that you are in the slightest danger,' Morton said soberly. 'She was taken as a hostage, to allow a murderer to escape.'

'But it is two days now! Why has he not let her go?'

'Those words go round and round in my head also ... Perhaps Mr Tranter could be persuaded to help.'

'Oh, he would if he could! He has said, over and over again, he would move heaven and earth to get her back!'

Morton smiled. 'That cheers me enormously,' he said. 'Could you ask him if he will see me now?'

A resolute look settled on her face. 'Indeed I will, Mr Morton. Indeed I will!'

71

She was as good as her word. In ten minutes he was in Tranter's office, shaking hands over his desk.

'Miss Marsden is a remarkable young lady,' Tranter said sympathetically. 'I can understand that you are desolated by events. But you should not despair. I suspect that she will continue to be able to write her own agenda for life.'

Morton frowned. 'What do you mean?' he asked.

'Why, that she is very determined and resourceful.'

'She will need more than those qualities, if she is to survive,' Morton said bleakly. 'Her abductor murdered Searle with as little compunction as you would swat a fly.'

'And have the police made no progress in rescuing her?'

'None. Our inspector in charge of the hunt for her believes that she has been taken outside the City police district. And I would not disagree with that . . . But he is content to let the Metropolitan police conduct the search for her.'

'Which you find difficult to accept.'

'Indeed! I would willingly resign from the force if I felt it would strengthen my hand, give me more scope for action . . .'

'I wish there was something we could do,' Tranter said earnestly.

'I am here, sir, precisely because I feel there might be.'

Tranter looked at him warily. 'I see. Well, we would consider any suggestion.'

'What is hampering our work', Morton said, 'is the fact that the public at large are not aware of the abduction. Or, if they are, they have no idea what Miss Marsden looks like. I have come to ask you to print a picture of her in your next edition.'

A look of alarm flitted across Tranter's face. 'A picture? Good heavens! I doubt if the directors would sanction such a departure. They regard the *City Press* as an informed commentary on the commercial scene, in what is the trading capital of the world. To my knowledge, no edition of the paper has ever carried a picture!'

Morton frowned. 'Very well, then. The front page of the paper is given over to advertisements by traders and members of the public.'

'Yes, indeed!'

'I recollect that there is a section for articles lost and found.'

'True.'

72

'Then I wish to place an advertisement for the return of a lost fiancée. And I want that advertisement to include a large picture of Catherine.'

Tranter blinked. 'I do not know,' he said. 'It might be regarded as setting an undesirable precedent.'

'So, to avoid that, you would allow one of your employees to be murdered. Is that what you are telling me?'

Tranter coloured. 'Of course not! But how do we know that would otherwise be the outcome?'

'Because the whole of the City police, and the Metropolitan force, have been looking for her for days! We have got to alert the wider public, before her captors kill her out of hand!'

'Would not publicity precipitate that very act?' Tranter asked sceptically.

'We do not know. It is possible. But it is the only course of action left open to us.'

'Oh, dear!' Tranter sighed. 'But, even were I to agree, we would need a block of her picture. We do not have facilities for making them here . . . In any case, it could not be in tomorrow's edition; that is already put to bed. I suppose that, if a block were in our hands by next Tuesday morning, we could include it in Wednesday's edition.'

Morton seized his hand. 'Excellent!' he exclaimed. 'And you can charge me ten times the normal fee! I will get you your block. You can rely on that!'

He took a cab to the West End, and walked to the studio of Aubrey Rivington, the society photographer. He went into the waiting-room.

'Hello! I am in the dark-room!' Rivington called in his mincing voice. 'You cannot come in!'

'James Morton. I need to see you urgently!'

'Ah! My very favourite policeman . . . And going to marry my most stylish debutante ever! . . . I will not be a moment.'

Morton wandered around the room, staring at photographs of young women; self-conscious or confident, pretty or plain – but wealthy all. He looked in vain for one of Catherine. But she was twenty-four now. It was two years since she had been presented at court. Gaggles of girls would have passed through this studio since then, to adorn its walls briefly and be eclipsed in their turn.

The dark-room door opened, and Rivington emerged. He was wearing a white coat, over a green shirt and yellow bow-tie. His golden locks were tied back with a thong.

'Ooh! You don't look very happy!' he cried. 'Don't say you have called off the wedding! I was so looking forward to it. As well as doing the photographs, Catherine promised she would invite me as a guest. That would make a change for me, I can tell you!'

Morton cut short his chatter. 'Catherine has been abducted,' he said. 'The man who took her had just murdered a shopkeeper. He took her as a hostage. But she has not been released.'

'Ooh! How dreadful!'

'I have bullied the editor of the *City Press* into putting her picture in next Wednesday's edition. But he says that I shall have to provide the block for the picture. I said that I would do so but, frankly, I have not the remotest notion of how to go about it. What I do know is that you have taken a good number of photographs of her, over the years. I hope you will be able to help me.'

'I have lots of lovely, lovely photographs of her!'

'I doubt if she will be looking much like a fashion plate at the moment,' Morton said grimly. 'But what I am concerned with is finding someone to make a printing block from your photograph.'

Rivington waved a limp hand. 'Oh, I can do that easily enough! Photogravure, they call it. You transfer a photographic negative on to a metal plate, and just etch it in.'

'Will it be a recognisable likeness, reproduced in a newspaper?' Morton asked.

Rivington looked offended. 'Of course it will!' he said. 'How big do you want it? Full plate size?'

Morton gave a relieved smile. 'Why not fill three columns with it? That should catch the eye on the front page!'

4

Next morning, Bragg walked through nearly empty streets towards the Temple. Saturday was a nothing of a day, he thought sourly. People were supposed to work in the morning. No doubt the junior clerks had to. But the big cogs in the machine could make their own rules. If they came in at all, it was only to socialise; maintain their contacts, make new ones. Places like the Gresham Club would do well on a Saturday. Everybody chattering, nobody listening . . . And, by now, nobody giving a toss about the murder of Searle. If it had happened to him, by the same token it had not happened to them. The instincts of the herd . . . Bragg wondered about Morton. He seemed to be bearing up well. But life had not prepared him for this. Up to now he had sailed through it, never even a squall . . . He was an oddity, and no mistake. Brought up in that great rambling house; his father away soldiering. An American mother, who wouldn't let her second son go the way of the first. Who'd had him tutored at home, rather than send him to Winchester School like his brother. Then off to Cambridge, where he spent his time playing cricket and such. It sounded like a recipe for an arrogant, self-indulgent wastrel. Yet here he was, full of idealism, wanting to serve his fellow man . . . No doubt there were plenty such. It was easy to be idealistic with bags of money in the bank. But not many would be prepared to start at the bottom, take orders from folk their kind looked on as peasants . . . He was a stupid donkey, all the same. If he had not spent so much time messing about, wondering if he was worthy of his lass, they wouldn't be in this mess now. That was where people of Morton's class suffered. In the Dorset countryside of his own childhood there was no buggering about like this. Life had to go on. The lads and lasses soon knew their place in the scheme of things. There was little choice, and damn all variety. They were all country cabbages, and made the most of it. And they were none the worse for that. As far as he could see, having a pile of money just gave you the chance to make a mess of things.

Thoroughly disgruntled, he knocked on the door of Sir Rufus Stone's chambers and went in.

The clerk regarded him with disfavour. 'Sir Rufus is in conference,' he said.

'How long will he be?'

The clerk shrugged. 'Who can tell?' he said. 'And it is Saturday morning!'

'Well, if no bugger wants to work,' Bragg said wrathfully, 'why the hell do they bother to come in?'

The clerk raised his eyebrows, then turned back to his work.

Bragg sat fuming for a good half-hour before Sir Rufus's door opened, and two men emerged. They seemed to be well pleased with the advice they had received. No doubt they would be paying a fat fee for the privilege.

The clerk looked across. 'You can go in now,' he said reproachfully.

The coroner was busy tying up a bundle of papers with green tape as he entered.

'Ah, Bragg! You are no doubt here to report on our rough diamond of a killer!' he said smugly.

Bragg did not respond to the sally. 'I am here because you sent for me, sir,' he said.

'Yes . . . Well, now, what progress are we making, eh?'

Bragg took the chair opposite him. 'Little enough, if I'm honest, sir. It is a bit different from the usual run of murders, because we believe it was done by a professional killer. So we are left with finding the person who wanted Searle out of the way.'

'I see . . . Someone who disliked him intensely enough to go to those lengths. But why is it necessary to postulate such an arrangement?'

Bragg tugged at his ragged moustache. 'I don't know about it being necessary. But Morton was there. He said it looked that way.'

'But your constable can hardly be relied on for a recollection of what we might call the nuances of the affair. After all, his young lady was abducted . . . Is there any progress on that front, sergeant?'

'Inspector Cotton has taken charge of that enquiry, sir,' Bragg said stolidly.

'Which is no doubt the primary cause of your very evident disgruntlement.' Sir Rufus stared at him coldly. 'In situations such as this, I regret the convention that the coroner should use a member of the police force as his officer. Internecine strife is not conducive to justice. Evidence coloured by rivalry or incompatibility is seldom secure.'

'Yes, sir.'

Sir Rufus glared at him. 'Well?' he asked.

'Well what, sir?'

'Why do you believe that this killing was procured at the hands of an underworld figure?'

'Two reasons, sir. First of all, Morton felt it was not really planned as a robbery. The murderer seemed to come in with the sole intention of shooting Searle. The stealing of the diamond looked to Morton like an afterthought.'

'A very profitable afterthought, at five thousand pounds a time!'

'Yes, sir. Almost in the same league as lawyers.'

Sir Rufus's lip curled. 'Keep your barrack-room wit for your peers, Bragg,' he said scathingly. 'You will not deflect me with such wiles . . . And your second reason?'

'Not long after the murderer had gone, forcing Miss Marsden to go with him, a known underworld figure burst into the shop.'

'Another villain? This beggars the imagination!' Sir Rufus looked at him with narrowed eyes. 'You are not baiting me, I trust,' he said coldly.

'No, sir. I swear it . . . One of the Blackwall gang, Tommy Potts. He took one look at Searle's body and legged it.'

'I take it that you mean he made a hasty departure . . . But there is nothing criminal in that. Violent death must be repugnant, even to someone brought up in the East End slums.'

'Maybe, sir. But he did not go into that shop to ask the price of a diamond tiara.'

'Hmm . . . And is that the extent of what has been discovered, Bragg?'

'Yes, sir. We are spending a lot of time looking for Miss Marsden.'

'I take it that your "we" does not indicate a less than whole-hearted pursuit of Searle's killer.'

'No, sir. It was he who abducted her, if you remember.'

'Hmm . . .' Sir Rufus swivelled round in his chair and peered out of the window. Eventually he swung back. 'I may have something of interest to you, Bragg . . . Not evidence, you understand, merely gossip. But gossip from a source that seems reliable. At least, my wife is prepared to vouch for it . . . which is, I suppose, some sort of a recommendation.'

'Lot's wife, sir.'

Sir Rufus frowned. 'As I remember it, she was turned into a pillar of salt, for looking back.'

77

'Ah. Sorry, sir. I had in mind the one of unblemished virtue. I was never very well up in the bible.'

'Huh! Well, if you will hear me without any further interruption, I will pick up the thread of my wife's discourse ... Lady Stone belongs to several women's groups – you know, church and charitable affairs. And they go in for a good deal of chatting over cups of tea. Recently they were discussing – informally, you understand – a family named Edgerton; or more precisely, a couple of that name. Mrs Edgerton was one of the Berkshire Willoughbys.'

'I cannot say that I am acquainted with them, sir.'

Sir Rufus's lip curled. 'Well, that is hardly surprising, is it? Anyway, the Willoughbys are a wealthy lot. And, a score or so years ago, the head of the family set up a series of family trusts for his children. Anthea Willoughby was one of his daughters. She was, and indeed is, both beautiful and charming. And she attracted the interest of several suitors, among whom was Edgerton. He was, and presumably still is, a socially presentable sort of chap. He trades as a ship-broker ... Baltic Exchange, that sort of thing. Must have seemed a reasonable catch. Of course, one now realises that he was principally after her money. But Willoughby *père* had seen to it that her trust was, to all intents and purposes, impregnable. When Edgerton realised that not even his wife could get at the capital for him, he took against her. The man is a thoroughgoing scoundrel and adulterer. As you can imagine, the marriage *per se* soon foundered.'

'Did they separate – divorce?' Bragg asked.

Sir Rufus pursed his lips. 'Now, there you put your finger on the crux of the problem – if that is not too much of a mixed metaphor. Edgerton needs his wife's money, in that it is her resources that provide the splendid house on Regent's Park, that enable them to live in some style. And, for some time, it suited both of them to conceal the emptiness of their relationship. But then his infidelities became gross. She discovered that he was keeping a mistress on her money.'

'So she wouldn't stomach that.'

'Apparently that was the breaking point in the relationship; but not in the marriage.'

'But surely she could not stay wedded to him after that?' Bragg said.

Sir Rufus cleared his throat. 'It is repugnant to me, Bragg, that

I must acknowledge a lacuna in our laws; concede that this noble edifice does not shelter all our citizens from wrongdoing and injustice ... When Mrs Edgerton looked to the law for relief in her plight, she found no remedy. Our worthy feminist sisterhood is perfectly right. The divorce law does indeed bear unequally on man and woman. If a husband can demonstrate that his wife is involved in an adulterous relationship, he can divorce her for it. But the wife has no such right. A woman can only divorce her husband if his adulterous relationship is incestuous. So the Edgertons are trapped in a loveless marriage; he by his financial circumstances, she by the inequalities of the law.'

'Where I come from,' Bragg said gruffly, 'she would have gone off with some other fellow. And serve the sod right!'

Sir Rufus snorted. 'Civilisation has laboured mightily to rise above such primitive posturing, Bragg. However, Mrs Edgerton is a woman of spirit, and she was prepared to give as good as she got ... In following this course, she formed a relationship – an admittedly adulterous relationship – with another man. Apparently this no longer means social ostracism, as would be the case with divorce.'

'And who was this man?' Bragg asked.

'A John Searle.'

'Our murdered jeweller?'

'The very same.'

Bragg frowned. 'Are you saying that Edgerton could have had Searle murdered?'

'It is not beyond the bounds of possibility, as I am sure you will allow.'

'But why? What would he have to gain?'

Sir Rufus shrugged. 'Perhaps he thought that, without Searle, he could rebuild a relationship with his wife. Perhaps the advent of a rival in her affections showed him starkly the error of his ways. Who can plumb the complexities of the human mind? It could be no more than a sense of having been diminished in the eyes of his cronies.'

'So, are you saying that I must investigate this possibility?'

'I think it would bear consideration, Bragg ... But we will not say as much to my wife, eh?'

*

Catherine gazed out of the window. A breeze was ruffling the new green foliage. It must be a cool breeze, for no one had ventured out into the grounds. She took a strange pleasure at being able to link cause and effect; to reason. Thank goodness she had realised that the tea was drugged. But she must be astute. If they found out, they would drug her food – or, even worse, inject it into her arm. She shivered at the thought. She could not bear hypodermic syringes near her!

She carried a chair to the window. Sitting here, she would naturally turn round when nurses came in. The light would frame her face, make it less easy to see her clearly. She opened the window and strained to hear the traffic. Perhaps the grounds were more extensive than she remembered; or perhaps it was Sunday. She could not guess. There had been a fuzzy period of merely existing. But now she could think again ... It had all begun with James's insistence that she should have an engagement ring like no other. As if she were Cleopatra, or Marie Antoinette! She ought to have stopped it at that stage. But she had been carried along by his excitement ... And her own, she might as well admit it. It had gone wrong because of that stupid man Searle; who thought she could be pressed into accepting a diamond the size of a pigeon's egg in her engagement ring. But James had not been free of blame. He must have realised that she hated the idea. Perhaps it was something in the male psyche. Certainly she could not see him deliberately flaunting his wealth in this way. It was natural that he should want the best for her. But even he should have seen that what Searle proposed was preposterous ... Poor man. He had certainly shuffled off the mortal coil untimely. The scene came back to her with frightening clarity. The door flung open; the figure of a man running in, his gun levelled. Then the sound of the shot; the pain of his hand on her wrist, dragging her to her feet. The blur of James backing to the depths of the shop; then, in a sudden moment of stillness, the click of the handcuffs closing on the stair-rail. It had stayed like a tableau for some seconds. Then the man had released her wrist, swooped on the wretched rough diamond and grabbed her again ... After that had come the dragging on her wrist, the urgings on, the muttered threats. Then the carriage ... But why? Why bring her here? What on earth had been gained? She compelled herself to live through the incident again. Ibbs down in the strong-room, Searle lying dead ... It was clear that the murderer knew James was a policeman. He expected him to have his handcuffs with him ... What if he had not; had left them at Old Jewry? Would he have been shot also? Her mind shied away from the thought. At least, he must be safe ...

Then had come the journey here. She still could not arrive at a reason for it ... Could it be that James's mother's hostility had taken a more active form? That she had contrived this means of separating them? She toyed with the idea for some moments, then dismissed it. To begin with, Lady Morton had no possible reason for such animosity ... Though it was true that – apart from Edwin's funeral – she had not been down to the Priory, to see the Mortons, since the wedding of James's sister Emily. That had been ten months ago. Catherine mentally chided herself for her thoughtlessness. Emily's marriage had left her parents marooned in that great house with only servants and a dying son. No wonder they felt resentful. But could that resentment have matured into a plot to remove her from the scene? To incarcerate her here for the rest of her life? ... No! The proposition only needed stating to be shown as preposterous ... Then who? The bars at this window were real enough ... And she had been expected here! Or, at least, a Miss Brown had been expected here. Her abductor had merely said a few words to the matron, and left. So it had all been arranged in advance. But by whom? What could possibly have been gained by it?

She heard the rattle of the tea-trolley in the corridor. She must be cautious, be rational or they would never believe her. The door opened, and one of the more amenable nurses came in.

'Good morning, dear,' she said cheerfully. She set a cup of black tea on the table, and began to straighten the bedclothes.

'What day is it?' Catherine asked.

'Saturday. This afternoon you will have a special tea, with fruit cake. That is something to look forward to, isn't it?'

Catherine looked calmly at her. 'Why am I here?' she asked.

The nurse smiled encouragingly at her. 'To get better, of course.'

'But who arranged for me to come here?'

'Why, your guardian, Miss Brown. And you are improving

every day. You are not violent, like you were at home. You are a very good girl . . . Now drink your tea!' She turned and locked the door behind her.

Bragg and Morton climbed the stairs to the offices of Edgerton & Co., ship-brokers, in Fenchurch Street. A young typewriter was sitting at her machine. She looked up as they entered.

'Is Mr Edgerton in?' Bragg asked genially.

She smiled. 'He is tied up at the moment. Would you like to wait?'

'Yes, we'll wait.'

They sat on bentwood chairs in a corner of the office. Perhaps Lady Stone's informant was right about Edgerton's need for money, Bragg thought. This set-up was a bit on the scruffy side. He watched the girl's fingers pounding at the keys of her machine. That was the big difference from when he had worked in a shipping office as a youth. Not many streets from here, either, though the building had been demolished years ago. In those days every letter had to be written by hand – and copied into a big copy-book. And the writing had to be legible as well. Be slipshod, and you could expect a clip round the ear. It was the typewriting machines that had brought young women into the offices. They could get their fingers around the keyboard much quicker than a man. And very pleasing they looked, while they were about it. Bragg looked across at the young woman, typing serenely away. If Edgerton was as lecherous as Sir Rufus made him out to be, he would not have been able to keep his hands off her . . . Steal up behind her, and . . .

A buzzer sounded, and the girl looked up.

'Mr Edgerton is free now,' she said brightly. 'Who shall I say wishes to see him?'

'City police.'

Momentarily she was startled. She got up and went out into the corridor. A couple of minutes passed. Bragg had a vision of Edgerton slinking down the back stairs; doing a bunk. Then the girl came back.

'Follow me, please,' she said.

She took them down the corridor and ushered them into a large office, whose windows looked across to the Ironmongers' Hall.

The man who rose from his desk to greet them was undeniably handsome, Bragg thought; with his brown eyes and wide smile. He would be used to turning the heads of silly girls.

'Sergeant Bragg and Constable Morton, detective division,' Bragg said curtly.

Edgerton smiled. 'Please make yourselves comfortable, gentlemen,' he said. 'Take off your jackets, if you like. It gets uncommonly warm in these offices.'

'No, thank you, sir,' Bragg said. 'We are all right as we are.'

Edgerton raised his eyebrows. 'Very well,' he said. 'And how can I be of service to you?'

'We are enquiring into the death of John Searle, on the afternoon of the eighth,' Bragg said flatly.

'Indeed? And how do you imagine that I can further your investigation, sergeant?'

'We have reason to believe that he had been friendly with your wife, if you understand me, sir.'

'My wife and I have many friends, officer. I would not regard Mr Searle as more than a slight acquaintance.'

'That is not how we have heard it, sir.'

'Then you have been given erroneous information.'

'I don't think so, sir. We believe that your marriage has broken down in all but name.'

'Rubbish!' Edgerton said angrily.

'Well, sir, if you would prefer us to make enquiries of Mrs Edgerton . . .'

'No! No . . . that will not be necessary.' He paused. 'I suppose there have been a few small problems. But nothing of consequence. And certainly, nothing which could remotely involve the police!'

Bragg smiled. 'Of course not. We have more important things to concern ourselves with than whether you are faithful to your wife or not.'

Edgerton sprang to his feet. 'I am glad to hear it,' he said angrily. 'In that case, I wish you good-day.'

Bragg looked calmly up at him. 'As I said, we are making enquiries into the murder of John Searle.'

'I heard you first time,' Edgerton said peevishly, slumping back into his chair.

'You knew Mr Searle, of course,' Bragg said evenly.

'Along with half a million of my fellow citizens.'

Bragg raised his eyebrows. 'You think as many as that, do you?'

Edgerton shrugged, and said nothing.

'Now, the way we hear it is like this. You are married to a beautiful, cultured woman, who is wealthy in her own right. One of the Berkshire Willoughbys . . . Right so far?'

Edgerton nodded.

'But you are a stupid, randy sod, who can't keep his hands off other women.'

Bragg paused, but this time Edgerton did not react.

'And, as is the way of these things,' Bragg went on, 'some kind friend let your wife know what was going on . . . This was the last thing you wanted. She has all that money, stuffed away in family trusts, out of your reach. Your business is not doing all that well. It is her money that funds the house on Regent's Park, the lavish way of life you enjoy. I bet you had the mother and father of a row; which might have cooled tempers, but solved nothing. No doubt you promised not to touch other women in future. But she would know, well enough, what that was worth.'

Bragg paused; still Edgerton said nothing.

'So what happened next was this,' Bragg went on. 'Being, as I have said, a high-spirited, determined woman, your wife went to see a solicitor and said: "I want to divorce this adulterous wastrel," or words to that effect. And the lawyer said: "Sorry, you can't! Not unless he is bedding his sister." Imagine that! Not fair, is it? He is more or less telling her that she's got to put up with you, and your vile treatment of her. So she says: "Bugger this! I can give the randy swine as good as I get!" And, do you know, she takes up with a diamond broker, name of Searle. A diamond broker who was shot dead in his shop on Wednesday last.'

Edgerton's face was ashen. He was gripping the arms of his chair till his knuckles showed white. 'It is not true!' he cried.

'Are you saying you were unaware of her association with Searle?' Bragg asked.

'That would be rather pointless, in view of what she has told you. But I was out of the country when Searle was killed.'

'Oh, yes? Where were you?'

'I was on the Continent.'

84

'That was far-seeing of you, sir. But we know Searle was killed by an underworld gunman. Somebody paid to get rid of him.'

Edgerton started to his feet. 'Get out! Get out!' he shouted. 'I will answer no more of your questions until I have my own lawyer with me!'

Bragg got to his feet. 'I would say that was very wise of you, sir,' he said. 'Very wise indeed!'

Out in the street, Bragg pulled out his watch. 'Do you think we have time to catch Searle's solicitors?' he asked. 'Before they pack up for the weekend.'

'They are in Bedford Row, sir.'

'That's not far. Get a cab, lad!'

Morton plunged into the traffic, bringing imprecations on his head from a score of drivers. One hansom practically knocked him down in an effort to get into another stream. He half wished that he was in the uniformed division again. He would have got a cab quickly enough then. Eventually he stopped an empty growler. It managed to force a path to the corner where Bragg was standing; but then it became wedged between a dust-cart and a brewer's dray. The dust-cart would move a few yards, until it came abreast of another collection of bins, then it would stop. This went on for twenty minutes; before a side street opened on their left, and they could escape from the procession. It was almost twelve o'clock before they reached the offices of Gribble & Oddie.

Bragg burst into the reception. 'Is Mr Vernon still here? Or has he gone to his country estate?'

The elderly clerk raised his eyebrows. 'I was not aware that he possessed any such thing,' he said.

'But is he in?'

'Oh, yes. He is in, sir.'

'Then can we see him?'

The clerk pursed his lips. 'Well, you have no appointment. And I happen to know . . .'

'I don't give a bugger what you know,' Bragg said irritably. 'Tell him it's the police!'

'Ah!' The clerk's face became grave. 'Are your enquiries of a personal nature? Or do they concern one or more of our clients?'

Bragg seized him by the lapels of his coat. 'I will have you in the bloody nick if you don't stop wasting police time. Now get on with it!' He gave the man a push, and turned to gaze angrily out of the window.

The man scuttled through a door at the rear of the office. There was a long pause, and Bragg began to prowl restlessly about. Then the clerk returned.

'Will you please come this way?' he said timidly.

They followed him up lino-covered stairs to an office on the next floor. It was positively Dickensian, Morton thought. Bookcases and presses lined the walls; tables were covered with untidy piles of files; bundles of documents overflowed on to the linoleum.

A balding, wizened man rose from his desk. He held out his hand. 'I am Vernon,' he said. 'I am sorry if my clerk appeared obstructive. It is no compliment to me, I assure you. I fear that I have reached the age where my subordinates are insubordinately determined to protect me. Whether that is necessary or not is something you can decide for yourselves.'

'It is a rather urgent matter,' Bragg said, mollified. 'We are investigating the murder of one of your clients – John Searle, of Furlonger & Searle.'

'I see ... Do be seated ... Yes, John Searle. A dastardly deed, officer. A great loss to the community ... One wonders who on earth could have done it.'

'I have to confess we are groping in the dark, sir,' Bragg said earnestly.

'Goodness! And you come to me! I very much fear that your expectations are about to be dashed. My relationship with Searle was strictly professional. Our firm had handled the affairs of his father, Alfred. When he died – and he could have been barely sixty-five – the son continued to consult us.'

'I see, sir ... Of course you will realise, from your long experience, that families fall out. We find that expectations are often the key to murder cases – or rather, expectations dashed ... Now, I admit we are clutching at straws on this one. The more so because we believe the killer was a paid assassin.'

'Great heavens!' Vernon exclaimed. 'How very Mediterranean!'

'We would like you to give us details of Searle's will, if you would.'

Vernon considered for a moment, frowning. Then he smiled. 'I can think of no conceivable reason why I should not ... Now, where on earth will the file be?' He glanced around the room in perplexity, then rang a bell on his desk.

The door opened as if the clerk had been waiting on the other side. 'Yes, Mr Vernon?' he murmured.

'You know John Searle, the diamond merchant?'

'Yes, Mr Vernon.'

'I seem to remember that we did some work for him recently.'

'Yes, sir. It was in regard of a new will.'

'Ah, was it? ... Yes, I remember now.'

'Mr Searle was to have attended, yesterday afternoon, to finalise his instructions, sir.'

'I see ... I was looking for his file. I am sure I had it recently.'

The clerk crossed to a table, and began to turn over the heap of files on it. Eventually he held one up. 'Here it is, sir.'

Vernon smiled in triumph. 'I knew it must be here somewhere!' he said. 'Thank you, er ... Yes.'

Bragg glanced across at Morton and raised a sceptical eyebrow. Then he turned to Vernon, who was thumbing through the file. At least something was making sense to him; his face was positively animated. Eventually he leaned back in his chair.

'I have to say that my client's untimely death has resulted in a state of affairs that he would certainly not have desired.' Having delivered himself of this utterance, the solicitor subsided into a reverie.

'Go on, sir,' Bragg said urgently.

Vernon took a deep breath. 'I was just considering the implications,' he said. 'But we can arrive at them as we go along ... The first occasion on which he consulted us about his testamentary dispositions was in July of 1890 ...'

'Five years ago.'

'Yes, almost five years ago. My file-note records that, up to that time, he had relied on an informal will made when he was a serving officer in the army ... You knew about that, I suppose?'

'The will, sir?'

'No! That he had been in the Second Dragoon Guards.'

'Yes, sir.'

'Good.' Vernon turned back to his file. 'Now, when he attained

87

the age of forty years, he decided to have a more formal will prepared. So he came to us.'

'That was in 1890 was it, sir?'

'Yes. As we have said, almost five years ago. In a sense it was a mildly odd proceeding, since the provisions of the new will were to be precisely the same as those of his informal dispositions.'

'So you could have told him there was no need to bother?'

Vernon gave a foxy smile. 'The wishes of one's client must always be paramount, officer,' he said. 'In any case, he was insistent. It seemed as if he would draw comfort from knowing that his affairs had received professional scrutiny. After all, he had been the sole proprietor of an important and prosperous business for five years, following the death of his father. It was an act of prudence on his part.'

'Right, sir. So what was to happen under that will?'

Vernon took a document from the file and perused it. 'The provisions are straightforward enough,' he said. 'A sum of five hundred pounds was bequeathed to a servant, should he survive the testator.'

'Who was that, sir?'

'A man named Thompson, who had previously been his batman.'

'We have met him, sir.'

'Good ... A further sum of two hundred pounds was to be spent on what he described as a celebratory dinner for the officers of the Queen's Bays, past and present ... I remember observing that it seemed an excessive amount for the purpose. But he inferred that I had scant conception of the capacity of dragoon officers in that regard.'

'And what was to happen to the rest of his estate, sir?'

'It was to be divided up between various regimental charities.'

'And that was the state of affairs at his death?'

'No! I am trying to tell you ...' Vernon said petulantly. 'He popped in on ... let me see ...' He consulted the file again. 'On Friday the twenty-sixth of April. He said that he wished to make a new will, and that he had destroyed the former one. He seemed to be quite exhilarated. He made an appointment to finalise his instructions on the tenth of May, at three o'clock in the afternoon.'

'Which was yesterday.'

'Yes, officer.'

'So he died intestate?'

'Yes ... I very much fear that we shall have to advertise for possible relatives. I know he had an aunt Amy, on the Searle side of the family. She may have left progeny. We shall have to see. This kind of situation is, regretfully, always difficult and prolonged.'

'But difficult and profitable for the solicitors, eh?' Bragg said with a grin.

An answering smile touched Vernon's face. 'The labourer is worthy of his hire, officer,' he said. 'Never forget that.'

As they reached the street, Bragg halted. 'I reckon you could do with some time to yourself,' he said gruffly. 'Why don't you get on with that family tree of the Searle lot. It might be useful, who knows? And I can tell that bugger Cotton you are working on it at home, or wherever. That way you will not have to drag yourself in when you are not up to it.'

Morton gave a weary smile. 'That is very considerate of you, sir,' he said warmly. 'I appreciate it immensely.'

'Don't thank me,' Bragg said gruffly. 'You are no bloody good to me when your mind is on that young maid!'

Morton spent the afternoon trailing round the streets again. This time he decided to concentrate on an area north of the City. He argued that, once he had made his escape, Catherine's abductor was likely to go a considerable distance. It would be pointless to go a mere hundred yards. By taking her further, it would cause the search area to widen, like a fan. That would be sound planning. Criminals were aware of the rivalry between the two police forces. They could well have calculated that the Met would only search a band close to the City boundary; and perfunctorily to boot.

He walked to City Road. He decided to search the area formed between it, Goswell Road and Old Street. It was an area on the outskirts of Finsbury, where there were large detached houses. He reasoned that Catherine's captors could not keep her in a street of artisans' dwellings without the residents becoming aware. When the Met search teams questioned such people, they would voice their suspicions. He suppressed his growing conviction that, by now, the Met would have abandoned the hunt; that everyone in this Metropolitan maelstrom kept their neighbours at arm's length. He criss-crossed the eastern end of the triangle, peering into windows, looking down into the basement areas. What a stupid idiot he was! He had seen her abductor; his face was imprinted on his memory. Why on earth had he not sketched him? He would have something to show to people then.

As he worked his way westward the houses became grander, with substantial gardens around them. A hundred years ago, London's merchant princes would have lived in them. Now, from the state of their gardens, most of them had been converted into apartment dwellings. An area in decline . . . He tried to break out of the depression that was enveloping him. Not everything was scruffy and dejected. The house he was approaching looked immaculate; the lawns neatly mown, daffodils brightening the flower beds . . . Yet it was not a private residence; there was a notice-board by the driveway. GREENLANDS SANATORIUM. If he did not get some kind of grip on himself, he thought, he would end up in some such institution . . . Well, he could do worse. It looked benign, with the sun on its brickwork. Perhaps he ought to go in, he thought sardonically. Book himself some rooms for his solitary old age; wither away in some elegance . . . He snorted. He was becoming maudlin! Letting self-pity overwhelm him, when he should be thinking of Catherine. He must take hold of himself, get on with the business of searching for her. He swung round and, with renewed determination, tramped off down the street.

It was early afternoon when Catherine conceived her plan. She knew it must be Sunday, because of the church bells. And there seemed to be very few staff on duty. Breakfast had been brought to her, but the dirty crockery had not been collected. Nor had the bed been made, or the commode emptied. One of the nurses had mentioned that Sunday dinner was a special treat. No doubt it was, if one was compelled to fast before it . . . The glimmer of an idea formed in her mind. She saw the electric bell-push. It was only for real emergencies, she had been told. If she pressed it frivolously she would be punished . . . Well, for her this was an emergency. Not that it would matter, once she had escaped . . .

She made herself sit in the chair, calmed her emotions, cleared her mind. Thank goodness her brain was working properly again. And she was sure she had deceived the nurses into thinking that she was still drinking the drugged tea. Without milk it was undetectable in the slops.

She went over to the window: some of the inmates were strolling on the lawns – the trusties, she thought sardonically. But they looked frail and bewildered; they would not hinder her. Indeed, they might serve as a screen ... She must not run, that would make her conspicuous. The porters could easily recapture her ... She thought through her plan again. Would it be better to wait until dinner-time, when the nurse brought in her meal? ... No. There might easily be someone else in the corridor. Almost certainly there would be more staff downstairs at that time ... So it must be now!

Trying to control her mounting excitement, she went over to the electric bell and pressed it. Somewhere in the bowels of the building a buzzer would be sounding. How long would it take them? ... Them? In her planning she had assumed that only one person would answer the bell – and that a nurse. Suppose that two people came; or, if one, a porter? Well, it was too late for second thoughts now. Catherine went over to the commode and took out the chamberpot. She emptied the carafe of water into it, to top it up; then she balanced it on the back of a chair. Standing as she was, she would screen it; and the nurse would have to come well into the room. It was then a matter ...

She heard the rattle of a key in the lock. The door creaked open. She tensed herself.

'What is all this about?' a woman's voice demanded. 'You know you are not supposed ...'

Catherine pivoted round and flung the contents of the chamberpot into the nurse's face. Then she ran through the door and locked it behind her. This was the critical time, she told herself. She must walk sedately down the stairs; not attract attention. Yet, at any moment, the alarm bell would sound downstairs. People would come rushing up. Her heart pounding, she slipped quietly down four flights of stairs. Now she was at the top of the main staircase from the hall. She could hear the alarm bell ringing. The clatter of feet approaching. A porter came pounding across the hall. Catherine turned her face away as he rushed by. She made herself walk slowly across the hall, through the door and out into the garden. She glanced around her. The gate was open. She stepped on to the lawn and drifted towards it. A quick glance around, and she was through! She picked up her skirts and ran. She could feel her heart pounding, but she could not stop yet ... Better if she could get into a side street; no one would see her then ... She had a pain in her side, she was gasping for breath ... But she had to keep going. At last there was a street on her left. She turned into it and slowed to a walk. She must try to keep going, get as far away as possible: then she could rest.

In the distance she saw the reassuring sight of a beat constable. She was safe! She stopped and leaned against the wall to get her breath back. He was approaching her at a measured pace. From his helmet, he belonged to the Metropolitan police. He cocked his head as he approached her.

'Hello, miss,' he said. 'Out for a walk, are we?'

Catherine felt like laughing, like throwing her arms round her rescuer's neck and kissing him.

'Oh, constable!' she cried. 'Thank heavens you have come! I have been abducted and incarcerated for days!'

'Abducted and what, miss?'

'Imprisoned, officer. Locked up!'

He frowned. 'Sounds serious,' he said. 'Do you know whereabouts?'

'Yes! In the Greenlands Sanatorium.'

'I know it,' he said. 'Well, you just come with me and we'll deal with your complaint properly – at the station.'

He took her arm and they set off in the direction from which he had come.

'What is your name?' he asked.

'Catherine Marsden. My father is William Marsden, the artist ...' The words were bubbling out of her, as if she had not spoken for a month. 'Do you know of James Morton?' she asked.

'The cricketer?'

'Yes! I am engaged to be married to him.'

'Very nice.'

They turned into a narrow walled street on the left, the constable keeping up a steady pace.

'James and I had gone to a City diamond broker, to choose a stone for my engagement ring.'

'I didn't know you could do that kind of thing, miss,' he said warmly.

'Ordinarily one could not. But Searle was intent on making a lot of money out of James.'

'I see, miss. Well off, is he?'

'Oh, yes. That does not matter to me, of course.'

'Naturally.' He looked at her quizzically. 'Well, go on with your story.'

'It all went wrong, constable. A man burst into the shop, shot Searle and dragged me off with him. I was forced into a carriage. The blinds were drawn. So that no one could see me.'

'Funny, I didn't hear anything about that,' the constable said. 'That's no way to carry on, is it?'

'Indeed it is not! And I have been incarcerated ever since.'

The constable looked down at her. 'Does that still mean locked up, miss?'

Catherine laughed. The tension and fear were draining away from her. 'Yes, it does, constable!' she said.

'And when do you say this happened?'

'On the eighth of May.'

'Four days ago.'

'Yes, but it seems much longer.'

His grip tightened on her arm. He stopped and beat a tattoo on a door in the wall. She was suddenly alarmed. This did not look like the entrance to a police station ... There came the rattle of a chain; the door creaked open. Framed in the aperture was one of the Greenlands porters. The policeman had betrayed her! He had merely walked her round to the back gate.

'This is one of yours,' he said. 'Or so she claims.'

The porter gave a malicious smile. 'She's one of ours, all right.'

'Then take more care of her in future.'

'We will, constable,' the porter said. 'We certainly will!'

Morton was slumped in his chair. He had no right to be here, he told himself. He ought to be out looking for Catherine. But he was bone-weary ... Yet he would not be able to sleep. He had no more than dozed since she was abducted. Even in his head, the word had a sinister finality to it.

93

There came a discreet knock on the door and Chambers, his manservant, came in.

'Will you be needing anything more tonight, Master James?' he asked.

'No, thank you,' Morton said. 'Off to bed with you!'

'My wife thought you might like some hot chocolate – to help you sleep.'

Morton sighed. 'She is very kind,' he said. 'But I fear I am beyond that stage. I would need a tumblerful of laudanum, I think.'

'Is there ... Is there any news of Miss Catherine?' he asked hesitantly.

'No, none.'

'Mrs Chambers and I would like you to know how sorry we feel; that this should have happened when you ought both to be so happy.'

'Thank you,' Morton said feelingly. 'I am certain that all will be well.'

'Very good, sir.' Chambers withdrew, closing the door quietly behind him.

He was fortunate, Morton reflected, to have these good people to look after him. They had come up from Ashwell over four years ago, uprooted themselves for his sake. To support him in his quixotic resolve to serve as a police constable. If they had thought it absurd, they had kept that to themselves. And now they were prepared to share in his sorrows. He thought wryly that, since their engagement, Catherine had been promoted from 'Miss Marsden' to 'Miss Catherine'. He wished he could be certain that she would one day be Mrs Morton ...

Seeking distraction, he took a piece of paper and began to sketch the face of her abductor – the face of a murderer ... Slowly the likeness began to emerge – the cold eyes, the long nose, the thin lips. Yes ... Even though he had only seen him with the light behind him, he was sure it was a good likeness ... But perhaps in his own mind only; and just in the split-second before the man pulled the trigger. Anyone else might see nothing memorable, nothing that would identify him beyond doubt. But, at least, he had done what he could ... The phrase had the baleful ring of failure. Something he would not contemplate while there was breath in his body.

Bragg had told him to construct the family tree of the Searle clan. He was loath to begin, for it had no obvious relevance to Catherine's abduction. Or, even if it had, it did not chime with his mood. Weary as he was, in body as well as in mind, he wanted to be physically active. It would almost be a betrayal to sit putting names in a framework on a piece of paper. Yet the sergeant had far more experience than he. His record as a detective was far better than anyone else's in the force; which was why Inspector Cotton had never been able to get rid of him ... Morton sighed. In truth he had no option but to trust in Bragg's flair. He himself had been rattling around for days; getting nowhere near to an explanation of what had happened, let alone rescuing Catherine. Perhaps something mechanical, like a family tree, might steady his mind; act as a palliative to his despondency. He took a sheet of paper, and began to list the questions he would have to address at the registrar's office.

Next morning Bragg and Morton took a train to Reading, then caught a Guildford line train to Blackwater. The day was sunny and clear. A light breeze stirred the new green foliage. In the back gardens, women were hanging out their washing. Well, it would dry all right, Bragg thought, on such a day ... But women were such hidebound creatures. Why had Monday to be washing day? He had known his mother set about washing with the rain pouring down – just because it was Monday morning. Have wet clothes hanging from the airing rack in the kitchen; draped over the back of chairs, getting in everybody's way ... Perhaps it was something to do with living in the country – in God's good air. Now, Mrs Jenks would do the washing when she knew she could get it dry. Though, like as not, she would be shaking smuts off it. Women were perverse creatures, no doubt about it.

He glanced across at Morton. The lad was worn out, for sure; his face haggard. From what little he had said, he had been tramping aimlessly round the streets – or if not aimlessly, then uselessly. It was a question now of how long he could keep going ... And he would get precious little sympathy from the rest of the force. He was popular, of course; not only because he was friendly and approachable, but because he was famous. But that was his weak spot, too. They were bound to feel that, coming from the top level of society, there was condescension in his electing to enlist as a constable. It was certainly not true. But the fact of it was, the other men treated him differently; deferred to his opinions because he had a quick mind, and could express himself clearly. The upshot of it was that he made the others feel inferior. They would gladly pull him down, then commiserate over the wreckage.

Morton looked across with a weary smile. 'I can at least add one piece of information to the file,' he said. He took a folded sheet of paper from his pocket and passed it to Bragg. 'That is a likeness of the man that shot Searle.'

Bragg took the drawing and stared at it. 'Nobody I know, anyway,' he said. 'We will put it up at Old Jewry; see if anyone recognises him . . . Perhaps you ought to do another for the Met.'

Morton gave a sardonic laugh. 'I have prowled around in their area for hours,' he said, 'and seen not the remotest sign that they are searching for Catherine.'

'Well, you wouldn't, would you? We do not exactly advertise ourselves when we are doing a search. It only makes our quarry move on.'

'I wish I could seize on that explanation, sir. But I feel that Inspector Cotton's vaunted relationship with the Met is worth nothing.'

'Ah! You underestimate him, lad,' Bragg said cheerfully. 'He will be aiming for that big spread in the newspapers: "Inspector Cotton Rescues Society Beauty". He would not pass up that chance lightly.'

'I can only hope you are right, sir ... I see a station in the distance. It must be Blackwater. Perhaps today's line of enquiry will yield something.'

'It is the only one we have got, lad. It's up to us now.'

They took a trap from the station to Sandhurst, and from there to Wellington College. As the twin towers of the school came into view, Bragg nudged Morton.

'You will have to watch my back on this one, lad,' he said. 'These nobby buggers stick together; and you have a better idea of what to expect than I have.'

Morton laughed. 'I only know what little my brother told me of public school,' he said. 'And his anecdotes were concerned more with other boys than with the teaching and administrative staff.'

'Hmm . . . I suppose it will be term-time.'

'Yes.'

'Then they will be making out they haven't time for us,' Bragg said darkly.

'I am sure that you will be able to persuade them otherwise, sir!'

Telling the cab driver to wait for them, they made their way into the school buildings and obtained directions to the office. It was a gloomy, sunless room. Its only occupant was an elderly clerk, wearing sleeve protectors. He was turning the pages of a large ledger. He looked up as they entered.

'Police!' Bragg said, flourishing his warrant-card. 'City of London police.'

A look of mild relief flitted across the man's face. 'Are you sure that you have got the right school, officer?' he asked. 'We have not had a trip to the capital since last October.'

Bragg smiled. 'It is not your current crop of scoundrels we are interested in,' he said. 'But someone long gone . . . A man name of Searle – John Searle.'

The clerk frowned. 'I do not recognise the name, officer. But what is the nature of your enquiries?'

'We want to find out as much about him as we can. He has been murdered.'

'Murdered?' the man repeated in alarm. 'We have not had a murder of an old boy for . . . oh, goodness knows how long! I have no idea what the procedure is.'

'The procedure', Bragg said firmly, 'is that you answer our questions truthfully, and give us all the help you can.'

'Yes . . . naturally. John Searle, you say?' He crossed to a book-shelf. 'Have you any idea when he was here?' he asked.

Bragg turned to Morton. 'How old would you say he was, constable?' he asked.

Morton frowned. 'I would say that he was in his mid-forties, sir.'

'That would mean . . .' the clerk gazed out of the window, frowning. 'He certainly should be in the register covering the later years of the fifties . . . Yes.'

He bent down, selected a book from the bottom shelf, and brought it to his desk. 'Searle, you say?'

'John Searle. And, as far as we know, his address would have been in the City of London.'

The clerk was now running his finger down a page of entries. 'Searle ... Searle,' he was murmuring. 'Here we are! John Searle, of Blomfield Street, London. Would that be your man?'

'Slap in the middle of the bull!' Bragg said genially. 'Well done!'

The clerk looked at him in bewilderment; then crossed to a wooden press, and began to pull out bundles of files.

'Can I help, sir?' Bragg asked after a time.

'No! No. You do not understand my system. You cannot possibly help.'

The clerk spent twenty minutes untying bundles, laboriously turning over the files, then tying them up again. Eventually he gave a cry of triumph.

'Here he is! I knew my system would not let me down! Now, what is it that you want to know?'

'Everything there is to know, sir,' Bragg said genially. 'For a start, when was he here?'

The clerk beamed. 'That I can certainly tell you,' he said. He opened the file and peered at a form pasted on the inner cover. 'He came here in the first year of the school's existence; that is 1859. And he left us in 1867 ... I have a note that he went to the Queen's Bays. Did you know about that?'

'Yes, we know about that, sir. What else can you tell us?'

The clerk pursed his lips. 'Our fees were paid promptly – by cheques drawn on the National Provincial Bank of England Limited – their branch at Bishopsgate Within ... Though within what I cannot imagine!' He allowed himself a weary smile.

'Inside the old walls of the City,' Bragg said brusquely. 'What else have you?'

He turned the papers in the file. 'He had measles in 1860 – December of that year. I see there was some debate about whether he would be fit to go home for the Christmas vacation. Eventually it was decided that he was ...'

'This is bugger all use to us!' Bragg broke in irritably. 'What we want to know is the sort of lad he was, what happened to him here, who his cronies were!'

'But it is all so long ago . . .' The clerk blinked nervously. Then his face cleared. 'I am sure that Mr Weston would have known him. He has been here since the beginning . . . You are fortunate, officer. He is retiring at the end of this term!'

'Right! Then go and fetch him!'

The clerk scuttled off and Bragg began to prowl angrily around the office.

'God Almighty!' he exclaimed. 'To think that the officers of our armies start off in this place. It's a wonder they have enough sense to wipe their arses. Or does their batman do that for them?'

Morton laughed. 'I am sure that my father's views would not be widely different from your own, sir,' he said. 'Though I hope he would express them more diplomatically!'

'Is that what I have got to be? Diplomatic? We have a murder on our hands! Your fiancée is in the hands of the bugger who did it! And all this silly old fool can tell us is that Searle caught measles! No wonder the country is going to the dogs, with your lot in charge! It's right what they say. It is time for a clear-out!'

Morton sat in diplomatic silence for some minutes, while Bragg prowled about the office. Eventually the clerk returned with a silver-haired man.

'This is Mr Weston,' he said. 'I hope he will be able to help you.'

Weston held out his hand. 'I gather that you are enquiring about John Searle,' he said. 'Is it really the case that he has been murdered?'

'That's right, sir. Constable Morton was on the premises when it happened.'

Weston shook Morton's hand in turn. 'That cannot have been a pleasant experience,' he said. 'And were you unable to apprehend the murderer?'

'He threatened to kill my fiancée. I was compelled to handcuff myself to some iron railings. So I was immobilised.'

'Great heavens! I trust that the young lady was not harmed.'

'We do not know yet. The murderer abducted her.'

'I am so sorry,' Weston said in a troubled voice. 'Naturally, I will give you all the information I can. However, I have to say that my knowledge of matters military is somewhat sketchy. I am here to teach the boys French.'

'French?' Bragg echoed. 'Whatever good is that to a soldier?'

'Apart from its cultural value, you mean? I suppose that they had been our traditional enemies for centuries. After all, when the curriculum was under discussion, the battle of Waterloo was still a recent memory. But you are wrong in assuming that the sole purpose of the school was to turn out potential army officers.'

'That is how it seems to us, sir.'

'I am not totally surprised. That is the modern conception of us. But the intention of Prince Albert – and he was chairman of the project to build the school – was almost the converse of that. Wellington was not only to be a fitting memorial to the nation's greatest soldier and statesman, but also an institution where sons of deceased officers of the British army and the East India Company army could be educated.'

'Deceased meaning killed in the course of their duties?'

'In practical terms, yes, officer. In a sense it was a concept that was already outdated. The battle of Waterloo, in 1815, ushered in an era of peace beyond the conceptions of the school's founders. Military orphans of school age were very thin on the ground. So, perforce, the school flung open its gates to the more general public.'

'But they would have to pay for the privilege,' Bragg said sardonically.

'Yes. And in return they received a general education which was second to none – or so we like to think!'

'I see, sir. And you were teaching them French right from the start?'

'Indeed, officer, together with elementary geography.'

Bragg sniffed. 'You see, sir, what I am trying to do is build up a picture of the man. For instance, why was he sent here in the first place? It hardly seems a breeding-ground for diamond brokers.'

The clerk intervened. 'I have the original application here, Mr Weston,' he said.

The master glanced through it. 'Ah, yes,' he said. 'I see that Searle had a military connection. His maternal grandfather was a Captain Thomas Furlonger. He had apparently distinguished himself at Waterloo. This is exactly the kind of connection the founders were looking for ... You know, as we talk my memory is being jogged. I am almost certain that I remember the boy. If I am right, he was a very gregarious chap, and a brilliant racquets player ... Yes, physically brave, but somewhat headstrong. It sounds like an ideal prescription for an army officer. But, if I am right, he was not always an influence for good. Well, there we are. I hope that has helped.'

'We have a better picure, thank you, sir,' Bragg said. 'But I am afraid we are no nearer knowing why he was murdered.'

From Wellington School, the cab driver headed off in the direction of Sandhurst where, he said, the headquarters of the Queen's Bays were. Bragg soon realised that the man was bamboozling them. His first job had been mucking out the horses in his father's stables – and him all of nine. At eleven he had been driving one of the small wagons between Bere Regis and Dorchester; finding his way to isolated farms. It was still second nature to keep an eye on the sun, to unconsciously gauge distance. Should he tell the driver he knew they were going out of their way? ... No. It was a pleasant day, and the police authority were paying. He took out his watch; knocking on two o'clock. No wonder he was feeling peckish! He directed the driver to find a nice country pub, where they could all have a chunk of cheese and a pint of yeasty ale.

It was almost four o'clock before Bragg and Morton were being shown into the office of the adjutant of the Queen's Bays. A wiry, sunburned man rose from his desk.

'Major Firth,' he said briskly, holding out his hand.

'Sergeant Bragg and Constable Morton, of the City of London police.' Bragg sat in a chair and wriggled his toes inside his boots. This trip had entailed too much tramping round schools and stations for his liking ... He had not bargained for this. He was breaking in some new boots, expecting he would be sitting down most of the time; thinking they would mould to his feet.

Firth was staring at Morton. Then he smiled. 'Of course!' he exclaimed. 'You are the cricketer! Son of Lieutenant-General Morton of the Life Guards. I am honoured to meet you, sir. How can I be of service?'

Bragg cleared his throat. 'You may or may not be aware that a former officer of your regiment was murdered in London last Wednesday. A John Searle.'

'As a matter of fact, we are aware of it, sergeant. His servant – formerly his batman – got in touch with us about the funeral. Said he knew of no relatives; felt the regiment would want to do the honours, and so forth.'

'And will you?'

Firth gave an uneasy smile. 'I imagine we will be doing something. Brother officer, and all that. Not my department.'

'Hmm . . . We are trying to piece together a picture of the man,' Bragg said, 'which might give us a better idea of who would want him dead.'

Firth shrugged. 'For all practical purposes we had lost touch with him. After all, he left us fifteen or sixteen years ago. Went to join his father in the family business – some shop or other.'

'Are you saying you cannot help us?' Bragg said irritably.

'Not quite.' Firth frowned. 'We had a Major Hurst dining in the mess a couple of nights ago. Retired now, but he had served with Searle. Naturally we got talking about the man.'

'Go on! And let's have none of this *de mortuis* shit!'

Firth looked at him uncertainly. 'Yes . . . Well, Hurst said that Searle was an exceptionally fine horseman. Strange, that, for someone brought up in the London streets. But, anyway, he was apparently reckless with it . . . As is often the perverse way of things, his men regarded him with affectionate awe: would follow him anywhere . . .'

'So, if we had been at war, Searle would have had an outstanding career?'

'Outstanding possibly; brief certainly.'

'And what did his fellow officers think about him?'

Firth pondered briefly. 'It is safe to say that they regarded him as an inveterate show-off, who would be a liability in real warfare – but, of course, there was none.'

'Hmm . . . This comes from that Hurst man, does it?'

'Mainly. Though there is a kind of regimental folk-memory too.'

'He reached the rank of major, we understand.'

'That is correct.'

'But he seems never to have used the rank in civilian life, as most ex-officers do.'

Firth shrugged. 'Perhaps that reflected the circumstances of his leaving us,' he said.

'And what is that supposed to mean?' Bragg said roughly.

'I mean that he resigned his commission, rather than retired from the army.'

Bragg frowned. 'Why did he do that, I wonder? His father was still a relatively young man – lasted another six years.'

Firth took a deep breath. 'I think he had been made aware that he had reached his ceiling – that no further promotion was likely . . . Also he had broken the code – had an affair with the wife of a fellow officer; been indiscreet.'

'The name of this fellow officer?' Bragg asked.

'That information is confidential, and will remain so.'

'I see. So the Queen's Bays don't go in for pistols at dawn,' Bragg said sardonically. 'Or was Searle the better shot?'

Firth's lip curled contemptuously. 'It was the general feeling that he should take up his destiny as a shopkeeper,' he said.

'I will have you know, it is one of the most important diamond broking businesses in Europe,' Bragg said angrily.

The adjutant was unimpressed. 'How interesting,' he said.

'Lots of people would think it was more worthwhile than playing at soldiers!'

Firth shrugged. 'No doubt,' he said soberly. 'But the way things are going in Germany, we may be more than playing at it before long!'

5

'When I got back to my rooms last night,' Morton said, 'there was a letter from my mother.'

'You told them about Miss Marsden, then?' Bragg asked.

They were trotting in a hansom along Portland Place, *en route* for Regent's Park.

'I wrote to them on Friday.'

'And how did they take it?'

'My mother seemed extremely anxious, almost distraught.'

'That should cheer you up a bit. At least you are all pulling together.'

'Possibly . . . But it is equally likely that her concerns are dynastic; that, if the worst comes to the worst, I shall never marry.'

Bragg snorted. 'You rich folk never give anybody the benefit of the doubt, do you?' he said. 'I suppose you don't have to. The rest of us, the real people, just have to get along with each other. If they harbour a grudge, it sours the rest of their lives.'

Morton forced a smile. 'Once Catherine has been found safe and sound, you may lecture me all you wish,' he said. 'But I find it almost unbearable to go through the motions of investigating Searle's murder, and have her abduction treated as a mere adjunct to the case, as almost an irrelevance.'

'Huh! Let Inspector Cotton hear that, lad, and he would stop even going through the motions ... We know there is a link. It may be a damn long piece of string, but we have hold of one end of it. And, as long as I am on the case, we shall not let go whatever anyone says. Now, liven up and keep your wits about you.'

The cab let them down in Cumberland Terrace. Bragg hammered on the door of the Edgertons' residence. A rather plain, pimply maid showed them up to a drawing-room overlooking the park. After some minutes she brought coffee, then disappeared again.

Bragg was becoming restive. 'I suppose Mrs Edgerton doesn't bother to get up in the morning,' he grumbled. 'Probably partying till the small hours.'

'These rich folk don't know how us workers live,' Morton mimicked him.

Bragg glared at him. 'That's enough of that, lad,' he said. 'If we were with that lot we saw yesterday, I could have you shot for insubordination!'

The door opened and Mrs Edgerton made an entrance. She was good-looking in a kittenish sort of way, Bragg conceded.

'Good morning, gentlemen,' she said. 'I gather from my maid that you are policemen. How exciting!' Her eyes were on Morton, her smile enticing. 'Do sit down.' She subsided languorously on to a *chaise-longue*.

Bragg sat down on his chair again. 'We are investigating the murder of John Searle, ma'am,' he said gruffly.

'I see ... Poor John! I was so sad to hear of it. Soon one will have no friends left,' she said with a pretty pout.

'We gather that he was a special friend of yours, ma'am – a very special friend.'

'How condemnatory you sound, officer! When one is a member of the Prince of Wales's circle, one must accept its mores.'

'So you do not deny that you were Searle's mistress?'

'Would there be any point in it?'

Bragg shifted uneasily in his chair. 'Let us say that I would not want to set off on a false trail.'

She cocked her head on one side. 'We were lovers, yes ... But I would hardly accept that I was his mistress. After all, that has connotations of dependence.'

'While you are a woman of means?'

'A lady of means, certainly.'

'I will stick to woman, ma'am,' Bragg said stolidly. 'In my book, "lady" has connotations of superiority.'

A look of irritation crossed her face. 'Well, what do you want of me, officer?' she asked.

'Just a few questions ... Did your husband know about your affair with Searle?'

'Of course. There would have been no point in an attempt to conceal it.'

'And what did he have to say?'

She shrugged. 'He was wildly angry, of course. He swore that Searle would never take me away from him ... That was pure melodrama on his part.'

'You mean that he could never afford to leave you?'

'Perhaps.' Mrs Edgerton shrugged. 'John Searle was lively, attentive, amusing – and very manly!' She gave a glance in Morton's direction. 'But he was too intense; he could become a little tedious.'

'Was your husband aware that you were only playing around with Searle?'

'Of course not!' she said with a pretty moue. 'That would have taken away most of the excitement.'

'I see ...' Bragg looked at her gravely. 'Would you say that your husband is capable of having Searle killed?' he asked.

'Over his association with me?'

'Yes, ma'am.'

She laughed. 'The idea both flatters and repels me,' she said. 'Frankly I have no idea ...' She considered for a moment. 'On the

105

whole, I think not,' she said. 'He is much too careful; perhaps that is what makes him so uninteresting.'

'Why does he need to be careful?' Bragg asked.

'His reputation in the City is the dominant element in his life. Some time ago I suggested that he should divorce me. That, at least, would have resolved the tension between us. But apparently the City would not have looked kindly on it.'

'We gather that he needs your fortune behind him.'

She raised her eyebrows. 'You are well informed, officer,' she said. 'Yes . . . He was aware of the family trusts when we married; but not aware of the restrictions placed upon them. You see, I enjoy the income from them in my lifetime. After my death, they become settled upon – in the quaint lawyer's phrase – the heirs of my body. But there will be no heirs of my body. I am unable to conceive children.'

'No children?' Bragg said sympathetically.

'No. Naturally I was not aware of this when I married – or, indeed, for a time after I married. At first my husband thought it reflected on him – until one of his mistresses became pregnant.'

Bragg frowned. 'I am sorry, ma'am,' he said. 'So what will happen to the trust monies?'

'In the event of my death, you mean? They will pass to my sister, and the heirs of her body – of whom there are three . . . In a sense, I ought to be grateful for my barrenness. Had I produced a child, I would have begun to fear for my life.'

'So you can see him killing a woman?'

Her lip curled. 'That is about his measure, officer,' she said.

Bragg and Morton took a cab to Waterloo station, then a train to Tunbridge Wells. Bragg was in an uncommunicative mood. He leaned back in his corner, puffing discontentedly at his pipe, and occasionally muttering to himself. As the train pulled into Tunbridge Wells station, he roused himself.

'This is a hell of a long way to come, lad,' he said.

Morton smiled. 'Equally, it is a long journey for a country jeweller to take to Searle's shop.'

'Yes.' Bragg knocked out his pipe and put it in his pocket. 'Something odd about that. Find us a cab, lad. I'll not walk further than I have to.'

Half an hour later they were in the Pantiles, peering into the shop window of Hurford & Co., Manufacturing Jewellers. So far as Bragg could see, there was nothing special about the articles on display. They were of good quality, certainly. But you could have seen their like in a score of shops in the West End of London. They pushed inside. A man with a gleaming bald head and ginger whiskers was behind the counter. He was engaged in wrapping a silver locket for an elderly man. Probably buying it for his granddaughter, Bragg thought . . . He would be a piece of the human flotsam that got washed up in places like this – family too well off, didn't want him around; moulder quietly out of their way . . . Eventually the old man shuffled off with his little parcel in his hand.

The shopkeeper turned to them with a practised smile. 'Yes, gentlemen? How can I be of service?'

Bragg put his warrant-card on the counter. 'Sergeant Bragg and Constable Morton, of the City of London police,' he said. 'You will be aware of the death of John Searle on the eighth of May.'

A puzzled frown touched Hurford's brow. 'John Searle?' he echoed.

'Don't tell me you have never heard of him,' Bragg said roughly. 'You were in his shop the day he was murdered.'

'There must be some mistake!' Hurford exclaimed.

'Oh, no. Searle told Ibbs you were coming; said he was looking forward to it. He was a nasty piece of work, wasn't he?'

Hurford swallowed. 'I decided not to go,' he said.

Bragg shook his head. 'It won't do, Mr Hurford,' he said. 'Ibbs saw you leaving as he came back just after one o'clock – and he is still alive to say so.'

The colour had drained from Hurford's face. He stumbled to a stool and sat down wearily.

'Right, sir,' Bragg said amiably, 'shall we start again? You have been a long-time customer of Furlonger & Searle. We have looked through your account with them. I also understand that you have had a serious dispute with Searle recently.'

Hurford took a deep breath. 'It was a trivial disagreement over a matter of business,' he said.

'A thousand pounds does not sound trivial to me, sir,' Bragg said cheerfully. 'I could live comfortably on that for the rest of my life.'

107

'I tell you, I was in this shop all day!'

'Oh no, sir. Apart from Ibbs having seen you, the eighth of May was a Wednesday. And, according to the notice in your window, Wednesday is your early closing day . . . Come on, now. You might as well make a clean breast of it.'

Hurford stared into space for a time, then he took a deep breath. 'There was a disagreement between us,' he said hesitantly. 'It was a matter of business ethics. He was clearly in the wrong, and I told him so.'

'How did it start, sir,' Bragg asked quietly.

'I had an American client . . . You will see from the door that we still manufacture jewellery here. It is a matter of pride to me. The factories in London and Birmingham have killed off nearly all the provincial makers. But there are still enough of the real gentlefolk here to support my one assistant.'

He seemed to drift into a reverie. Then he began again. 'My wife would say it was greed on my part, sergeant. I would say it was no more than legitimate professional ambition . . .'

'What sort of ambition?' Bragg prompted him.

'Why, ambition to create something of value, something of beauty, something enduring.'

'Go on, sir.'

Hurford stared into the distance. 'It was early in March that it all started,' he said dully. 'Before our season really began. An American gentleman, named Harvey Bernstein, leased a large house on the outskirts of the town. It belongs to a wealthy local family. But it had become too much for the old couple; and their children had moved away. When the wife became ill, they decided to go and live in the Mediterranean sun. So the house has been rented out to a succession of long-term visitors. The most recent was Mr Bernstein. His wife had some medical condition or other. Or said she had. It, at least, provided the excuse for her to go from one place in the world to another . . . However it be, they came to England. And Mrs Bernstein realised that any town with "Wells" in it meant a spa. And spas are places where sick people go to be cured. In this very pleasant town she found her spa, and a grand house available for rent.'

Hurford clasped his hands, and looked up as if in prayer. Then he began again, his voice more animated.

'Bernstein came into the shop one day. His watch needed

regulating. He became intrigued at our claim to be manufacturing jewellers. And I took him into the workshop, so that he could see my man at work. He said that his daughter was coming to join them, and he would like to give her some jewellery for her birthday. He thought that a piece made locally would intrigue and amuse her. We looked at various items, and he seemed to settle on a pendant – but something considerably grander than anything I could show him from stock. I said that I would make some drawings for him, and we arranged that he should come back in two weeks' time ... I want to make it clear, sergeant, that I was only trying to give substance to his thoughts ... Anyway, he duly came back again – and we had put in a fortnight's work on the project! He came in, and he was very taken with a design which had a large central diamond surrounded with filigree white gold. Money seemed to be no constraint. I am still convinced it was not the cost ...'

'So, what happened then?' Bragg prompted him.

'Why, I went up to London to see Searle, who was my usual supplier ... My grandfather had known Thomas Furlonger. Anyway, I bought a large brilliant-cut diamond, which was priced at one thousand pounds, and brought it back with me.'

'That is a great deal of money!' Bragg said. 'Did you pay cash for it?'

'No. I paid by cheque, which was duly honoured.'

'So, the diamond was yours, at that stage.'

Hurford frowned. 'I think it would be clearer if I tell the story in my own way.'

'Sorry, sir. Go on.'

'I brought the diamond back, as I said. Then I waited for Mr Bernstein to come in again. But nothing happened. I saw them walking about the town, but they never came in. I became a little anxious; but in this trade one cannot harass one's customers. After all, no one needs jewellery.'

'That is quite an admission, for a jeweller,' Bragg said genially. 'So what happened?'

'Why, I kept the diamond in my safe and waited ... Then I heard a rumour that the Bernsteins were leaving. I went to see him at his house. He said his wife had heard that mountain air was good for her condition, so they had rented a chateau in Switzerland. I protested that he had ordered a diamond pendant from me. He said he had done no such thing; he had signed nothing. Furthermore, he said that I had done no work beyond the drawings, and I still had the stone.'

'And was that true, sir?'

'Yes, sergeant, it was all true . . . I blame my pride in my work and a certain amount of human greed for my predicament . . . However, I shrugged the matter off. As he said, I still had the stone. It would be easy enough to return it to Furlonger's, and I would be back where I started . . .' He drifted into a grim-faced reverie.

'So, did it not work out that way?' Bragg asked.

Hurford looked up. 'No, it did not, sergeant. I went up to London, and pressed Searle to take back the stone. He said that it would be against the law to set aside the bargain! Think of that, between two traders! He said the City of London was a market overt – yes, a market overt. Something to do with its medieval past. Then he gave his cocky, sneering smile and said: "Of course, I am speaking as the principal of Furlonger & Searle. But if I put on my other hat, and address the problem as an individual – as merely John Searle – why, then, I might be able to help you. I will offer you five hundred pounds for it." That was half of what his firm had charged me for it! I tell you, sergeant, I was seething with anger. I protested, of course; and he told me to try and get a better price elsewhere . . . And he was smiling! Smiling at my discomfiture.'

'An unpleasant fellow,' Bragg said mildly. 'What time did all this happen?'

Hurford frowned. 'I was in Furlonger's by half-past twelve. I suppose it was all over by one o'clock.'

'And is there anyone who could vouch for it?'

'Bernstein is staying at the Dorchester in London. He would vouch for it!'

Bragg smiled. 'No, I was thinking of your trip to Furlonger's.'

'There was no one else in the shop, if that is what you mean. But Ibbs can vouch for my visit. You have said so yourself!'

'Right, sir . . . And what time did you get home?'

'I was back in Tunbridge Wells at half-past four.'

'Hmm . . . The half-past three from Waterloo? That would have given you plenty of time.'

Hurford frowned. 'Time for what?'

'Well, you see, sir,' Bragg said mildly, 'we are of the opinion that Searle was murdered by a professional killer.'

'Are there such people?'

'Oh, yes, sir. Hang out in the East End . . . If you left Furlonger's shortly after one o'clock, you would have had plenty of time to get in touch with them, arrange to have Searle knocked off, and still catch your train home.'

'But this is absurd!' Hurford cried. 'Why would I even contemplate such a thing?'

Bragg cocked his head on one side. 'It is not for me to speculate,' he said. 'But I suppose you might have thought you would get a better deal from Searle's executors.'

'Nonsense!' There was a note of panic in Hurford's voice. 'I tell you I had nothing to do with his death!'

'Hmm . . . I suppose you might find, say, a nice waitress, who would remember that you were sitting in her café from half-past one to three . . .'

'No, sergeant,' Hurford said glumly. 'I was just walking the streets, wondering how I could face my wife.'

Bragg got back to Old Jewry, to find a note from Inspector Cotton demanding his presence. He went along the corridor, tapped on his door and went in.

Cotton looked up from the report on his desk. He gave Bragg a hostile stare, then went back to his reading. Bragg stood for several minutes before the inspector placed his initial at the bottom of the last page and tossed the report into a tray. Then he looked up.

'What is it, Bragg?' he asked coldly.

'You left a note for me to come and see you, sir.'

'Oh, yes . . . Where the hell have you been? I was looking all over the bloody place for you!'

'I was down in Tunbridge Wells, on the Searle case, sir.'

'Tunbridge bloody Wells? How do you justify a jaunt like that?'

'Searle was putting the screws on a jeweller from there. The man had bought a diamond, worth a thousand pounds, for an American customer; but he welched on the deal. Hurford took the stone back to Furlonger's; but Searle only offered him half of that.'

'So is he our man?'

'Possibly. In fact, I would welcome your advice on this one, sir,' Bragg said earnestly.

Cotton looked at him warily. 'Out of your depth, are you?'

'Certainly, I have never come across this situation before.'

Satisfaction chased suspicion across Cotton's face. 'Well, sit down, then! Get to the point.'

'Do you mind if I smoke, sir?'

'Yes, I bloody do! Your room smells like a four-ale bar. I'm not having mine the same! Get on with it!'

'Very good, sir ... As you know, Morton and his young lady were present when the crime was committed ... By the way, is there any progress on the abduction?'

Cotton's eyes narrowed. 'We have done all we can in our own area,' he said shortly. 'It's down to the Met now.'

'I see ... Well, now, Morton witnessed the shooting of Searle. He says there was no hesitation, no bluster. Not a word was said. The man burst into the shop, gun in hand, took three or four paces straight to Searle and shot him in the head ...'

'Go on, man. I haven't all day!'

'Well, he clearly knew Morton was a policeman; expected him to have his 'cuffs on him ... He was on top of the situation right from the start. It was all very expert.'

'What do you mean, expert?'

'We believe that he was a hired gunman. If so, we are also looking for the person who set him on.'

Cotton's lip curled. 'You always want to complicate things, don't you?' he said contemptuously. 'It was a straightforward armed robbery. Nothing more!'

'The coroner won't have it so, sir. And once Sir Rufus gets an idea in his head, he won't let it go.'

'Huh! So where does he think the rough diamond is now? Some charity box for poxy whores?'

'Antwerp, probably.'

'Why not Amsterdam, where it came from?'

'Precisely because it came from there – it could possibly be recognised.'

'Why doesn't the coroner mind his own bloody business! He is concerned with the murder, that's all!'

'Try telling him that!'

'So, what do you want of me?' Cotton asked suspiciously.

'Well, you are the liaison officer with the Met, sir. They ought to have an idea if there are professional killers around.'

'Right. I will have a word. I'll gee them up on the young woman at the same time.'

When Bragg got back to his room, he found Morton sitting disconsolately at his desk.

'What have you been up to?' he asked genially.

Morton gave a ghost of a smile. 'I have been over to Edgerton's office. His secretary is a very pleasant and helpful young lady, as you will remember.'

'I remember she had her eye on you, all right!'

'I doubt it ... Anyway, I pretended that I had forgotten something Edgerton had told us at our interview. As a result I got a good look at his diary. From that it is clear that Edgerton was at a meeting in London at the time Searle was murdered. But, interestingly enough, he had no appointments at all for the following days.'

'Where are we, lad? The murder was on Wednesday the eighth.'

'Yes, sir. Edgerton was away from the office on the Thursday, Friday and Saturday.'

'And Sunday too, of course.'

'Yes. His secretary said that he had taken a short holiday on impulse ... Yet his diary is usually full well in advance.'

'Not on impulse, then, even if he didn't tell his secretary. So what are you thinking?'

'That in three days – or four if you include the Sunday – one could easily pop over to Antwerp with a rough diamond in one's pocket.'

'Well done, lad! Your brain is not completely addled! ... Try and put a bit more flesh on it. I would enjoy twisting that bugger's tail.'

There came a knock at the door, and the duty sergeant poked his head inside. 'A young chap from Sir Rufus Stone's chambers popped in, Joe,' he said. 'The coroner wants to see you.'

'What, now?'

'I expect so. Yesterday if you can manage it!'

Bragg and Morton strolled in the warm spring sunshine towards the Temple. To Bragg, Morton's dispirited walk and downcast air were becoming an irritation, a constant reproach. And none the less so, because unspoken. Bragg tried to put himself in his shoes. He thought back to his marriage; to his pride in his comely young wife; the way she was overwhelmed by the metropolis, country lass that she was. But she had had guts. Most of the wives had been townies. Some of them had made fun of her ways. But she had shrugged it off. She was proud of her husband; proud, too, of their little home. And when the baby was on the way, it seemed as if she would burst with happiness . . . That it should all be destroyed in an hour! And him not even there. Of course, everybody had been sympathetic. He could hardly spend a minute on his own, before bedtime. And it had helped – the comradeship, the support . . . He must have seemed ungracious at the time; with the anger and grief straining to burst out of him. Morton must be going through the same. He deserved all the sympathy that was going.

'Oh, I forgot!' Morton checked in his stride. 'We had a message from the Met.'

'When was that, lad?'

'While you were with Inspector Cotton.'

'Then why the hell did you not tell me before now?'

'I . . . I'm sorry, sir. I simply forgot.'

Bragg frowned. 'You are bloody simple if you forget things like that! What was it? Have they found Miss Marsden?'

Morton looked startled at the force of Bragg's reaction. 'Alas, no,' he said. 'It was a telephonic communication; they are holding Tommy Potts for us, on a charge of attempted murder.'

'Good! That will do to be going on with,' Bragg growled. 'Where is he?'

'Stepney police station.'

'Right. He can stew there for a few hours . . . I hope to·God Sir Rufus hasn't got some wild notions we have got to follow up.'

'We could hardly describe the Edgerton lead as a wild notion,' Morton said sharply.

114

'No . . . No, you are right, lad.'

They turned in strained silence into the Temple; in silence they crossed Pump Court and mounted the stairs to Sir Rufus Stone's chambers. His clerk seemed harassed.

'He is upsetting everyone today,' he complained. 'I cannot think why! He had a most successful case yesterday.'

'Getting above himself, is he?' Bragg asked genially.

The clerk looked startled, then a smile touched his lips. 'I am sure that he would not concede it was possible,' he said.

At that moment Sir Rufus erupted from his room. 'Have you seen my Stevens' *Mercantile Law*?' he called to any and all in earshot. 'I had it yesterday!' He checked. 'Ah, Bragg!' he said. 'You come at an inconvenient moment.'

'I expect you could fit us in, sir, while your subordinates are searching for your Stevens.'

Sir Rufus glared at him. 'I suppose that your laboured witticism deserves a modicum of my time!' He turned on his heel and stalked back to his room.

'Well, sit down!' he ordered. 'Tell me why you are thus disturbing what little time I am left to earn the pitifully small emoluments my clerk sees fit to accept for my labours!'

'You sent for me, sir,' Bragg said quietly.

'Did I? Ah . . . Yes, the jeweller case. How are matters progressing? I assume that they are not; since I have a distinct impression that you have been avoiding me!'

'Not at all, sir. You can tell Lady Stone that her Edgerton lead looks very promising.'

'I shall do no such thing, Bragg. My good lady is opinionated enough, without needing encouragement!'

Bragg smiled. 'Nevertheless, it has been very useful, sir. At the moment he is top of the list. We suspect he might have gone to the Continent, with the rough diamond, last weekend.'

'Suspect? What good is mere suspicion, Bragg? You must give it substance!'

'We will, sir.'

'Huh! And what about the young lady journalist? Has she been found yet?'

'Inspector Cotton is dealing with that, sir,' Bragg said stolidly.

'Ah! Do I detect dissatisfaction, resentment in your tone?'

'No, sir.'

115

'Come, Bragg! I cannot conceive that you would be content to sit back, and take no action in the matter!'

'We are probing about a bit, yes, sir.'

'But not to the detriment of the Searle investigation, I trust.'

'Of course not, sir . . . By the way, we came across an odd legal point the other day. Perhaps you could explain it for us.'

Sir Rufus gave an expansive smile. 'Are you sure you can afford my fees, Bragg? Meagre as they are.'

'Oh, it is to do with the Searle case, sir. We went down to Tunbridge Wells, to interview a suspect. It turns out that Searle was trying to diddle him over a diamond.'

'You have a bad attack of alliteration, Bragg,' Sir Rufus observed coldly. 'It does nothing to commend your observations to me.'

'Sorry, sir . . . We saw this Hurford man this morning. He has a jeweller's shop in that town. It seems he took a bit of a chance with a customer. This was a wealthy American; and our man thought he could make a killing by manufacturing a pendant for his daughter.'

'I would not have thought that particularly reprehensible,' Sir Rufus observed.

'No, sir. Not at all . . . What happened was that Hurford went up to Furlonger's, and bought a diamond for a thousand pounds. As it turned out, the project fell through. So he takes the diamond back to Searle, and asks for a refund of his money.'

'And what is strange about that?' the coroner asked impatiently.

'Nothing, sir. But Searle refused. He said that the law would not allow it; the bargain had to stand. He apparently quoted something about a market overt.'

'Ah!' Sir Rufus raised his eyebrows in surprise. 'Goodness me! How interesting . . . If you want a truly authoritative opinion, Bragg, you will have to go to a commercial lawyer . . . The phrase, of course, simply means an open market – almost market day. By extension, it describes the law appertaining to such markets.'

'Well, I can see that somewhere like Billingsgate, or Leadenhall market might fit the bill. But hardly a diamond broker in Poultry,' Bragg said.

'Ah! That is where you are enmeshed in your own ignorance,

Bragg. In the City of London, every day is market day for this purpose – excepting Sunday, that is.'

'So Searle was on the right side of the law, was he?'

'There is one restriction, I seem to remember . . .' he said. 'Ah, yes! It is necessary that goods should be exposed for sale to the public.'

Bragg glanced at Morton. 'He seems to have had everything in apple-pie order, does our Mr Searle,' he said. 'There was a little display of silver and jewellery in one of the windows.'

'Then that would have sufficed,' Sir Rufus said. 'And I suppose that, for some people, a thousand pounds is worth killing over . . . Certainly Hurford would have been well able to make use of the diamond stolen by the murderer.'

From the Temple, Bragg and Morton walked to Poultry. It struck Morton that there was no indication of the tragedy in Furlonger's window. There were the silver pieces, the pendants and bracelets displayed in the window; but not a trace of the black crepe that would normally have marked the death of the proprietor. Perhaps it was because there were no women employed in the business; that would usually be their prerogative . . . Surely that was odd in itself, Morton thought. If Searle had been an inveterate womaniser, would he not have set out to employ young women; forced his attentions on them? Even if shop girls were not of his social class, such a man would surely have derived some satisfaction from seducing them . . . On the other hand, Sergeant Bragg might have completely the wrong idea of the man.

When they entered the shop, Ibbs was negotiating with a customer. He seemed admirably patient, unflustered by the man's indecisiveness. Eventually the parcel of jewels was assembled, the two shook hands, and the customer hurried out.

'People are always in a rush to get out of here,' Bragg observed with a smile.

'Hardly surprising, is it?' Ibbs said. 'Coming out of that door, anybody is likely to have valuable gems about him.'

'But not valuable cash when he is coming in?'

'Not often.'

Bragg allowed a pause to grow, then: 'We have been down to see Mr Hurford, in Tunbridge Wells,' he said.

'Oh, yes?'

'According to him, Mr Searle treated him disgracefully.'

'I knew they had a disagreement, yes.'

'You saw Hurford leave the shop. Did Searle say anything about the incident?'

'He seemed rather amused by it.'

'Hmm . . . This market overt business. Do you agree with it?'

Ibbs gave a surprised half-smile. 'Whether I agree with it or not is of no consequence,' he said. 'It is the law under which we trade . . . It gives us finality, which is essential. After all, gemstones are a very valuable commodity. It is essential to know where one stands.'

'Has Searle ever allowed a customer to take a diamond on approval?' Bragg asked.

'No, never.'

'Right . . . Now, Mr Hurford confirmed that you were not on the premises when he came in.'

'Indeed. I only saw him leaving, as I came back from lunch.'

'Did Searle give you any details about his conversation with Hurford?'

Ibbs frowned. 'Yes, I remember! He remarked that he had sorted Hurford out.'

'What did he mean by that, do you think?'

'I took it that he had prevailed in some dispute between them. I thought no more about it.'

Bragg and Morton had a bite to eat in a pub, then took a cab to Stepney police station.

Bragg went over to the desk sergeant. 'You have a Tommy Potts for us,' he said. 'Attempted murder.'

The sergeant smiled smugly. 'You will never get it to stick,' he said. 'Attempted, maybe; but he has never succeeded in anything, all his life.'

'Funny sort of law you have out here,' Bragg said gruffly. 'Real Salvation Army stuff. Pat them on the head and say: "There, there! Don't do it again!" I thought you in the East End were a hard lot.'

The sergeant snorted. 'Anyway, from what he says, all he did was go into a shop and out again. Funny sort of attempt at murder.'

'Well, he will have to tell his story to the City magistrates. They are not Salvationist do-gooders.'

The sergeant took a key from his desk, and they followed him down to the cells. He unlocked a door. 'Someone to see you, Tommy,' he said genially, and went upstairs again.

Potts looked at Morton. 'Blimey!' he exclaimed.

'So you remember where we last met?' Morton said coldly.

'I dunno about met.'

'It was between four o'clock and half-past four on Wednesday last; in the premises of Furlonger & Searle,' Morton said.

Potts shrugged, and said nothing.

'A murder had just taken place. We have reason to believe that you were a member of the gang.'

'Here!' Potts cried in alarm. 'You can't fit me up for that!'

'Don't bet on it,' Bragg growled.

'All I know is I got inside and there is this bloke lyin' on the floor dead. 'Course I hopped it!'

'That hardly seems the action of a concerned citizen,' Morton said.

Potts did not reply.

'Why did you turn tail, knowing that a man was dead?'

Potts snorted. 'Because, with my record, you would try and pin it on me . . . And I was right, wasn't I?'

'No,' Morton said in a level voice. 'I saw the murder. I know you did not fire the shot. But we think that you were sent to confirm that Searle was really dead; that you were privy to the murder.'

'I don't know about no privy; and I didn't do no murder!' Potts cried. 'You're trying to fit me up!'

'Then what were you doing in that shop?'

Potts looked down at his fists. 'I was going to buy something.'

'What?'

'A bracelet for my god-daughter's christening.'

Bragg gave a guffaw of laughter. 'You deserve to get away with it for your bloody cheek!' he said. 'But it won't stand up, will it? You cannot afford Furlonger's prices! Thinking of turning the place over yourself, were you?'

119

'No! There was a little silver bangle in the window.'

Bragg gazed at him in silence. Then: 'All right,' he said. 'You can go for the moment. But I want something in return.'

'What's that?'

'The man who shot Searle also kidnapped a young woman, name of Catherine Marsden. I want to know where she is being kept.'

Potts shrugged. 'I ain't heard nothin' about that,' he said earnestly.

'Then bloody well make it your business to find out!'

By five o'clock, Morton was at the door of Aubrey Rivington's studio. A haughty-looking woman admitted him.

'It is the usual chaos here,' she said with a cool smile. 'Still Aubrey is the best, so we must perforce endure!'

He followed her into a waiting-room, where two doting mothers were shepherding debutante daughters. They looked up at him briefly, then turned away. Morton hoped that he was not at the end of the queue. From what Catherine had said of her own experience, Rivington was quite capable of spending an hour over the taking of one exposure. He glanced at the young women. They looked unsure of themselves, really rather insipid. But the four months of the Season would transform them. They would be shuttled from garden party to ball, from dinner party to opera. And in the course of it they would endeavour to acquire confidence and style. Above all, they would hope to meet unattached young men, who might be charmed into offering them the only future that society had prepared them for – marriage.

The door opened and Rivington ushered a strained-looking young woman back to her mother.

'They will be ready in one week,' he said in his mincing voice. 'Not a minute before!'

His eye caught Morton's. 'Will you come through, officer,' he said.

One of the mothers started to her feet rebelliously.

'This is an official matter,' Rivington said tartly. 'Did you not know that I do work for the police?' He led the way to his studio.

'I am not sure that your clients will be pleased to hear that,' Morton remarked.

'What? Oh, that! Well, if they wish they can go elsewhere,' he said waspishly. 'I can hardly cope with all these ladies wanting their ugly ducklings turned into swans.'

He crossed to a table and picked up a metal plate.

'Be careful with it,' he said. 'I would hate it to be damaged.'

Morton looked at the etching on it. 'So this is my betrothed, is it?' he remarked.

'Oh, yes! I made an impression from it. See!'

Morton took the print from him. It was Catherine to the life! A little younger, a little less self-possessed, but recognisable certainly. 'This is absolutely splendid, Aubrey,' he said warmly. 'Only you could have done it! And, tomorrow morning, it will look out from the front page of every *City Press* on the streets!'

6

Bragg sat at his desk, next morning, irritably cleaning his pipe. 'Why is it, lad, that nothing ever stays the same?' he asked. 'Here am I, forty-five next month; been smoking thick twist for thirty of them, and suddenly I cannot get it any more! I am told it's old-fashioned!'

'Who told you that, sir?' Morton asked in amusement.

'My local grocer. I have been buying it from him for over twenty years! Suddenly I have to put up with dried camel dung!'

'Then change your tobacconist! Sleuth out a satisfactory supplier!'

'Huh! I had enough of Sir Rufus and alliteration yesterday. I don't want you taking the piss!'

'Nevertheless, I am convinced that, somewhere in this Metropolitan maelstrom, everyone can achieve their heart's desire.'

'You mean, if I go far enough into the tumble-down reaches of Wapping, I might cadge a length of twist from a pig-tailed Chinese seaman?'

'Not at all, sir. Quite the contrary. When something becomes *démodé*, one should seek it in an establishment which can afford to stock the unusual.'

'So?'

'You ought to go to one of the better tobacconists in the City.'

'When I want my leg pulled, lad, I'll unscrew it for you to play with!' Bragg said gruffly.

'I am serious, sir,' Morton said. 'I am even prepared to make a small wager with you.'

Bragg's moustache twitched disapprovingly. 'I don't bet, lad, as you well know. Nor should you, if you know what's good for you!'

'Very well, sir. Then let me merely suggest that you should go to, say, Frankau's in Gracechurch Street, or Klingenstein's in St Mary Axe.'

'Don't be daft, lad! They supply boxes of cigars to the nobs! Have you never looked in their windows?'

'That is precisely why they would be able to afford to stock less prestigious lines.'

'Huh! If they did, they would charge an extra ha'penny an inch!'

There came a tap on the door, and the Commissioner wandered in.

'Ah, Bragg,' he said. 'Constable Morton . . . I am sorry that your young lady has not yet been liberated,' he remarked diffidently. 'But Inspector Cotton seems confident . . . quietly confident . . . Yes.'

'I am relieved to hear it, sir,' Morton said coolly.

The Commissioner turned to Bragg. 'And how are things progressing on the murder and robbery aspects of the case?'

'Progressing might not be the right word, sir. Up to now, we seem to have done no more than confirm what we already knew – or guessed, I suppose.'

'But you have a suspect, surely? After all, Constable Morton saw the murder!'

'Yes, sir. But we believe the shooting was done by a professional – a hired killer.'

'I gathered that. Though how firmly based the supposition is I cannot guess. Perhaps Inspector Cotton will be able to substantiate it. I understand that he is trying.'

Bragg gave a contemptuous snort, but said nothing.

'Yet, even accepting your thesis, Bragg,' Sir William went on, 'someone must have planned the whole episode, set it afoot.'

'Yes, sir. We have one candidate. A man named Edgerton.'

'Do you look to be able to charge him?'

Bragg sniffed. 'It all depends, sir.'

The Commissioner frowned. 'On what does it depend?' he asked irritably.

'Well, sir. At some stage we might have to well and truly stick our necks out. If we are right, the man who set up the murder will have been very careful to give himself an alibi. We shall find he was at an official function, or was chatting to the Bishop of London at the time . . .'

'Well, go on!'

'It's just that, with top people in the City as suspects, and the City's top policeman known to be directing the investigation, we cannot afford to go blundering around.'

Sir William cleared his throat. 'I take your point, Bragg. It is axiomatic, of course, that we cannot arrest without adequate evidence . . . Yes.' He turned and wandered out.

'Poor old bugger,' Bragg said feelingly. 'We are out of our depth, but he's way over his head! Right, lad. You try to put a bit more flesh on the Edgerton side of it, while I poke about some more.'

Bragg wandered along Cheapside and turned into Foster Lane. The heavy iron gates of Goldsmiths' Hall were open. In the vestibule a commissionaire was standing, his hands clasped about his paunch. On seeing Bragg he scowled.

'You here again?' he said querulously. 'Stirring up trouble.'

Bragg smiled. 'There was no trouble last time, and there will be none this; not for your lot, anyway.'

'Huh! Who do you want?'

'The top man, of course.'

'Not a chance! None of the Wardens are in this morning.'

'Then who will know about the members?'

The commissionaire pursed his lips. 'They will have a list of their names and addresses in the office,' he said.

'No. That is not what I am after. I am more concerned with the running of the company, the politics of the place.'

The man shook his head. 'I don't know . . . unless you were to see the Prime Warden's secretary. He must know about everything. Though whether he will talk about it is another matter!'

'Very well. Tell him I would like to see him.'

Bragg strolled into the inner hall, admiring the polished columns of pink marble, the great dome. Projecting from one wall was a banner with a heraldic device – two covered cups and two lions' heads, quartered. Just the same as the plaque in Searle's office. He had been proud to belong to this lot ... Well, why wouldn't he be? It was the top of the tree for him; a family tradition. Yet it seemed, from what he was learning of Searle, that he would want more out of it than he put in. It would be a means to an end.

He heard footsteps approaching. He turned and the commissionaire beckoned him. He took Bragg down a corridor on the ground floor, towards the back of the building. He tapped on a door, and led the way into a small office.

'Sergeant Bragg, of the City police,' he said loudly, then withdrew.

A grizzled man in his fifties rose from his desk, and held out his hand. 'My name is Betts, Alfred Betts,' he said. 'I am afraid that the Prime Warden is away at the moment.'

Bragg sat on the chair opposite him. 'I am sure you will be the very person I need to talk to, sir,' he said amiably. 'Prime Wardens come and go, but you go on for ever, eh?'

'Something like that, sergeant,' he said. 'I do hope that our members have not caused offence to anyone. I admit that our banquet last week was, well, a little more festive than one would wish, but ...'

'I am not concerned with rowdiness in the street, sir,' Bragg said with a smile. 'I cannot see who, around here, would complain anyway ... No, I am interested in one of your members – or rather, one of your late members.'

'I see. Who is that?'

'John Searle.'

A cautious look spread over Betts's face. 'I see,' he said. 'I knew of his tragic end, of course.'

'Yes,' Bragg said drily. 'Not quite the way for one of your lot to end up, was it? Now, I gather that he was not the first member of his family to belong to the Goldsmiths.'

'No, indeed,' Betts said equably.

'I believe that Thomas Furlonger, his grandfather, reached the dizzy heights of Second Warden. But what I want to know is why John Searle never got any further than a foot-soldier.'

Betts looked uncomfortable. 'Of course, he was a diamond broker, not a goldsmith by trade,' he said.

'Yes. But so was Furlonger. And we both know that it has precious little to do with it. I bet you could find me a score of members who have no connection with the trade at all.'

Betts shrugged and said nothing.

'So you see,' Bragg went on, 'I am curious. At the same time I don't want to put a whole team of detectives in here to find out whether I am right or wrong. They are apt to cause a bit of a mess. And, being inquisitive souls, who knows what they might want to pry into.'

Betts was frowning. He stared out of the window for a space, then he turned back to Bragg.

'It is true that his progress was limited. That was because of an unfortunate incident. His advancement was, in effect, blocked by one of our members.'

Bragg raised his eyebrows. 'They can do that, can they?' he asked. 'A member of the company can just pass the word, and that's it?'

'The individual concerned was more than a mere member of the company,' Betts said.

'An officer, then. But what is Searle supposed to have done to upset him?'

Betts hesitated. 'The details of the matter were never made clear. There was no need. The complainant was a man of stature and integrity. His word was accepted ... Moreover, a lady's honour was involved.'

'A relative?'

Betts shook his head. 'I can say no more.'

Bragg jumped to his feet with sudden anger. 'Searle has been murdered!' he shouted, leaning across the desk, his face inches away from that of Betts. 'I don't give a tuppenny bugger about the niceties of a lady's honour! For all I know – and you too – this man of integrity and stature didn't stop at having Searle black-balled. I want to know who he is, and where he lives.'

Betts blanched. 'Very well,' he mumbled. 'I can only ask you to receive it in confidence.'

Bragg drew back. 'Thank you, sir,' he said amiably. 'Jot it down for me, will you?'

He waited calmly while Betts consulted a book, then wrote a name and address on a piece of paper and handed it over. Bragg read it with interest.

'Colonel Sir Thomas Porteus, eh? I shall enjoy having a chat with him . . . And the lady?'

'His daughter, Avril.'

Morton went into a café and ordered a cup of coffee. He was living in a perpetual daze; his mental faculties had atrophied. He seemed to have been standing outside himself; listening to his endless enquiries: 'Do you deal with the travel arrangements of Edgerton & Co.?' A baker's dozen of ticket agents; as many shaking heads. What did it matter any more? The waitress brought his coffee.

'You look as if you had lost a pound and found a penny!' she said coquettishly.

Morton looked up at her cheerful face. 'I am sorry,' he said. 'I am somewhat obtuse today.'

'I expect you could get something for it at the chemist's,' she said pertly, and passed on.

She was right to chide him, he thought. However great his personal misery, he had no right to foist it on others. He sipped at the scalding liquid, then left it and marched out of the café. It was too inactive, too passive. He could not just sit in a coffee shop while his life crumbled about him. Outside the Bank of England was the pitch of a news vendor.

'City Press . . . Get your City Press,' he was calling.

Morton sprinted across. He fumbled in his pocket for change. 'Give me a copy,' he gasped, pushing a half-crown into the man's hand. He took the paper and walked away.

'Your change!' the man called.

Morton walked on unheeding until he got away from the crowds. Then he unfolded the paper. Catherine's face gazed out at him, serene, self-possessed, beautiful. He felt tears pricking at his eyes; a sob forming in his throat. He wanted to dash among the passers-by, seizing their arms, demanding of them if they had seen her . . . But it would add nothing to the effect of her picture. They had only to read the heading:

They would not need the plea to contact the police to feel the horror of her plight ... By nightfall, hundreds of copies would have been distributed – thousands even. Would find their way to the suburbs for a score of miles around. People sitting in trains would look across, and see her picture in the paper of the person opposite. At last, matters were not solely in the hands of Inspector Cotton, and a Met reluctant to co-operate with the City police. Buoyed up with hope, he resumed his quest.

The trouble was that there were so many ticket agents. And often, travel arrangements were left to secretaries or junior clerks. No doubt these people would receive inducements to deal with a particular firm; especially if it were located in some back alley ... But it would not have to be too far from Edgerton's office.

He hurried back to Fenchurch Street. He had been over this ground already, but not systematically ... There was the Iron-mongers' Hall. And along the western side of it an alley that he had not been aware of. Fishmonger Alley. That was strange in itself, since Fishmongers' Hall was down on the Thames. Perhaps he was becoming light-headed ... He walked down it, and emerged in Billiter Square. And there, on the corner, was a ticket agent's shop. He took a deep breath to steady himself, then went inside.

'I believe that you deal with the travel arrangements of Edgerton & Co., the ship-brokers,' he said.

The girl smiled. 'Yes. Have you had a problem with tickets?'

'City police. I would like some information, please.'

The girl's face fell. 'Just a moment,' she said. 'I shall have to ask my boss.'

She was away for several minutes. Morton felt frustration building in him. Sergeant Bragg would have known how to deal with this. He would be over the counter and into the back office, threatening the direst of penalties, even physical violence. Morton well knew that he could never bring it off: that if he tried the same approach, it would probably end in a complaint to the Commissioner. Yet there could be situations where it was the only course open. He was just screwing up his resolve to vault over the counter and storm the office beyond, when a bespec-

127

tacled, meek-looking man appeared. He was holding a sheaf of papers in his hand.

'I believe that you are enquiring about Edgerton's account,' he said in a concerned voice.

'That is so, sir.' Morton laid his warrant-card on the counter.

The man peered at it. 'Well, I have had a quick look at it,' he said. 'I can see nothing wrong, constable.'

'We are concerned about a recent trip to the Continent – last week in fact.'

The man put down his bundle and began to flip through the papers. 'Would that be on the ninth of May?'

'That sounds right.'

'Yes. Mr Edgerton himself. Two tickets for the train to Dover and back; two return tickets on the ferry from Dover to Ostend.'

'In Belgium.'

'Yes. Out on Thursday the ninth of May; back on Saturday the eleventh of May.'

'Do you know who went with him?'

'Why, Mrs Edgerton, I presume.'

'I see. And could they travel on from Ostend to Antwerp?'

The man frowned for a moment, then picked up a large red-bound book. He thumbed through the pages for some moments, then looked up in triumph.

'Yes, indeed!' he said. 'The trains leave Ostend every hour and a half, during the day. One has to change at Ghent. According to the timetable, at least, one could get there in an hour and a half.'

Bragg pushed the ledger away from him, and looked through the glass screen at Ibbs bustling round the shop. Somehow trade seemed to have slackened off. Perhaps the sensation-seekers had been sated; yet the trade buyers had not come back . . . He ought to find out what was going to happen to the business now. Though that would be up to whoever administered the estate. He got up and went to the door in the screen.

'Do you think you could close up the shop for a bit,' he said. 'There are one or two matters I would like to mention.'

'Of course, sergeant.'

Ibbs took a bunch of keys from his pocket, crossed to the door and secured it at top and bottom.

'Like a fortress,' Bragg remarked, as Ibbs sat gravely in the chair opposite him.

'Exactly,' Ibbs said. 'Of little use when the other side use guns.'

Bragg put his pipe in the ashtray. 'You have been working for Mr Searle for many years,' he said.

'Indeed, sergeant, and for his father before him.'

'That was Alfred Searle?'

'Yes. A real gentleman he was.'

Bragg sniffed. 'They all are . . . So, when did you start?'

'In 1877; eighteen years ago.'

'And you had worked for a time in your family's business in Clapham.'

'Yes. That was retail, of course.'

'Whereas the retail here is only a device, so that customers cannot change their minds.'

Ibbs shrugged and said nothing.

'I see, from the records, that John Searle joined his father in 1879; two years after you.'

'Yes.'

'But he was a partner right from the start?'

'Of course, he was family.'

'In the army he had the reputation of being a bit wild; a womaniser; not quite a gentleman.'

Ibbs looked shocked. 'I would not know anything about that,' he said.

'We have picked up a rumour about Searle and a Miss Porteus. Her father is a member of the Goldsmiths' Company.'

'Oh, yes?'

'The old man seems to have got the notion that Searle's intentions were a good deal less than honourable. He saw to it that Searle was kept out of any office in the guild.'

'I know nothing about that side of his life, sergeant.'

'Hmm . . . Still, it's interesting, don't you think?'

'Perhaps.'

'And when did John Searle come into his own?' Bragg asked. 'When did Alfred die?'

'Oh, ten years ago, I would say . . . 1885.'

'So John would have had five or so years to learn his trade.'

'Yes. But he picked it up quickly. He was a natural.'

'He is interesting,' Bragg said blandly. 'I'll give you that . . . There is one small thing we might get out of the way. January 1889. There is an entry in his drawings account. "Pendant £30". By the side of it there is what seems to be "C1" – though it could be "CI". Have you any thoughts on that?'

'I think that must be the pendant he gave to my wife, Clara. It was the first occasion on which she acted as hostess at our Christmas reception.'

'What, the previous December?'

'Yes. It was held at the Viaduct Hotel in Holborn. Quite a small affair. Naturally, not many of our customers were able to bring their wives. But those that came seemed to appreciate Clara's efforts. And, after all, in the jewellery trade the whims of the ladies are all-important!'

'No doubt! . . . There was just one oddity about it. You had been made a partner the previous year. But the cost of the pendant was all charged to Searle's drawings. I would have expected that one eighth of the cost would be charged to your drawings.'

Ibbs smiled. 'He was insistent that he should bear the whole cost. He said that I had more burdens than he had, and slender resources.'

'What did he mean by that, do you think?'

'Well, for one thing I was married, with a young son. And, when I became a partner, he had asked me to move from Clapham to somewhere nearer the City.'

'This was when you went to live at Islington, was it?'

'Yes, sergeant.'

'I see. Then that's sorted out . . . There is one other conundrum that you might be able to help me with. This rough diamond that was stolen – or rather the insurance on it.'

'What do you want to know?'

Bragg shrugged. 'There is probably nothing in it,' he said. 'But I get the impression it was insured twice over.'

Ibbs looked perplexed. 'That would have been Mr Searle's department,' he said. 'But I am sure there would have been an explanation for it.'

'Hmm . . . Well, we know that Searle took out a policy with Lloyd's, to cover the trip from Amsterdam to London and back.'

'Yes. I am aware of that.'

'Then take a look at this invoice.' Bragg pushed it across the desk. 'It appears that, when Searle picked up the diamond from Moeller's, in Amsterdam, they presented him with this invoice. If you look at it, there is the cost of the rough diamond, and under it an insurance premium. All written out in English, so Searle knew precisely what he was paying for.'

Ibbs frowned. 'I know precious little about insurance,' he said. 'But, on the face of it, it does seem odd . . . It looks as if Mr Searle implicitly accepted the total amount shown on this invoice.'

'But why would Moeller's insist on insuring the diamond themselves – even though they were going to pass on the premium to Mr Searle?'

'I can only suppose that it is a practice based on experience. I have not seen anything quite like it before. But, normally, a parcel of stones would be brought to us by Moeller's. Mr Searle had never, to my knowledge, gone to bring a stone back before.'

Bragg frowned. 'I still don't see it,' he said. 'This is an invoice which Furlonger & Searle have yet to pay – on the face of it, anyway.'

Ibbs shrugged. 'I can only guess . . . But, if the stone were lost in transit, they would have ensured that its value would be recovered.'

'Not if the insurance premium had not been paid, it wouldn't!' Bragg said triumphantly.

'Ah, but Moeller's would have paid the premium themselves. On this invoice they are merely passing on the burden to the purchaser.'

'So, you are saying that Furlonger's were paying a hefty insurance premium, just for the privilege of dangling a bloody great diamond in front of Miss Marsden's nose . . . The things some people will do to screw the rich!'

'So you think Edgerton is our man?'

Bragg and Morton were walking through the dejected streets of the East End, towards Foxy Jock's pawnshop.

'I would say it was virtually a cast-iron certainty,' Morton said buoyantly. 'We have a motive, in that Searle had seduced his wife. And, if we postulate a hired killer, means and opportunity are no longer relevant!'

'Hmm ... I wonder how many men we could hang on that reasoning.'

'Probably none who, immediately after the killing, crossed to the Continent and took a train in the general direction of Antwerp.'

'Yes ... You know, Searle was as bent as a nine-bob note. Unless I have missed something, he had set up an insurance fraud.'

'Really?'

'Well, insuring the same risk twice over looks like a fiddle to me ... If you remember, Searle took out a special all-risks policy with Lloyd's, before he set off to fetch the diamond. Yet, when we look at the invoice from Moeller's, there's a damn great insurance premium tacked on to the bill, for Furlongers to pay. In my book that's fraud. Lose one stone, collect the cost twice over.'

'That presupposes he had foreknowledge of both the Dutch insurance and the raid.'

Bragg grunted. 'One thing he had no foreknowledge of was that he was going to get shot.'

'I am sure', Morton said, 'that there is a system for sharing the risk, where there is multiple insurance.'

'How do you mean, lad?'

Morton laughed. 'I am out of my depth here, I admit. But, where several Lloyd's syndicates insure, say, a merchant vessel, each would take a proportionate share of the risk and of the premium paid.'

'Maybe. But they know who else is taking a slice. Here we have a rough diamond that Moeller's make sure is insured. And they see that the customer pays the premium. Fair enough. But Furlonger's are in another country. And Searle insures the same stone with insurers in England ... Now, let us say the stone goes missing. Moeller's don't get the stone back, but they claim on the Dutch insurers. So they are happy. Searle does not have to pay the invoice now, because that would invalidate the Dutch com-pany's insurance claim. At the same time, Searle goes to his insurance broker, and makes a claim on the English insurer.'

'Certainly, someone seems to be getting five thousand pounds for nothing,' Morton said. 'But surely there would have to be a conspiracy between Searle and Moeller's, to make it work?'

'I don't know, lad.' Bragg sighed. 'This is a real sod of a case . . . Anyway, let us see what old Jock can tell us.'

They went into the pawnshop, and Bragg banged the bell on the counter. The curtain at the back was carefully parted, and a bloodshot eye observed them.

'Come on, Jock!' Bragg cried. 'Let's bloody have you!'

'Ah! Mr Bragg!' Jock pushed through into the shop. 'And the nice young constable, too.'

'What is the news about the rough diamond?' Bragg demanded.

Jock nervously licked his lips. 'Nairy a word, sergeant. Quiet as the grave!'

'But you must bloody know!' Bragg blustered. 'A kid can't get his Saturday ha'penny pinched without you know!'

Jock shook his head slowly. 'Not this time, Mr Bragg. And it's not for want of asking.'

Bragg snorted angrily. 'Then what about the killer? The man who knocked off Searle.'

'Gone to America, they say. Straight to Euston, and a train to Liverpool.'

'What ship? We could telegraph America!'

'Don't know. And I daren't be too nosy.'

Bragg turned to the door. 'Keep listening out!' he said.

Once in the street, he nudged Morton. 'America, eh?' he said. 'What was the name of that supposed customer of Hurford? Bernstein, wasn't it? I reckon he would bear looking at a bit more closely.'

Catherine was staring dully out of the window, watching the grey clouds floating over the roof-tops. Now she was being watched more closely. When her food was brought, or her room was being tidied, there were always two maids. She wondered if they had found another way of drugging her. Certainly a lethargy had settled on her. But her mind seemed clear. Perhaps it was no more than despair . . . The absurdity of the phrase struck her. Despair was the stage before surrender, and she would never do that! She was conscious that she had stopped wondering why she had been brought here. Her will was set on a narrower goal – that of staying sane. To speculate on the future was self-destructive.

She just had to have faith that she would be freed. After her abortive attempt to escape, the whole world seemed to be against her. But James would rescue her, she was sure of it.

She was just about to lie on her bed, to seek oblivion in sleep, when she heard a key in the lock. One of the porters came in.

'You come with me,' he said gruffly.

'Why? Where are you taking me?'

'To Matron.'

'Why does she want to see me?'

The man shrugged. 'I dunno,' he said. 'But she's not for taking any chances . . . So behave yourself.'

He took a firm hold on Catherine's arm, and marched her down the stairs to the ground floor. He led her along a corridor to the back of the building, knocked on a door and pushed her inside. Matron turned from the window, her face grim.

'Sit down,' she ordered.

She picked up a newspaper. It looked like a *City Press*, Catherine thought. The typeface, and the layout of the back page were familiar. Matron was staring at the paper, then at her, then back to the paper. She put it down, and Catherine could see a picture on the front page. This was a new departure! Matron hastily turned the paper over.

'You are leaving here,' she said abruptly.

'So you believe me at last!' Catherine exclaimed.

'I only know what I was told when you were committed,' Matron said sharply.

'At all events you are sending me home!'

Matron's stare was troubled, almost resentful. 'You will be going at three o'clock,' she said.

Catherine could feel relief and excitement flooding through her. 'I realise that you are not at fault,' she said, 'that you were misled into thinking that I am unbalanced.'

Matron ignored her. She rang a bell on her desk and the porter came in. 'Take her back to her room!' she ordered.

To Catherine it was perplexing still to be guarded as she made her way upstairs. They obviously had no intention of treating her with respect and courtesy. But she had run away once; and this was certainly not the moment to complain.

She sat on her bed, wondering what time it was. There was no clock in her room; no church clocks nearby to tell her. She looked out of the window, but there was no sun. Well, it was some time since she had eaten lunch . . . And she would need to change into her proper clothes. Her glance fell on the emergency bell-push. She would not dare to press that again! Not for something as trivial as having her clothes brought. She thought back to her abortive escape attempt. To have been committed here was like a prison sentence. The Metropolitan police constable had not doubted for a moment that she was insane. And ever since that incident she had been treated with hostility and mistrust. But now she would be going home! Her parents must have been riven with anxiety. And James . . . poor James! The image formed in her mind of her last glimpse of him – handcuffed to the stair-rail, his face grim. At her feet the lifeless body of Searle; a look of surprise, incomprehension, somehow frozen on his face. It was all hideous! But she must forget it. She was going home; back to the certainties of her old routine. Back, also, to the prospect of a new life with James. She would soon be able to put this incident behind her; to look forward, to plan the future with him.

There came the clump of boots in the corridor. Two porters came in, their faces impassive.

'Come on,' one of them said. 'You are going with us.'

'But I have to change into my proper clothes,' Catherine protested.

'Never mind about that!'

Her arms were seized; she was dragged protesting out of the room, and down the corridor.

'Are you going to walk, or shall we have to carry you?' one of the men demanded harshly.

Resentment and apprehension gripped Catherine. 'I shall walk, of course!' she said.

'Then hurry up!' She was conscious of the incurious stares of other inmates as she was hustled down the stairs. A growler was drawn up at the front door. Catherine was bundled inside. One man sat beside her, still clutching her arm. The other was opposite, scowling at her, daring her to escape. As the carriage pulled out of the driveway, he jerked down the window blinds. Catherine had a sensation of the carriage turning left, going towards the City. She tried to follow its course in her mind, but soon lost track of it. Certainly the streets were busier. She could hear news vendors calling, the rumble of heavy drays. They must

135

be going south. After twenty minutes or so, she sensed that the cab had turned off the main thoroughfare, was picking its way through side streets. As it slowed to a halt, the man opposite released the blind beside him. She had a glimpse of a shop window bearing the legend BENSON'S DIVAN.

The man next to her seized her wrist. 'You keep your mouth shut, or there will be trouble!' he growled menacingly.

Then she was being hustled across the pavement, through an ornate doorway and across a tiled lobby. There was a wrought-iron staircase on the back wall. Catherine was dragged up it, conscious of the mingled odours of tobacco and cheap scent. On the next floor one of her escorts went over to a desk on the landing. He spoke briefly with a be-rouged, middle-aged woman. She nodded her head, then handed him a key.

He hurried back. 'Number seven, top floor,' he said.

Then she was being pulled again, up flight after flight of stairs, her wrist stinging. At last they reached the top landing, brighter because of the skylight. She must try to remember what the men looked like, she thought. They were part of this monstrous conspiracy against her. They stopped at a door, and one of the men unlocked it. Catherine was pushed inside.

'Keep quiet, if you know what is good for you,' she was admonished. Then the door banged shut, the key was turned in the lock, and she was left alone.

Bragg and Morton took a cab to Chelsea. They found the house of Charles Drewin in a quiet little street near the Thames. A maid showed them up to a sitting-room at the rear of the house. Morton strolled over to the window.

'What a splendid view!' he exclaimed. 'The grounds of the Royal Hospital, and then the river. Who would expect this in the heart of Westminster?'

'There must be plenty of money about,' Bragg said darkly. 'But then, there would be if he has had prosperous businesses like Furlonger's as clients.'

'I thought you said that it was in decline, sir.'

'I mean years ago. Remember, Drewin goes back a long way.'

The door opened and a lined, balding man came in. His shoes

were gleaming, his frock coat well brushed. He gave a pixie-like smile.

'It was well that you sent a message,' he said brightly. 'I normally play bowls on a Wednesday afternoon.'

'Sorry to inconvenience you, sir,' Bragg said.

'Not at all! Citizen's duty, you know.' He waved them to chairs. 'Do you know, in all my years of practising accountancy in the City, this is the first time that the police have sought my help.'

'You will have read about the murder of John Searle, sir.'

'Yes, yes. A dreadful business! One can only be grateful that he had no family. It must be terrible for the nearest and dearest when something so shocking happens.'

'Yes, sir. Now, you were the auditor of the Furlonger & Searle business for many years. So no one will know it, and the people involved in it, better than you.'

Drewin raised an eyebrow. 'I fail to see how that can be of help in what, I understand, is a simple case of robbery with violence.'

Bragg nodded. 'It may come down to just that,' he said. 'But for the moment we are keeping an open mind. Now, their diamond broking business goes back a good long time.'

Drewin smiled. 'Yes, indeed! It was originally Furlonger & Sons. It was set up in the 1760s by the grandfather of Thomas Furlonger.'

'He's the one with the nose?'

Drewin chuckled. 'Yes. The Furlonger nose is a very prominent family feature! Acceptable in a man, I suppose, but a distinct handicap for a woman. Interestingly enough, his daughter did not inherit it.'

'That was Louisa, who married Alfred Searle,' Morton remarked.

'Yes. The mother of John, now sadly deceased . . . And he inherited his own father's nose.'

'Tell me about the Searles,' Bragg broke in impatiently.

Drewin frowned. 'Well, we did not act for them. Their business had been set up in the previous generation, by David Searle; and they had Chetwynd's as their auditors.'

'We understand from Ibbs that it was Alfred Searle who amalgamated the two businesses.'

137

'Ah, yes. Wilfred Ibbs. How is he? A sound fellow; reliable.'

'He is being just that – sound and reliable ... Am I right in thinking that the Searles had traded from Hatton Garden?'

'That is correct. They not only traded as brokers; they had a small retail business also. Rather quixotically, Searle continued that in the new business at Poultry.'

'Ah,' Bragg said. 'So it was not just a matter of market overt?'

Drewin looked puzzled, but said nothing.

'Is it the case that Louisa was Thomas Furlonger's only child, sir?' Morton broke in. 'I am endeavouring to construct a family tree.'

Drewin frowned. 'To the best of my knowledge and belief, she was. I certainly know of no other.'

'Thomas Furlonger must have been disappointed not to have a son to carry on the business.'

'Well, perhaps. But the Furlongers seem always to have had an equivocal view of parenthood. He himself had been bundled off into the army; out from under his father's feet. I think the Furlongers always found it difficult to share authority with others.'

'A good thing too,' Bragg said with a smile. 'We might not have beaten Napoleon otherwise ... Now, old Thomas was well respected in the City and beyond. Even to becoming Second Warden in the Goldsmiths' Company.'

'Indeed! A very sound man, very stable. It must have been a deep disappointment to him that his wife did not bear him a son. But he seems to have made the best of it. He certainly saw to it that Louisa married within the trade.'

'But outside the City, nevertheless,' Bragg remarked.

Drewin smiled. 'I suspect that the mystique of the City was not something Thomas bowed down to, or even admired,' he said. 'He had experienced a wider world, had fought for king and country. No, I think that he would have died content.'

'And, knowing what you do, would you say that John Searle would have disappointed him?'

Drewin looked out of the window with a frown. 'You mean, on the presupposition that he would have expected his policies to be continued? ... Well, both Alfred and John have perforce modified the business in accordance with modern demands. For instance, there was little or no call for coloured diamonds in Thomas's day.

138

But wholesaling in any form has to respond to the demands created by retailers ... No. His only disappointment – and a major one – would be that John Searle has left no children; that the business, if it survives, will pass out of the family.'

On getting back to the City, Morton went to the Guildhall and asked directions to the office of the Registrar of Births, Marriages and Deaths. Soon he was confronted with a range of shelves bearing great, dusty tomes. He selected one at random. He was relieved to find that most of the pages were blank. With such a small population residing in the City, the entries were bound to be few in number. So what should he look for? Perhaps he should start with John Searle; begin with his beginning. He guessed that he would be in his mid-forties at the date of his death. So he could have been born around 1850. He took the register for that year to a table, and began to scrutinise the pages ... No. There was no mention of a Searle. Which way to go, then? Backwards or forwards? He mentally flipped a coin – backwards! He took the register back to the stacks, and brought out that for 1849. He carefully turned the pages ... names that meant nothing – names with a resonance in the modern City – names that ... He had almost missed it! John Searle, born on the seventh of April, at number three, Blomfield Street. Father Alfred Searle; mother Louisa Searle. Father's occupation diamond broker; name of informant Alfred Searle.

Well, it was a start. One strand was already in place, because Louisa had been the daughter of Thomas Furlonger – Tommy the Nose, as Bragg liked to call him. And surely the house in Blomfield Street had been the family home of the Searles for generations? So their history ought to be here also. He settled down to go through the registers since 1800. It was a mammoth task, but there was no point in undertaking it at all, and then skimping it.

Births, marriages, deaths; all of human life. Births, marriages, deaths; 1818, 1819, 1820 ... Jackson, Tolly, Benson, Searle ... Searle! The birth of Alfred Searle, on the twentieth of June 1820! David Searle had registered that; the father of the child – a broker. Very coy about the kind of broker, but that was understandable in a public document. Anyway, the address was three, Blomfield

139

Street. There could be no doubt. He went back to the stacks for more registers.

By now Morton was becoming adept at his task. His finger would swoop down the page, his eyes probing the entries. Fortunately there were not too many names beginning with the letter S. But he must maintain his concentration, or he would be wasting his time ... Samuels ... Short ... Simpson ... Searle! The birth of Amy Searle on the eleventh of December 1828. The informant David Searle, of three, Blomfield Street. So there had been a daughter? ... Alfred and Amy, son and daughter. Both beginning with the letter A. If there had been another child, Morton wondered idly, would its name have begun with the letter B?

A clerk was standing at his elbow. Morton looked up.

'We shall be closing in half an hour,' he murmured.

'But it is vital that I carry on my search!'

'Sorry, sir. We are open again tomorrow, at ten o'clock.'

'I am afraid you do not understand. I am a police officer. I am investigating the murder of the jeweller, last week. I simply have to keep going.'

The clerk looked at him dubiously. 'Can you prove that?' he asked.

'Of course.' Morton laid his warrant-card on the table. The man picked it up and scrutinised it.

'The trouble is, constable, that there will be no one on duty to see that the place is locked up.'

'There will be cleaners, surely?'

'Yes. But they will be gone by eight o'clock.'

'Then, can you give me a key? I will promise to bring it back to you in the morning.'

The clerk pursed his lips. 'Well, I suppose these are exceptional circumstances. Very well, here is my key. And, if you switch on any of the electrical lights, be sure to switch them off again before you leave.'

Morton smiled at the clerk's retreating back, and went to the stacks for some more register books. At least he was half-way through the century now; more than half-way through his task. He opened the register for 1851. He was conscious that his concentration was waning. His eyes were blurring with fatigue

140

as they followed his finger down the page ... Marriages ... the same surnames recurring. Was it reincarnation, he wondered. The same handful of christian names. Alfred ... Edward ... Mary ... Alice ... Searle ... Searle! He was suddenly alert. The marriage of Amy Searle, on the sixth of May 1851 ... to Samuel Ibbs, of Church Road, Clapham! The bride's address was given as three, Blomfield Street, in the City of London.

At first Catherine sat on a chair, utterly dejected. The terror induced by those two brutes was ebbing away. But she was still imprisoned; still not in control of her life.

Why had she been moved? she wondered. Had they in some way found out that she was connected with the *City Press*? ... There had been a picture on the front page of the matron's newspaper – in the advertisements section. Most strange! Mr Tranter would be horrified at the idea; outraged. Had he been replaced as editor? Or had he been placed under unprecedented pressure? ... The matron of Greenlands had certainly looked at her, then back to the newspaper. It must be! It was her likeness that was in the paper. James must have arranged it! The thought surfaced that it had to be an act of near desperation on his part, but she suppressed it. There was hope! She had been moved from the sanatorium because people had seen her; the staff and some of the inmates. But who would believe the inmates? How many of the staff would risk their jobs?

She went over to the window, and tried to empty her mind. She stared out over the roof-tops. This was a tall building, as her aching thighs attested. Her room was at the back; facing south, if the hazy sunlight was any guide. She mentally shook herself. This was not her room! She must not drift into a passive acceptance of what was happening to her. She was not a piece of worthless flotsam on the sea of existence! She turned to examine her cell. After all, prisons were to be broken out of!

It was a strange room, she thought. The building could once have been a hotel; outmoded by the marbled grandeur of modern competitors. There was a table and two chairs, a double bed with a heavy silk cover. The carpet was worn in places, yet the curtains were of heavy brocade. But how odd! There was no chest of drawers, and no wardrobe. Not even hooks on the wall! Was, say, a commercial traveller expected to drape his coat over the back of a chair? Leave his clean linen in his valise?

Certainly, only a man could bear to sleep here, and a heavy smoker to boot! The smell of stale tobacco was revolting. She pitied the poor woman who had been here recently; who had obviously sprayed perfume around in an attempt to mitigate it.

One corner of the room was curtained off. Catherine went over and pulled back the curtain. There was a wash-hand basin ... and a bidet! She had only once seen a bidet in all her life; and that had been in Paris. How strange! Perhaps this was a hotel owned by a French company ... Yes, the French were inveterate smokers, even some of the women. And they loved perfume! Oh, well, it hardly mattered ... And yet, worrying away at the problem had somehow lifted her. Not exactly restored her self-esteem, certainly not amused her. But it had reminded her that she was a sentient being, not an inert clod. She would regain control of her destiny; the opportunity would come. She crossed to the door. Perhaps, in this strange place, the lock would not function. She might just be able to walk out ... But no. The key had shot the bolt; the door was unyielding. She was imprisoned.

She lay down on the bed, and watched the blobs of cloud move slowly over the fading blue of the sky. After a time she heard footsteps outside, a key turn in the lock. She sat up, as a man came into the room with a tray.

'Supper,' he said gruffly. He placed the tray on the table then went out, locking the door behind him. Catherine became conscious that she was hungry. She got up and crossed to the table. At least the food was a considerable advance on that at Greenlands Sanatorium. There were potted shrimps and thin fingers of toast; asparagus spears, beef consommé that was still hot, and a dish of vanilla cream. After her long abstinence it tasted like a banquet. It must have been brought in from a good restaurant.

When she had finished, she lay down on the bed and drifted into a light sleep. She dreamed that she was at Covent Garden ... the first act of *Carmen*. The dancers were swirling around the stage in their brightly coloured skirts. The trumpets were blaring, the drums beating ... Thump, thump, thump! Suddenly

142

she was awake. Someone was hammering on the door; there were men's voices, boorish laughter. She got up and crept to the door.

'A new girl,' one of them was shouting. 'Fresh from the country. Virgo intacta!'

'Come on!' another chimed in. 'Show yourself, sweetheart! Whet our appetites!'

Catherine crept back to the bed and huddled, terrified, in the corner.

'I have proposed we should auction the chance to be first,' said another voice. 'The kitty to go on a binge for us all! I have put in a bid of ten pounds. Jumbo has gone to twelve. Any advance on twelve?'

'I have a better idea,' another called. 'Why not have a raffle? A fiver a time, and the losers get to watch the performance!'

Catherine pulled the bedclothes over her head, to shut out the vile clamour. Why was this happening to her? How had she deserved this?

Late that evening Morton went to Park Lane. For some reason the curtains were drawn in the sitting-room of Catherine's house, and the bedrooms above. They might have been drawn against the evening sun, but it looked like a house in mourning. He rang the bell. The door was opened by a red-eyed maid.

'What has happened?' he said fearfully.

'Nothing . . . That's just it, isn't it? When is she going to come back to us, Mr Morton?'

Morton tried to smooth the tangle of his own emotions. 'You must try to keep cheerful, for her parents' sake. They need your support at this time. After all, you are closer to them than anyone except Miss Catherine.'

'But how can we keep cheerful? Not a word from her for a week!'

'I am convinced that she is safe.' Even as he spoke the words, Morton wondered if he still believed them.

'I do hope so, sir . . . They are in the drawing-room. Will you go through?'

As he entered the room, William Marsden got up and shook his hand perfunctorily. 'Is there any news?' he asked.

143

Mrs Marsden was watching them, hope fading in her eyes.

Morton shook his head. 'I am sorry,' he said.

'Well,' William said bleakly, 'I am sure that you are doing all you can.'

'This merely serves to demonstrate how powerless the so-called forces of law and order are,' Morton said bitterly. 'Believe it, or believe it not, the sum total of my achievement today has been to demonstrate that John Searle and his assistant Ibbs were cousins. Which advances the investigation not one whit!'

'And Sergeant Bragg?'

'He was over at Furlonger's. He feels the key to Catherine's abduction lies there.'

'But this is absurd!' William blustered. 'Why are there not men on the street asking about her, knocking on doors?'

'Because we are still convinced that she has been taken outside the City area. Inspector Cotton is keeping in touch with the Met's operation.'

'Convinced? Who are you to be convinced you need do nothing?' William demanded angrily. Then his head dropped. 'I am sorry, my boy,' he mumbled. 'It is just that I fear . . . we may never see her again.'

Mrs Marsden was dabbing at her eyes with a handkerchief. 'If only we knew where she is,' she said shakily. 'Even that would be a comfort.'

7

'You are late, lad,' Bragg said, as Morton entered his room next morning.

'I am sorry, sir,' Morton said wearily. 'I only dropped off to sleep about four o'clock.'

'Hmm . . . Well, I reckon we should get away from here as soon as we can. I passed the Commissioner in the corridor just now. He was looking a bit broody.'

'About the Searle case, you think?'

'Well, it is hardly a shining example of an investigation. If you asked Inspector Cotton, he would say we'd got bugger all!'

'Which is precisely what he has achieved in his much-trumpeted search for Miss Marsden.'

'Yes, lad. But believe me . . .'

There was a knock on the door, and Sir William Sumner came in. He cleared his throat diffidently.

'Ah, Bragg,' he said. 'The Searle case . . . My presence was requested at a meeting of the Watch Committee last night. Requested, in this context, meaning required . . . They were expecting, nay, demanding progress – an arrest. It is never easy to explain operational complexities to a lay audience, particularly to one which is openly hostile.'

'Baying for blood, were they?' Bragg asked.

'Indeed they were. And not yours!'

'It's the kind of situation, sir, which shows the wisdom of having a distinguished military man at the head of the force,' Bragg said earnestly. 'Someone who can see the larger picture, someone who can deal with pressure.'

Sir William gave an uneasy smile. 'Yes . . . Quite,' he said. 'But also someone who can recognise the moment for withdrawal – even if it means sacrificing one of his units.'

Bragg's face dropped. 'You would never do that, sir, surely?'

'Under extreme pressure, certainly. We must both hope it will not come to that . . . Now, where are we?'

Bragg sighed. 'Jock McGregor thinks we are right, sir.'

'McGregor. Is not that the fence in Spelman Street?'

'That's right, sir,' Bragg said admiringly.

'Hardly an immaculate fount of information!'

'He has never misled us before – at least, not knowingly.'

'Hmm. And what particulars has he confirmed?'

'He said it was a hired killer. He also said that the man went straight to Euston, took the train to Liverpool and a ship to America.'

'I see . . . Taking the diamond with him?'

Bragg hesitated. 'Well, no, sir. We think that the diamond found its way to Antwerp.'

Sir William raised his eyebrows. 'By whose intervention?' he asked.

'We think the ship-broker, Edgerton. We know that he bought

145

tickets on the Ostend ferry from Dover, for the day after Searle's murder.'

'I see.'

'They were two return tickets, out on Thursday the ninth of May, back on the Saturday.'

'But why two tickets?' Sir William asked.

'We think it was a blind, sir.'

'A rather expensive blind, Bragg!'

'Not if you have a gemstone worth five thousand pounds in your pocket!'

'Hmm . . . So you think he is your man?'

Bragg hesitated. 'I reckon he could be, sir. You see, with a hired killer, we are left with identifying the man who set him on. So we have to ask ourselves, who would commission a murder? The answer has to be someone who has been done down by the victim, somebody nursing a grudge, an intolerable sense of shame and outrage.'

'But still with enough cupidity to dispose of the diamond to his advantage?'

'We see that as secondary, sir,' Bragg said.

'And this Edgerton man fits your theory on both counts?'

'Yes, sir. Searle was shafting his wife.'

'Ah! Hmm . . . I see.' The Commissioner gave a sly smile. 'It is well that every man in Edgerton's position does not resort to murder! But, as far as I can see, you have no more than circumstantial evidence against him.'

'That's right, sir. If it was a hired killer, that is all we can ever hope to get.'

Sir William sighed. 'You bring me little comfort, Bragg,' he said. 'I do not know what I shall say to the Watch Committee . . .' He wandered disconsolately out.

Bragg pulled out his watch. 'Right, lad,' he said. 'I have an appointment with a man at Goldsmiths' Hall. Find yourself something useful to do.'

Bragg sauntered through the sunlit streets. This was an unrewarding case, he thought. If Morton had not been in the shop when Searle was shot, if he had not actually seen the killer, it might in some ways be easier. That sounded stupid, even perverse. How often was a detective lucky enough to be a witness

146

of a murder? Lucky enough? That was hardly a phrase Morton would use, with his fiancée still held as a hostage. Yet that side of it was not quite right either. There had been no messages from her captor, no demands made. On the other hand, her body had not been dumped in an alley. It was perplexing.

He went into Goldsmiths' Hall and approached a porter.

'I have a meeting with Colonel Sir Thomas Porteus,' he said.

The man looked at him condescendingly. 'And who might you be?' he asked.

'Sergeant Bragg, City police.'

'Oh, I see. Right. I will find out if he is in the building. The man turned on his heel and strode off. Bragg wandered over to the leather-covered porter's chair. It might be pleasant, passing your days sitting here, he thought. Watching the toings and froings of the City's rich and powerful, answering the odd question; taking a message somewhere in the City, with time for a pint on the way back ... But touching the forelock would go against the grain for him. And there would be plenty of it.

The porter returned and took Bragg to a room at the back of the building. A grey-haired man rose as he entered, and held out his hand.

'Porteus,' he said crisply. 'And you must be Sergeant Bragg.'

'Yes, sir. I will not take up much of your time.'

'Nevertheless, we will do so in comfort.' He gestured towards a chair. 'Now, how can I assist you?'

'I am investigating the murder of a man called Searle, sir. John Searle.'

Porteus was suddenly watchful. 'And do I know this John Searle?' he asked.

'I am sure that you do, sir,' Bragg said. 'He was a member of the Goldsmiths' Company.'

'Ah, that John Searle. I had no idea he was dead.'

'Really, sir? You must be the only person in London who doesn't know. Quite a *cause célèbre*, as they say.'

'I have been away, sergeant,' Porteus said tersely.

'Right, sir. Now, this is not the easiest of cases, because we think that someone paid to have him killed.'

Porteus lifted an eyebrow. 'I see. On what is that supposition based?'

'One of our constables was in the shop at the time. He saw the shooting. We think the killer could have been paid by someone with a grudge against Searle.'

'That would appear to be logical,' Porteus said drily.

'Yes . . . Now, we know that Searle was a member of the Goldsmiths', as were Searles back through the generations.'

'Correct.'

'But John Searle was not as highly regarded as his forebears. One of them even became Second Warden – as I believe you were, sir.'

'Third Warden, sergeant. That was the pinnacle of my particular mountain.'

'I see, sir,' Bragg said blandly. 'You had no inclination to go higher?'

'No. My health . . .'

'Ah! Well, you look very fit again, sir . . . Now, we have got the notion that John Searle was kept back by someone in the company – someone who had no great opinion of him.'

'Every candidate for high office must be thought worthy by his peers, sergeant,' Porteus said mildly.

'Of course, sir. Very proper too. But the impression we have is that most of the members would have gone along with Searle's candidature. We are all hypocrites in some measure, aren't we?'

'I would not presume to pontificate about other people's conduct, officer,' Porteus said brusquely.

'Not as an individual, I am sure. But as Third Warden of the Goldsmiths' Company you might . . . Was that the reason you never got to Second Warden, sir?'

'I told you, I was ill!'

'Yes. And I would never doubt it, sir. Your daughter having got involved with someone like Searle!'

The blood drained from Porteus's face. 'That is a lie!' he shouted. 'A villainous lie!'

'We do not think so, sir. You see, we are holding the other end of the string, so to speak. We are investigating Searle and his goings-on. You would be surprised at the odd bits and pieces we are picking up.'

'Searle was scum!'

148

'Indeed he was, sir. Yet, as so often happens, he had a way with the ladies. Your daughter was not the only one to be deceived by him.'

Porteus sprang to his feet. 'I do not deny that I was glad to hear of his death,' he said angrily. 'If you think I had a hand in his death, then go ahead and prove it!'

Morton went into Furlonger's shop. Ibbs was behind the counter, but there were no customers.

'Trade seems flat,' he remarked.

Ibbs shrugged. 'After the murder there were sensation-seekers coming in. Now I expect people are waiting in case the business collapses.'

'And will it?'

'There is no reason why it should. But that is not up to me.'

'Even as a partner?' Morton asked.

'As a mere one-eighth partner, certainly not. It was never more than a gesture, anyway.'

Morton took the skeletal family tree from his pocket. 'Your mother's name was Amy, was it not?' he asked.

'Yes, why?'

'She was the sister of Alfred Searle?'

'That's right.'

'So, you and John Searle were cousins?'

'Yes. I only went to work at Furlonger's because of that.'

Morton frowned. 'How could you possibly be content with a one-eighth share in those circumstances?' he asked.

Ibbs laughed ruefully. 'Whenever has a City business passed through the female line, if there was a male inheritor?' he asked. 'I was glad even to get a job there. It's a deal better than selling silver-plated trinkets to hard-up clerks, as they have to in Clapham. Diamond broking is at the top of the tree; you are someone of consequence.'

'And if this business collapses?' Morton asked.

'I expect I would get a job elsewhere. Furlonger's has always been the best.'

'Good.' Morton spread out the family tree on the counter. 'I wonder if you could help me fill in the missing names in this,' he said.

After lunch, Bragg and Morton went to Edgerton's office. They had to wait for about half an hour before he returned. He glanced in the waiting-room as he passed the door, but affected not to recognise them. Eventually his secretary came and ushered them to his office.

'Still on the trail, sergeant?' he said in a bantering tone.

'Yes, sir,' Bragg said stolidly. 'You seem to be in better form than when we last met.'

'Indeed, officer?'

'Yes, sir. I would say that on that occasion you were under stress.'

Edgerton shrugged. 'The pressures of business life, officer,' he said.

'Which was no doubt the reason for your mistake.'

'Mistake? What mistake?'

'You said that you were out of the country when Searle was murdered. We now know that you did not leave London until the day after his death.'

Edgerton frowned. 'Really? Well, you could be right. But since you have, as I remember it, a theory that Searle was killed by a hired gunman, it scarcely seems significant.'

Bragg smiled. 'A good point, sir ... Of course, you will be aware that a valuable rough diamond was stolen by the murderer.'

'That rumour is going around the clubs, sergeant.'

'Yes ... Now we ask ourselves, when the murderer had passed over the diamond to the man who employed him, what does he do? – The employer, not the gunman.'

'I did manage to untangle it,' Edgerton said sarcastically.

'Good. How about attempting an answer for us, sir.'

Edgerton frowned. 'I know nothing about diamonds, rough or smooth. People are saying that it would be valueless outside the trade, after all the publicity.'

'They can be very astute, people can,' Bragg said. 'I expect they are saying that a really clever villain would have that stone over on the Continent before you could say "Jack Robinson".'

Edgerton shrugged.

'And here you are,' Bragg said blandly. 'A great one for Continental travel . . . Just happening to go to Ostend on the day after the murder. An easy trip from there to Antwerp; off-load the diamond, and you have a couple of days to enjoy yourselves . . . It was your wife you took with you, wasn't it, sir?'

Edgerton's face was grim, his eyes watchful. 'It was . . . a lady friend,' he said.

'I see, sir. And, since she was a lady, there would be nothing untoward in it . . . But she would help to create the illusion of a happy family outing, I can understand that.'

'She is my mistress.'

'I see. One of the many? Has she got a name, this mistress?'

Edgerton dropped his head. 'Mrs Arabella Tilson,' he mumbled.

'Address?'

'Ten, St Martin's Lane. Over the pie shop.'

Bragg raised his eyebrows. 'In the West End?' he exclaimed. 'Right in amongst the theatres. Would she be an actress, then?'

Edgerton said nothing.

Bragg stood up. 'Peter Edgerton, I am arresting you for procuring the murder of John Searle. You are coming with us.'

'I wonder if we could drop in at the *City Press* office,' Morton said. 'There may be some responses to my advertisement in yesterday's paper.'

'Of course, lad. It's a fine day. And we don't often walk along Aldersgate.'

Edgerton had been safely deposited in the cells at Old Jewry, and they were on their way to interview his mistress.

'I had an interesting morning,' Morton remarked. 'Perhaps not profitable, but it brings matters into clearer focus. Do you realise that Ibbs is a cousin to the late John Searle?'

'Related?' Bragg exclaimed. 'Why did he not say as much before?'

'Presumably because the matter did not arise. He certainly did not conceal it. Indeed, he has been most helpful in filling in the blanks on my family tree.' Morton took the document out of his pocket and gave it to Bragg.

151

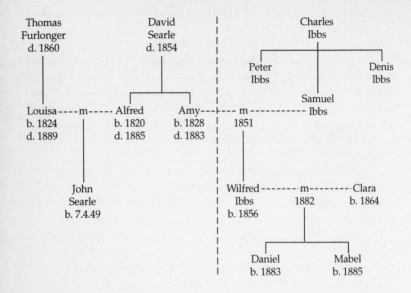

'So Amy Searle married an Ibbs ... I suppose it makes more sense now; it never seemed to click somehow – a retail jeweller coming into diamond broking.'

Morton smiled. 'He described his family's activities as selling silver-plated trinkets to hard-up clerks.'

'Well, he has saved you a deal of trouble.'

Bragg turned to pass the document back to Morton, and checked. There, not ten paces ahead of them, was a sign, sticking out over the pavement.

THE TOBACCO COMPANY

Bragg bit back his exclamation of surprise. It was probably only offices. And he did not want to look a fool before young Morton. He gazed over to the other side of the street as they neared it, affecting to be absorbed in the antics of some men trying to rear up an electric lighting standard. Then he glanced out of the corner of his eye. It was a shop, all right.

At the same moment Morton caught sight of it. 'This is exactly the kind of establishment that we were speaking of the other day,' he said.

'I know, lad,' Bragg said gruffly. 'Full of boxes of cigars, like I said.'

Morton smiled. 'But surely there is nothing to be lost?'

Reluctantly Bragg pushed open the door. To him it smelled more like a Turkish brothel. He was out of his depth here. His measure was the bludgeoning reek of a four-ale bar, not this nancy perfumed rubbish. But he would have to go through with it. He ought to have had a bet on with Morton. Five bob would have bought a few more pounds of that cat's piss flake he had to smoke.

An assistant approached Morton. 'Can I be of assistance to you, sir?' he asked with an obsequious smile.

'To me, no,' Morton said. 'But to Mr Bragg I most fervently hope that you can!'

The man turned to Bragg. 'And what is sir's pleasure?' he asked.

'Thick twist,' Bragg said defiantly. 'The stronger the better.'

'Certainly, sir.' The assistant turned on his heel and stepped lightly behind the counter. He opened a drawer and took out a rope of tobacco. 'How much does sir require?' he asked in as matter-of-fact a voice as if Bragg had been asking for the finest Turkish.

'Ten yards! Give me the lot! I can't get it where I live.'

The man pursed his lips reprovingly. 'I could hardly advise it, sir,' he said. 'Even in ideal conditions, it would be bound to deteriorate before you could use it all.'

'But suppose it disappears again?'

The assistant gave a superior smile. 'Our customers could always be assured of a regular supply, sir,' he said.

Bragg was conscious of Morton's eyes on him, the assistant awaiting his decision. In a place like this he was sure to be fleeced . . . But he had made such a fuss about it, he could hardly draw back.

'All right,' he said. 'Give me about six inches. I can easily come back if it is to my taste.'

'Very good, sir.' The assistant gravely laid the rope of tobacco across a cedar-wood block and cut a length off the end. 'That will be two shillings, sir.'

Bloody hell! Bragg thought. Half a day's wages for a labourer. Didn't even bother to weigh it! Not the thing in a place like this ... He put his hand in his pocket and passed over a florin. It was all right for Morton, standing there as pleased as punch. He didn't even need to count his sovereigns. He heard himself saying: 'Thank you very much; I will certainly come again.' It was a pretty pass when a craving for tobacco could reduce you to a fawning, lying wastrel! But he would get his own back on Morton somehow.

He walked on in a dudgeon, listening to Morton's teasing self-congratulatory chatter. Then it dried up. Bragg realised that they were outside the office of the *City Press*. Morton led the way up to the editor's office, and knocked on the door.

'Come in!'

Tranter was sitting at a desk on which pieces of manuscript, letters and newspapers were in a confused jumble. He looked up, and a shadow crossed his face.

'Ah, Mr Morton ... and Sergeant Bragg also ...'

Morton held out his hand. 'I am hoping for good news,' he said.

Tranter took it limply. 'I am sorry to say, Mr Morton, that we have had not a single reply to your advertisement. Not a single one ... But I do not think you should despair. We have a restricted circulation. And, as I warned you, it was a new departure.'

Morton turned away. 'Thank you for trying,' he said, and walked despondently out of the room.

When they got outside Bragg stopped a cab, and directed the driver to take them to St Martin's Lane. Morton said not a word during the journey, though Bragg could see his hands clenching and unclenching. He would not like to be in the shoes of Miss Marsden's abductor if Morton got hold of him. Likewise the person who had planned it.

They were set down in front of the pie shop, and Bragg found a door next to it. He beat a tattoo on the knocker, then turned to gaze at the traffic. It was even more tangled here than in the City. But then, the ordinary commercial activities had shifted west-wards a hundred years ago. He watched with sardonic amuse-ment as a Met constable tried to back a furniture van to create a

154

gap. A yard would do it. But the back of the van was only a foot from the horses of an omnibus. Why would drivers insist on following so close? He heard the squeak of a lock, and turned as the door opened.

'Mrs Arabella Tilson?' he enquired.

She was holding a thin wrap around her shapely body.

'Yes.'

'Sergeant Bragg and Constable Morton, of the City police.'

'Can you prove that?' she asked. 'Only, a girl has to be careful.'

Bragg showed her his warrant-card. 'Right,' she said. 'What do you want?'

'Just a word.'

'What is it, then?'

Bragg shook his head. 'Not standing in the street, madam,' he said.

She hesitated, then led the way upstairs, into a room overlooking the street.

'Just a moment,' she said. 'I was still in bed . . . I will slip some clothes on.'

She would not look at all bad without, Bragg thought. Full breasts to lay your head on; wide, welcoming hips. A deal more comely than Bertha at the pub as well. He walked over to the window to clear his mind. The traffic was flowing again. The Met constable must have been less inept than he looked. Maybe it was just that he had not been brought up with horses . . . Not that they would last much longer, by the sound of it. The papers were saying that the future lay with electric trams. Well, at least they would not stink the streets out in the summer . . . There he went, alliterating even in his thoughts. Perhaps Sir Rufus was right, his brain was becoming addled. He heard the door open, and turned back to the room.

She had put on a bright yellow blouse, lacy down the front, and a bright green skirt. Her hair had been combed, there was a trace of lip-salve on her mouth.

'Now, gentlemen,' she said coquettishly, 'what is this word you want to have with me?'

Bragg cleared his throat. 'I believe you are acquainted with a Mr Peter Edgerton,' he said, sitting on a sofa under the window.

She smiled at him. 'Yes. He is a friend.'

'A very good friend, I believe.'

'There is no need to be embarrassed, Sergeant Bragg,' she said archly.

'I believe that you have taken a trip with him recently; a trip lasting several days.'

'That is so.' Her eyes were sparkling with amusement.

'We have just arrested him for murder.'

The brutal sentence wiped the smile from her face. 'Murder?' she said, aghast.

'We believe that you were part of an elaborate plan. Whether knowingly, is what we are here to establish.'

She frowned. 'I was part of no plan!' she said firmly. 'I just went to enjoy myself.'

'Did you have a permanent relationship with Edgerton?' Bragg asked. 'He referred to you as his mistress.'

She shrugged. 'If he wants to use words like that it is up to him. He certainly did not own me.'

'Or keep you?'

'No. He did give me presents from time to time.'

'Right.' Bragg allowed a pause to develop, then: 'I would like you to tell us about the recent trip, in your own words,' he said.

'Who else's words would I use?' she said, suddenly waspish.

'Very well. Start from when you left home. That was on the morning of Thursday, the ninth of May, I believe.'

'Yes,' she said mulishly.

'What happened then?'

She shrugged. 'He came for me in a cab. I had only my valise and my handbag ... We drove to the station, and took a train to Dover. It was cold there – much colder than London. I had to put a shawl round me at the docks. But, once we were on the boat, it was warm enough.' She gave a bright smile. 'We had lunch on board. I have never had a proper meal on a ship before! Then we just sat around, watching the seagulls.'

'Yes, all right,' Bragg said irritably. 'We don't want it down to the last grunt and gasp. Where did you disembark?'

'Ostend. Or so Peter said.'

'And from there?'

'We took a train to a little place called Bruges. We stayed in a hotel that had been a nunnery once. The rooms were all white-washed, and the furniture was really old . . . It made you wonder what they got up to in those days.' Again a smile for Bragg.

'Do I take it that you shared the same room?' he asked.

'Of course we did! Why do you think he took me?'

'What was the name of this hotel, madam?'

'I think . . . Yes, the Hôtel de la Poste.'

'And how long did you stay there?'

'Thursday and Friday nights. We started back first thing on Saturday.'

'Hmm . . .' Bragg mused. 'Why not come back on the Sunday? It seems a waste of a day.'

'We had to. You see, Peter is a churchwarden at St Ethelburga's.'

Bragg suppressed a smile. 'So, were you and he together all the time?'

She shook her head. 'No. He had to go to somewhere on the Friday. He left at noon, and only got back at ten o'clock that night. I thought it was a bit of a cheek, really; dragging me all that way, then leaving me in a strange town. But he made up for it.'

'In bed, you mean?'

She smiled. 'Well, that too! But he brought me this little pin back.' She crossed to Bragg, leaned over him, and presented her bosom for his inspection.

Bragg peered at the pin. It was a tiny diamond, with four gold leaves surrounding it. 'Very nice,' he said.

'Yes. My men friends often give me presents.'

'No doubt . . . And did he mention the name of this place he went to?'

She wrinkled her nose. 'He did say. But I was a bit cross, so I didn't pay much attention.'

'Could it have been Antwerp?'

She considered for a moment, then shrugged. 'It could have been,' she said slowly. 'Yes, I am almost certain it was.'

Catherine went over to the window and gazed out. In the real world it was sunny and warm. In the sinister world she was caught up in there was silence, desolation. Her menacing gaoler had brought her breakfast, and taken away the remains of her supper. After that there had been silence. Oddly enough, she had not felt loneliness. Perhaps that was an emotion born of tranquillity. And she was by no means tranquil. Inside she was raging at the treatment meted out to her. In some totally obscure way, it was part of the raid on the jeweller's shop. Her abduction had obviously been planned in advance ... Until the moment when the matron had seen the picture in the *City Press*. Now they were improvising, panicking ... Did that mean that she was in even greater danger?

To divert her thoughts, she tried to open the window. Even London's polluted air would be preferable to this tobacco-laden fug. She pulled down at the top window, but it refused to budge. No wonder! It was encrusted with paint. Someone had tried to open the bottom one. There were chisel marks along the sash. But there were no sash cords. They must have rotted away; their weights plunging to the bottom of the frame. She crouched, then pushed upwards with all her might. The window moved! When she stepped away, it did not drop back. There was a narrow gap between the bottom of the window and the frame. She went in search of something to wedge it open. In the fireplace there was a poker; it would make a splendid lever! She took it to the window ... The gap was too narrow to admit it. She took a deep breath, then pushed up at the window with all her strength. It would not budge even a fraction. She felt tears pricking at her eyes, but she fought them back. She had succeeded, she told herself. A little fresh air was seeping in, to mitigate the smell of tobacco ... She would never have been able to escape through the window anyway. But it had been a minor triumph, something to set against the vile jeering of the night before.

The mere memory of it frightened her. Bestial men! And were those creatures the very same that one met at society receptions? Who were so considerate, so entertaining with their pleasantries? If so, was James like that? ... No! The very idea revolted her. He was kind, considerate, a gentleman ... But her tormentors would claim the same distinction, be accepted as such. To escape her thoughts, she went to the wash-basin and plunged her stinging hands into cold water. Then she lay down on the bed and drifted into a doze.

She was awakened by the sound of a key in the door. Her heart jumped with fright. But it was only her gaoler, bringing her lunch. When he had gone, she went over to the table. It was a plate of cold meats, and a fruit jelly. Surprisingly, the sight of it made her feel hungry. Animal appetites, she thought ruefully. So inevitable, yet so pleasurable in the right circumstances. Not that these could be the right circumstances for anything ... Was civilisation such a thin veneer? She dismissed the speculation from her mind, and began to eat.

When she had finished, she lay down on the bed again. In truth, there was nothing else to do. At least, by resting she was conserving her strength. And it was a comfortable bed. Presumably it would have to be ... She tried to empty her mind of speculation. She would not even try to imagine what it would be like with James ... But he could never be like those oafs. He would be considerate and gentle; his hands would ...

Again there came the sound of a key in the lock. Catherine jerked upright, ready to defend herself.

A young woman whisked into the room, and locked the door behind her. She laid a finger across her lips, and walked quietly to the bed.

'Is it true that you are here against your will?' she asked quietly.

'Yes,' Catherine whispered. 'I was abducted from a jeweller's shop. The man who took me had just murdered the owner.'

'What are you doing here?'

'I was taken to the Greenlands Sanatorium. Then I was brought here. I think the matron realised that I had been kidnapped.'

'I see ... The girls here go to Greenlands; for a rest as they say, when they are unlucky. I have been there myself.'

'What do you mean, unlucky?' Catherine asked.

'When they pick up a dose of clap ... Venereal disease.'

'I see.'

'Do you want to get away?' the woman asked. 'Have you anywhere to go?'

'Yes, yes!'

'Right. I will help you. I owe the old cow one. I have a room of my own, on the first floor. My own regulars and, up to now, the pick of the casuals. But she is saying I am getting past it. No one is asking for me any more, she says. Lying bitch! She's trying to get me out on the street again. I can still bring the punters back here, she says ... Hey! Shouldn't you get the coppers on to it? Get her charged with abduction? That's serious!'

'No! That is the last thing I want,' Catherine whispered urgently. 'My fiancé is a policeman. I would not want him to know of this – ever!'

'Hmm ... That is a tricky one.'

'Why do you have a key to this room?' Catherine asked suspiciously.

'One of the maids left a pass-key in a lock. I got it copied. I can get into every one of the rooms now ... But nobody knows.'

'Very well. When can you help me to escape?'

The woman thought for a moment. 'Not now,' she said. 'Later, when there are plenty of people about. When it's getting dark. You won't be noticed then.'

'I am in your hands,' Catherine whispered. 'But, if I escape, I shall see that you are rewarded.'

The woman snorted. 'It will be enough that you have got away. They will be scared out of their wits ... Now, be ready as soon as it starts to go dark.'

Bragg and Morton went to the Dorchester Hotel after lunch. The desk clerk confirmed that Mr Harvey Bernstein was indeed staying at the hotel. In fact, he had just come in and picked up his key. Bragg scribbled a note, then beckoned a page and asked him to take it up to Bernstein's room.

'Don't I get a tip?' the boy complained.

'It's police business,' Bragg said curtly.

'But nobody's paying me for taking it up!'

'Is that a fact?' Bragg delved into his pocket and brought out a penny. 'Here you are,' he said.

The boy looked at it scornfully. 'It's usually threepence,' he said pertly.

Bragg aimed a playful cuff at the boy's head. 'Hop it!' he said. 'I am not an American millionaire.'

The boy scowled, then shrugged his shoulders and disappeared.

Ten minutes later, Bragg had begun to think that he had misjudged the lad. How would it look on his expenses sheet? 'To messenger boy for not delivering a message – 1d.' Of course he

160

would never put in a claim ... In a way that made it rankle even more. Then he saw a thick-set man, in a check morning coat and trousers, approaching the desk. He went over.

'Mr Harvey Bernstein?' he asked.

The man swung round. 'Indeed I am, sir. You are the police officers, I take it.'

'Yes, Sergeant Bragg and Constable Morton.'

'Right!' He turned to the clerk. 'Where can we talk?' he asked.

The clerk led them to a small sitting-room off the foyer.

'We will not keep you long, sir,' Bragg said. 'But we think you might have some information which could help us in a murder case.'

'That seems in the highest degree unlikely, officer,' Bernstein said. 'We have only been in London a short time.'

'It relates to your period of residence in Tunbridge Wells, sir.'

Bernstein frowned. 'I see. Well, go on.'

'I believe that, when you were there, you got to know a man called Hurford.'

'The jeweller?'

'Yes.'

'I would not regard him as an intimate, sergeant. But we had business dealings, yes.'

'Would you like to tell us about the pendant, sir?'

'Ah! The pendant.' He frowned. 'Up to then, officer, I had regarded him as an inoffensive country shopkeeper. But, over that, he was more than a trifle sharp.'

'I see. Trying to defraud you, was he, sir?'

Bernstein pursed his lips. 'Defraud is a big word,' he said. 'I guess he was just trying to railroad me. You meet that in business, sergeant. But I did not expect to find it in a small town in Kent County, England.'

'So, what happened?'

'I guess I am not familiar with English ways. You might say that I miss the nuances. I went into his store because my watch was losing time ... I guess he could have told me it needed an overhaul; so there is that in his favour. He said it needed regulating. He just took off the back, adjusted the lever in the mechanism. And that was that! No charge. Well, I was impressed by that. Real old-world courtesy. We started to converse, and I made a remark about his claim to be a manufacturing jeweller.

He had some fine pieces in there, many of which had been made on the premises – or so he claimed.'

'Did you find cause to doubt that, sir?' Bragg asked.

Bernstein gazed across the room, where a waiter was dusting the tables. 'No, I did not,' he said firmly. 'At least, he convinced me that jewellery was made on the premises. We had a long discussion. I remember that Hurford presented it as a kind of challenge. He would make a piece at his shop for me. I said that my daughter was coming over, and that I might consider some jewellery as a birthday present for her . . . The next time I passed his store, he beckoned me in and showed me some drawings of pendants. I guess I showed a preference for one over the others. And that is how it was left. At no time, sergeant, did I enter into any contract for a piece of jewellery to be made. If he was determined to misconstrue our conversations, it must be entirely his affair.'

'So, how did it all end, sir?'

'Well, my wife decided that small-town life was a little constricting. And she had heard that a chateau near Geneva was for rent. She had read in some book that mountain air would be good for her. She has a medical condition . . . So I cabled the rental agency and we did a deal. I have rented it for June through September. We are here to do a little shopping, before going over.'

'And you took the pendant affair no further?'

'That is so, officer. In view of our change of plans, my daughter has not even come to England. I told Hurford that I no longer wished to pursue it. He became agitated, a trifle heated. I guess he had set some store by making good his claims. But we parted friends, kind of.'

'Did he threaten you at all?' Bragg asked.

Bernstein considered for a moment. 'No,' he said finally. 'There was nothing he could threaten me with. But he was mighty disappointed.'

'It seems he was so confident of making the pendant for you that he went to London and bought the central diamond for it.'

Bernstein raised his eyebrows. 'Well, he had no contractual basis for taking that step,' he said.

'I believe that Hurford would agree with you,' Bragg said

soberly. 'Anyway, he took the diamond, worth a thousand pounds I believe, back to the broker he got it from.'

'A thousand English pounds, eh? Our friend Hurford is quite an operator . . . Or, in view of your involvement, should that be "was"?'

'Oh, Mr Hurford is still alive . . . but the broker refused to take the stone back. He is now very dead.'

'Wow! . . . Guess I am well out of that place! Tunbridge Wells . . . It sounds so quaint, so old-worldly. Wait till we get back home!'

Catherine was sleeping when, through her dream, she heard the sound of a key in the door. She choked back a scream as a man came in . . . It was only the porter with her dinner. He gave her the briefest of glances, picked up her lunch tray and went out. He would be well accustomed to seeing young women reclining on beds, she thought, but not often alone. She got up and ate her meal. She felt like an infantryman in the Crimean war – a last bite before going over the top! But could she trust the woman? She had not even given her name. Yet if she refused to go with her, what then? She remembered the cruel jeering voices of the men outside her door. She had no alternative but to trust her.

She washed herself and tried to tidy her hair. Without a comb or brush it was difficult. The woman had said there would be plenty of people about. She doubted if she could pass for a light woman in her sanatorium dress – or even a fallen one! But she did look rather like a maid. She felt an excitement building in her. She was no longer a piece of flotsam. She glanced in the mirror. No . . . A maid would have some kind of uniform cap; an apron too, possibly. Well, the apron was out of the question. But there was a white napkin on the dinner tray. She folded it and secured it to her head with her hairpins. Yes, that would help, particularly if she kept her head modestly bowed . . . If only she were not so tall!

She gazed out of the window at the clouds, tinged red by the setting sun. When it is getting dark, the woman had said. That sounded comforting. But she had also said that there would be plenty of people about. That meant clients of the girls here; louts like the boorish oafs who had hammered at her door. She was suddenly afraid. What if she were discovered, stealing down the stairs? The woman might try to protect her. But she could not succeed against men like that ... And her revenge relied on an undetected escape. If her actions were discovered, she would certainly be out on the street! But was it more subtle than that? Was the woman a decoy? Sent to lure her into a life of prostitution? She would never be able to leave then; never go home, never see James again! She dug her nails into the palms of her hands. The pain brought her spiralling panic down to earth. Brothel-keepers would not be so cunning. There could hardly be a grosser way to earn a living. Their customers were ... There was the sound of a key in the door-lock. The woman slipped inside, her finger to her lips.

'Are you ready?' she whispered.

'Yes.'

'That little cap on your head is a good idea. Now, follow me. Keep your head bowed a little. Take no notice of the people around you. We will go down the stairs, across the hall and out into the street. When we get there turn left, and run! Are you ready?'

'Yes.'

The woman opened the door, poked her head outside and beckoned. She locked the door behind them, then walked down the corridor to the stairs. Catherine followed her. She could hear the sound of men's voices coming from below, women's laughter. Now a couple were coming up the stairs, the woman chattering brightly. From the corner of her eye she saw that the man was portly, with a red face and greying whiskers. Ugh! They passed Catherine without a glance ... Now she was nearing the ground floor. There was the heavy smell of cigar smoke. Catherine felt it catch at her throat. She wanted to cough. But that would be the very thing to cause people to look in her direction. Now her guide had reached the bottom of the stairs, and was beginning to cross the lobby. Catherine hurried after her, head bowed. She reached the doorway, felt the cool air of the street. Her heart leapt to see omnibuses, hansoms, people walking carefree on the pavement. The woman had turned left, then stopped. Catherine went up to her.

'I can never repay you for this!' she whispered.

'No need,' the woman said. 'I did it for myself, not you. Now, go down this street. There is a Methodist meeting-hall on the left. They will look after you.' She turned away and hurried back.

Catherine walked on, determined to avoid recapture at any cost. She was conscious of curious looks. She dare trust no one. Not even a policeman now. On her left was a large brick building with lancet windows ... stone steps leading to oaken double doors. One was ajar. She could hear singing:

> *All hail the power of Jesus' name,*
> *Let angels prostrate fall.*

This was where she had been told to go. She hurried up the steps and into the hall. There were rows of wooden benches. People in the front ones, standing and singing lustily. Facing them, on a dais, was a bewhiskered, round-faced man with bright eyes. He managed to maintain a smile, even as he sang. His glance held Catherine's momentarily, as she sidled into a pew. The woman already there turned to share her hymn book with Catherine, even pointing out the verse with a stubby finger.

To Catherine it was fantastical. One minute stealing out of a brothel, the next singing the praise of God. But slowly the conviction was growing in her. She was safe! She only had to win over these good people and she would be restored to her family. But she would have to gain their trust. She had no money, her hair was unkempt, her clothes poor. If she claimed to be the daughter of a famous painter, to live in Park Lane, they would think she was demented. Instead of being taken home, she might find herself in another institution. She must make them want to help her.

The hymn came to an end, and everyone knelt down. The man on the dais said a short prayer, then walked solemnly down the steps and into a room at the back. As the congregation rose to its feet, the woman next to Catherine turned and smiled.

'Welcome to our meeting,' she said, holding out her hand.

'I was late ...' Catherine said foolishly. The room was suddenly hazy. She tried to focus on the woman's face, was conscious of a look of alarm, then all went black ...

165

She was first conscious that her elbow was hurting. She was lying on something hard; she could hear voices, someone was holding her wrist. She opened her eyes.

'She is coming round,' a man's voice said.

'A good thing you were here, doctor,' a woman remarked.

Catherine opened her eyes and saw a circle of concerned faces above her.

'You fainted,' a woman assured her. 'That is all. The doctor says that you will be perfectly well in a few minutes.'

They lifted her, and put her in a chair brought from the minister's room.

'Where am I?' she asked.

'In the Methodist hall. You came in during the last hymn.'

'I escaped,' she said. 'I was told you would help me.'

'Escaped?' the woman echoed. 'Where from?'

'Benson's Divan.'

There was a shocked silence. The woman drew back, as if fearful of being contaminated.

Then the minister raised his arm. 'Alleluiah, brethren!' he cried fervently. 'Let us praise God that one of our fallen sisters has been brought back to the fold!'

There was a moment of hesitation, then a ragged chorus of 'Alleluiah!'

'Let us ask His grace that her feet shall be set on the path of righteousness.'

'Amen!'

'That she shall be delivered for ever from her former way of life. And that, by His goodness, she shall be forgiven her manifold sins and wickednesses.'

'Amen! Amen!'

Catherine felt light-headed. It was as if she was taking part in a stage play, a farce. But everyone was very earnest. She could hear the minister talking to another man.

'What are we to do with her?' he was saying.

'I want to go home, please,' she said as loudly as she could.

The man who had been holding her wrist bent down by her. 'Where is home?' he asked.

'Near Hyde Park.'

'Will there be anyone there?'

'Yes. My parents.'

The doctor went over to the minister. They seemed to be having an animated discussion about her. The minister was determined not to allow her to relapse into her former way of life. But the doctor was insisting that her parents would be the best people to look after her in her present state. Eventually the doctor prevailed, and another member of the congregation went to find a cab. Catherine hoped that he would succeed, before there was a collective change of heart. But they were good people ... good people ...

When she regained consciousness again, she realised that she was in a cab. She could hear the horse's hooves, the noise of steel tyres on the road. She was propped between two people. She moved her hand.

'Ah! She is conscious again,' a man's voice said.

She opened her eyes and saw street lamps, stretching like a necklace into the distance.

'You said that you lived near Hyde Park,' the doctor said gently. 'So we are heading in that direction. Will you be able to show us the way to your house?'

'Yes,' Catherine said.

'You see! Her voice is stronger already,' the doctor said. 'I think it was no more than exhaustion.'

A silence fell. Hazy as her mind was, Catherine knew she had to do something – say something – or her life would be ruined.

'You must say nothing to my parents,' she said.

'What was that?' the minister asked.

'You must not say that I was in Benson's Divan.'

'But that is the truth, is it not?' he asked suspiciously.

'Yes.'

'I am a minister of the truth,' he said firmly.

'I am not a fallen woman. I was held captive there by criminals.'

'Is she feverish, do you think?' the minister asked.

She felt a cool hand on her brow. 'I would say not,' the doctor said.

'What is your name?' he asked her.

'Catherine Marsden ... I am engaged to be married to James Morton, the cricketer.'

In her dulled mind she knew that it was a mistake ... It always was.

'I see ... What county does he play for?'

'Kent . . . And England too.'

'Indeed he does! You must be very proud of him!'

'Yes, of course I am!' She was becoming cross.

'He is a very fine cricketer,' the doctor said in an indulgent tone. 'Tell me, how many runs did he score in the Melbourne test last winter?'

He was trying to trick her again. But she knew the answer. Although James was not aware of it, she had been keeping every newspaper cutting about his cricket that she could get hold of . . . It was a game that England had won. And James had been their top scorer . . . 'One hundred and seventy-three,' she said.

'My God! She is right!' the doctor said. 'She is not indulging in fantasies.'

'So what now?' the minister asked.

'Why, we take her home just the same.' The doctor turned to Catherine. 'Can you give us a more precise address?' he asked.

'In Park Lane. Just past Deanery Street, going north.'

'Is that your parents' house?'

'Yes. My father is William Marsden, the painter.'

'Does that mean anything to you, Walter?' the minister interrupted pettishly.

'Why, yes! We are rescuing a young woman; but not, I believe, a fallen one.' The doctor put his head outside the window. 'Cabby! We are going to Park Lane. The house just beyond Deanery Street.'

A silence fell inside the carriage. Catherine sensed a resentment in the minister at being baulked of his triumph. But everything was going to be all right . . . She was being taken home!

The thought seemed no sooner to have formed in her mind than it became a reality. The carriage stopped outside her house. The doctor got out and went up the steps. There was a silence, then the sound of a door opening. A snatch of conversation, then the clatter of boots, her father's arms round her.

'Thank God! Thank God!' he was saying. 'Come in! Come in!'

She was carried into the drawing-room and laid on a sofa.

'Your daughter came into our Methodist meeting-hall in Bloomsbury,' the minister said. 'She was in some distress, so we thought it best to bring her home.'

'Thank you, sirs,' her father said. He plunged his hand in his pocket and pulled out a fistful of coins. 'Please accept this for your church funds,' he said, 'as a token of our gratitude. You can have no conception of the relief and joy you have brought us!'

When the men had gone, Mrs Marsden put her arm around Catherine's shoulder. 'Oh, my dear,' she said. 'We have been so anxious ... James was very good. He came almost every night, trying to keep our spirits up ... And now you are back with us! Are you well? You must have suffered so.'

Catherine smiled. 'Oh, yes! I am well now,' she said. 'But I do not want James to see me like this.'

'Then we will not let him know you are back until tomorrow,' her father said. 'A night's sleep will work wonders.'

8

Catherine slept fitfully. She had left the curtains open, so that the light from the street lamps shone in. She could see all her familiar things around her. Yet no sooner did she close her eyes than she was back in Benson's Divan, the vile, jeering voices in her ears. With the first glimmer of dawn she fell into a deep sleep. She was awakened by the stealthy opening of the door. She curled up in fright. But it was only her mother, with a breakfast tray.

While she ate they sat and chatted inconsequentially. Who had been seen at what party with whom; what social events were going to take place that day. Gradually Mrs Marsden became reassured that her daughter was sound as well as safe. She considered renewing the assault, trying to persuade Catherine that she should give up her career at the *City Press*. After all, she could say Catherine's engagement to James meant marriage, domesticity, children. Even if she could combine them with a career, it was not fair to James. But now was not the time, after goodness knows what she had been through ... She tried to pump her about what had happened; but got a very snappy refusal. Well, there was at least something that should please her.

'Papa received a very special letter this morning,' she announced teasingly. She paused, and watched a smile grow on Catherine's face.

'A letter that makes me feel prouder of him than ever. Though,

169

if anyone had asked me yesterday, I would have said it was not possible!'

Catherine gave a laugh. 'Mamma! You are chaffing me. What is this letter?'

'It came from the Queen's chamberlain. Your father has been asked to paint a portrait of the Queen! It will hang in the state dining-room at Buckingham Palace.'

'Goodness! How absolutely marvellous! I assume that he will accept.'

'Well.' Mrs Marsden's smile faded. 'He merely tossed it on the table for me to read . . . He has been so shocked by your abduction that he has done nothing for a week.'

'But he must! I am home now, safe and sound. Everything will be just as it was.' Catherine felt her spirits rising. 'I will have a long bath, and wash all the unpleasantness away. Then I must write a note to James. It can go by street messenger.'

'Perhaps you would write to Lady Lanesborough also. She has been very anxious about you.'

'I will do better than that, mamma. I will go to see her. I can think of no better tonic!'

Once downstairs, her father embraced her warmly, swore that he would not be able to concentrate on his work for a week, and volunteered to take her letter to Old Jewry. Not once did either of her parents question her about her experiences . . . But James would be another matter. Well, one thing she was resolved on; she would not make any mention whatsoever of her incarceration in Benson's Divan.

An hour later Catherine was being shown into Lady Lanesborough's boudoir. Her godmother embraced her with unaccustomed warmth. Obviously, removal from the scene served to enhance the esteem in which one was held. Enhanced also was a determination to worm out every detail of what had occurred. She must scotch that!

'The doctor says that I must try to wipe it from my mind,' she said. 'Otherwise I will never fully recover. I have not even told my parents.'

'But you must have told them something!' Lady Lanesborough said in an accusatory tone. 'It cannot do much harm to repeat it to me.'

'I will only do so if you promise me faithfully that you will never, never tell anyone else.'

Lady Lanesborough frowned. 'Oh, very well,' she said irritably.

Catherine smiled. 'There is nothing at all sensational,' she said. 'I was taken to a sanatorium, and locked up in one of the rooms.'

'A padded cell?'

'Not quite, godmother! Though I am sure that several people regard me as overdue for one.'

'But why?'

'I have not seen James yet, but I imagine he will tell me that it was merely to cover the murderer's escape.'

'Hmm . . . There are some unsavoury rumours going about concerning that man Searle,' Lady Lanesborough said with relish. 'One of them relating to that rather insipid Porteus girl. What is her name? Avril, I think . . . Her father is some kind of dealer in bullion. Eminent in the Goldsmiths' Company, one gathers. It is said that Miss Porteus met Searle at some Goldsmiths' occasion or other . . . I cannot think what her mother was about, even allowing her to be introduced to the man. I grant she is plain, and a trifle gauche, but it is no excuse for casting her adrift on society's waters.'

Catherine interrupted. 'What happened?' she asked.

Lady Lanesborough leaned forward conspiratorially. 'As I said, this Avril girl met John Searle at some social occasion.' She paused. 'You must have met him also . . . After all, you were there when he was . . . well, murdered.'

'Yes, godmother,' Catherine said shortly. 'I hope to be allowed to forget it.'

'Of course, child . . . But you must have formed some view of him . . . I mean, one does, does not one?'

Catherine laughed. 'There is very little to worm out of me, ma'am. I suppose I spent less than twenty minutes in his company; and, of course, I was with James.'

'But . . .?' her godmother prompted her.

'But I felt his manner was objectionable, insinuating . . . really rather odious.'

'Yes . . .' Lady Lanesborough seemed to savour Catherine's description. 'I am sure the Porteus family would agree with you.

But this wretched Avril became quite besotted by him. They eloped together. Went to France. I gather that they travelled down the valley of the river Loire, visiting the sights, indulging in goodness knows what excesses! Then they went to Paris. By then whatever romance had existed between them was dead. Searle left her destitute, in a hotel on the Left Bank – the Left Bank, mark you. She had to telegraph for her family to come and rescue her ... Of course, the girl's prospects are ruined. Within her own class, she is unmarriageable ... I gather that her parents sent her to Worcester – to the ends of the earth, one would think! She formed an attachment with a moderately presentable young man. An accountant, I believe. But he somehow got to hear of her escapade with Searle, and withdrew from the liaison.'

'How unfortunate,' Catherine said.

'Indeed! One gathers that her father was beside himself with rage. Vowing revenge against Searle! But one cannot think that any society person would go to the lengths of having him killed, can one?'

'I gather that there is to be a memorial service for Searle next Thursday, sir,' Morton said moodily. 'The City grandees closing ranks against the inevitability of fate!'

Bragg put down his pipe. 'When is the funeral? That is what interests me more.'

Morton gave a tired smile. 'Is this your theory that a murderer always attends the funeral of his victim?' he remarked.

'I would not want to be seen to be absent,' Bragg said.

'According to the newspaper, it is to be at Battersea cemetery this afternoon. And it is to be a private ceremony.'

'Huh! Just because some poor bugger has been murdered, there is no call to shove him in a hole, cover him over, and get away as quickly as you can.'

Morton smiled. 'I think that his old regiment will ensure there is more ceremony than that,' he said.

Bragg sighed. 'You know, lad, I wish I knew where that American fitted in.'

'Bernstein, you mean?'

'Yes.'

'Are you saying that we should consider him a suspect?'

172

'I don't know, lad. Americans are a violent lot. You only have to read the newspapers ... And that Bernstein looked as if he was used to getting his own way.'

Morton laughed. 'As I understand the situation, that was precisely what he got!' he said.

'But we don't know, do we? We only know what he wants us to know.'

'Hardly that,' Morton objected. 'In large measure, Hurford's and Bernstein's stories corroborate each other.'

'Maybe ... But a hired killer seems American to me.'

Morton pondered. 'Of course, the whole edifice of our specu-lation may be without foundation. It could be no more than a single thug with a gun.'

'You can't believe that, surely?' Bragg exclaimed. 'If so, why was Searle shot? Why was Miss Marsden taken? ... More particularly, why has she not been released?'

There came a knock at the door, and the desk sergeant poked his head in.

'A solicitor to see you, Joe,' he said. 'Name of Middleton.'

'What does he want?'

'One of your guests is his client.'

'I only have one; though I reckon we ought to pick up a few more.'

'Edgerton. He was making a fuss this morning ... saying it was Friday. If he didn't get bail today, he would be in over the weekend.'

'God Almighty! He is not in for picking pockets! He's on a murder charge.'

The sergeant shrugged. 'I had to let him send a message to his lawyer,' he said.

'All right. Bring him in.'

Bragg sat staring grimly out of the window until there was a tap at the door. A diffident-looking man in his late twenties was ushered in. He held out his hand.

'Middleton,' he said, 'of Leggett & Crowe.'

Bragg shook his hand. 'I gather you want to see us about Peter Edgerton,' he said.

Middleton sat down opposite him and moistened his lips. 'I understand that he was arrested yesterday by you,' he began.

'That is correct, sir,' Bragg said genially.

'May I have particulars of the charge?'

'Murder, sir.'

'I see. And what is the name of the person of whose murder my client is alleged to be guilty?'

'John Searle, sir.'

Middleton blinked. 'But I understand from the newspaper that Searle's death occurred during the afternoon of Wednesday, the eighth of May.'

'That is correct, sir.'

'Sergeant, it can be demonstrated that my client was at a meeting in Fenchurch Street during the whole of that afternoon!'

'Yes, sir. We accept that.'

Middleton frowned. 'In that case, you must also accept that your charge is baseless.'

Bragg pursed his lips. 'I imagine that you are not all that familiar with the criminal law,' he said.

Middleton gave a tentative smile. 'Well, we are better known as commercial lawyers,' he said. 'But one would hardly need to be any kind of lawyer to see that my client's innocence is a self-evident truth!'

'Not really, sir ... You see, if two or more people put their heads together, and plot to get rid of another, they are all equally guilty of his murder. What is the Latin tag for it, constable?'

'*Malitia praecognitata*, sir. Evil intended beforehand.'

'So you see, sir,' Bragg said smugly, 'Mr Edgerton could have been with the Archbishop of Canterbury that Wednesday afternoon. He would be just as guilty as if he had pulled the trigger.'

Middleton frowned. 'But what evidence is there of such a conspiracy?' he asked.

'No direct evidence, sir. It is hardly surprising, is it, when you have gone to the lengths of employing an assassin?'

'But you cannot erect a gallows of conjecture, and hang my client upon it.'

Bragg pursed his lips. 'I like that, sir,' he said. 'It's one of those phrases you wish you had the wit to put together yourself ... But it is not conjecture that a valuable rough diamond was stolen by the murderer. And when we go into it, we find that your client, Mr Edgerton, had booked two tickets on the Ostend ferry for the day after the murder.'

'I was not aware of that, officer,' Middleton said.

'Now, for some reason, your client elected not to take Mrs Edgerton. Perhaps he was not certain that he could rely on her loyalty ... But he did take a female companion. You might say that he was going out of his way to make it look like a family outing.'

'Who was this lady, sergeant?'

Bragg frowned. 'I think perhaps I ought not to give you that bit of information, sir,' he said pompously. 'Your client might think it was prejudicial.'

'He could hardly think', Middleton retorted, 'that any information given to us would damage his cause.'

Bragg shrugged. 'Very well, sir. She was a Mrs Arabella Tilson. He had booked two tickets – and this was before the actual murder ... Two tickets on the ferry from Dover to Ostend and back. We have been told that, from Ostend, this apparently married couple went to stay in Bruges. In a former nunnery, would you believe! ... That should have added a little spice to their goings-on.'

'There is no need for derogatory innuendo, sergeant,' Middleton said irritably.

'No, sir. I agree that he has managed to destroy his reputation quite well enough on his own ... Not that we are interested in that. Perhaps his wife deserves him. But what we are interested in is that, while he was staying in Bruges, he took a trip to Antwerp. He did not take his female companion with him – which you might think is strange in itself. I would not know if Antwerp is the kind of place foreign visitors would want to goggle at. But I do know that if you have a rough diamond in your pocket, and you want to turn it into cash, then Antwerp is the place to go.'

The bumptiousness had gone out of Middleton. 'It would appear that you are resolutely opposed to bail, officer,' he remarked.

'Indeed, sir. As you know, you can apply for it when Edgerton comes up for the committal proceedings. But the magistrates are not noted for their leniency. So I would not bank on it.'

Morton escorted the lawyer back to the street. As he started back, the desk sergeant called him over.

'A gent left this letter for you, Jim,' he said. 'Grinning from ear to ear, he was. Said you would know what to do about it.'

Morton looked at the superscription. 'It is from Catherine!' he shouted exultantly. 'Dear God! It is her writing!'

He sprinted down the corridor and into Bragg's room. 'I have a letter from Catherine!' he cried. 'It was left at the front desk!'

'Thank God!' Bragg said. 'Well, aren't you going to open it?'

Morton slid his finger under the flap, and tore open the envelope. He pulled out the letter and read it avidly. 'She is safe and sound, she says . . . At home with her parents once more . . . She is longing to see us . . . She specifically says "you and Sergeant Bragg", so she must have information for us.'

'When can we go, lad?'

'We are bidden after lunch,' Morton said buoyantly. 'So, if we have a pie and a pint in a pub, we can be there inside an hour.'

'There is one thing,' Bragg observed smugly. 'Nobody can say alliteration is bad luck today.'

By two o'clock Morton was ringing the bell at Catherine's home. Her father had evidently been looking out for them, because he came bounding down the steps to greet them.

'It is absolutely marvellous!' he cried. 'I could scarcely sleep a wink last night; I was so overjoyed and relieved.'

'She got home yesterday?' Morton asked, crestfallen.

'Late last evening. She was brought home by some Methodists! She had apparently gone to their meeting-hall . . . Come in, come in. She is longing to see you!'

He led them into the sitting-room, where an unseasonal fire was blazing in the hearth. Catherine stood up as they entered, and Morton embraced her warmly.

'Thank God you are all right!' he said fervently.

'Yes,' Catherine said. 'And I really am safe and sound.'

Morton scrutinised her face. 'You look very tired and strained,' he said.

'Perhaps. But it will soon pass. After a few days, it will seem to have been only a bad dream.'

'But what on earth has been happening to you?'

Catherine laughed shakily. 'I suppose that I have been experiencing some rather radical nursing care,' she said.

Morton frowned. 'What on earth do you mean?' he asked.

'When I was abducted by Searle's murderer, I was taken by carriage to a private sanatorium.'

'Sanatorium?'

'Yes. Greenlands Sanatorium.'

'Good heavens!' Morton exclaimed. 'I went past it in my search for you.'

Catherine smiled at him. 'If only I had seen you,' she said.

Bragg intervened. 'Under what pretext were you taken there?' he asked.

'No one gave me any pretext. My abductor dragged me into the building, threatening that he would kill me if I made a sound. The matron looked briefly at me, exchanged a word or two with him; then I was whisked away upstairs and locked in a room.'

'She did not ask your name, and address?'

'No, sergeant. My abductor gave my name as Miss Brown.'

'So you were expected . . . It had all been arranged in advance.'

'I suppose it must have been.'

'And you have been in that place ever since?'

Catherine had a sudden pang of apprehension. 'Until I escaped,' she said.

'You should have seen the clothes she was wearing!' Mr Marsden broke in. 'Our scullery maid would turn up her nose at them. My wife is insisting that we should go there, and reclaim her proper clothes.'

'Perhaps we will go ourselves, and find out what it was all about,' Bragg said. 'After all, the man who took your daughter there had just murdered John Searle.'

Catherine flinched. 'It was all so hideous,' she said.

'Nevertheless, I would be grateful if you would try to remember a few things,' Bragg said. 'Young Morton and I are supposed to be investigating Searle's murder.'

'It hardly seems to matter now,' Morton said apologetically. 'Nevertheless, it is so.'

'Can you bear to think back to that afternoon you were taken, miss?' Bragg asked.

'I have thought of little else, sergeant.'

'I am sorry to put you through this,' Bragg said. 'But we have Morton's recollection of it. I want to compare that with yours.'

177

Catherine smiled at Morton. 'Of course I will try, sergeant. I have lived with the memory of it for what seems like a century!'

'Good. Start, if you will, from the point where the two of you are going towards the shop.'

'Very well ... I remember thinking that the premises looked more like a fortress than a shop,' Catherine said. 'There were bars at the windows and door. It seemed, if not sinister, at least unwelcoming.'

'I think', Morton broke in, 'that your memory may be coloured by your subsequent experience.'

'Keep out of it,' Bragg admonished him. 'It's Miss Marsden's recollection I am interested in now.'

Morton grinned. 'I consider myself suitably admonished,' he said.

'Go on, miss ... You did not care for the outside of the place.'

'I recollect that John Searle was behind the counter, leaning over a ledger ... some kind of account book, I suppose. He looked a little surprised as we entered. He glanced up at the clock on the wall, as if he had lost track of time. Then he began fussing around me, referring to me as the future Mrs Morton, and so on. He embarked on a long explanation of how diamonds were formed, where they came from, the colours obtainable. He seemed totally uninterested in my views on the matter!'

'A big-head, was he?' Bragg asked.

Catherine smiled. 'He was certainly absorbed in his own expertise,' she said. 'Perhaps I am unjust to him. But it all became a little tedious ... Then he condescended to share with us his own thoughts on what would be appropriate for my engagement ring! He called out to an assistant, who was down in the bowels of the earth. He came up the staircase like a gnome, put a packet in Searle's hand and went down again.'

'That would be Ibbs?' Bragg asked.

Morton nodded.

'At least now Searle seemed to be paying some heed to my wishes,' Catherine went on. 'For this was at least a white diamond, in the rough. But its size was grotesque! I have never seen a diamond so large, except among the crown jewels in the Tower of London! I tried to tell him that it was too big for the purpose; that I wanted a working ring! But he would not listen. It was as if he had been wound up, and had to keep going until he stopped! . . . Then he was saying that the stone would have to be cleaved into smaller pieces; trying to persuade James to have a pair of ear-rings made out of the others . . . I could see that James was taken with the idea. Yet it was so absurdly, hideously expensive. I began to wish that I was anywhere but there . . .' She stopped, her lip trembling.

'I am sorry, my dear,' Morton said contritely. 'You are right. It would have been foolishness. Perhaps Searle was a better sales-man than we have given him credit for.'

'Is this when the gunman came in?' Bragg asked.

'Yes.' Catherine shivered.

'I want you to be especially careful from now on,' Bragg said. 'We never know what will prove important.'

'I assure you, sergeant, every detail is imprinted in my brain. I fear that I shall never be able to forget it!'

'Take your time, miss,' Bragg said gently.

'I was sitting at the table with my back to the door. James was opposite me.'

'Facing the door?'

'Yes . . . And Searle himself sat between us, with his back to the counter.'

'I see . . . And Ibbs?'

'He had retired to the depths again.'

'Right. I have it.'

A shadow had come over Catherine's face. 'I was feeling increasingly irritated,' she said. 'I wanted to break into the conversation, say I felt faint – anything to get away. I looked up as the gunman burst through the door. In the fraction of a second that followed, I saw Searle glance up at the clock. Whether it was surprise or irritation on his face at the interruption I cannot say for certain. There was an explosion, Searle toppled over . . . and the man took hold of me . . .'

'Take your time, miss,' Bragg said gently.

Catherine sat quietly for a few moments, then she began again, her voice low.

'It was like a nightmare . . .' she said. 'I can still feel the barrel of the gun, hard against my temple . . . See James handcuffing himself to the railing, his face a grim mask . . . Then I was being jerked along; scared of tripping, because I feared for my life. The streets seemed unnaturally empty, as if all normal life had

179

deserted me. There was a carriage near Mercers' Hall, with its blinds down. I was bundled inside. The driver must have known his destination, for no words passed. As he set off I tried to estimate the distance we were travelling, but it was hopeless . . . Then the carriage turned off the road into the driveway of the sanatorium. My abductor threatened that he would kill me if I uttered one word.'

'This abductor,' Bragg interrupted, 'did he have an American accent?'

Catherine gave a puzzled frown. 'No, his accent was English; not cockney, but of London I would say.'

'Thank you, miss. Go on.'

'When the carriage stopped, the man put his gun in his pocket and took my arm. He marched me down a long corridor, to an office at the rear of the building . . . The matron of Greenlands was sitting at her desk. The man introduced me as Miss Brown; said that I was expected. He told Matron that I was violent, and given to screaming. Then two of the nurses took me to a room at the top of the building. I was given some institutional clothes, and made to put them on. My own were taken away. They still have them.'

'And what happened after that, miss?' Bragg asked.

'The days came and went . . . nothing happened. I was just a prisoner . . . until I escaped, yesterday evening. I overpowered a maid, took her key and slipped out of the building.'

'She was brought home by some splendid Methodists,' Mr Marsden said buoyantly. 'She managed to get into their meeting-hall, and obtained their protection . . . And now, I think she needs my protection from you!'

'Nonsense, papa!' Catherine said. 'I am perfectly recovered.'

'I'll tell you what,' Bragg said. 'I would like to go and see the matron at the sanatorium. What was its name?'

'Greenlands, sergeant.'

'Yes . . . A visit there might well be profitable.'

'And I will come with you!' Catherine said firmly. 'After all, they have a rather nice skirt of mine.'

Morton went outside and waved down a cab. Soon they were trotting northwards. Looking at the strong, composed features of the men, Catherine found it hard to imagine the terror she had experienced during her abduction. But as they turned into the driveway of Greenlands she felt a sudden pang of fear. James must never be allowed to know about Benson's Divan! She would have to dominate the conversation from the first.

As they got down from the carriage she was given a few curious looks, but there was no recognition in the faces. That was good. She led them down the gloomy corridor to the office of the matron, and knocked on the door.

'Come in!'

Bragg opened the door, and allowed Catherine to precede them.

'Miss Brown!' the matron exclaimed, fear in her eyes.

'Yes,' Catherine said emphatically. 'When I ran away, yesterday, I left my clothes behind. I have come to collect them. Also, these police officers wish to ask you some questions.'

The matron gasped.

'I am afraid that I have left the clothes I ran off in at home,' Catherine went on. 'I will send them to you.'

'Thank you.' The matron seemed to be regaining her composure. 'Let us say that you discharged yourself, not ran away.'

Bragg cleared his throat. 'We would like to know a bit more about how Miss Marsden – that is her real name ... How she came to be in your sanatorium at all.'

'Well,' the matron said hesitantly, 'she was committed by her guardian. He came with a doctor, who confirmed that Miss Brown was mentally deranged, and needed confinement in an institution. I was paid three months' fees in advance. It all seemed perfectly normal and professional.'

'When was this?' Bragg asked.

The matron went over to a press and brought out a slim file. She opened it and consulted a sheet of paper. 'On Friday the third of May,' she said. 'It was arranged that Miss Brown would be brought in on the afternoon of the following Wednesday.'

'And did you not ask any questions about the Miss Brown you were admitting?'

'Of course! How would we have known what treatment to give her otherwise?'

Bragg stared at her coldly. 'Well?' he asked.

The matron looked uncomfortable. 'I was told by her guardian that she was a young society woman, who had delusions. She had been cruelly wronged by a personable man, who had turned

181

out to be married already . . .' She glanced at Catherine's incredulous face. 'He said her mind had gone,' she went on doggedly. 'She had made up a family for herself. She would tell us that she worked for a newspaper as a reporter, and was going to marry a famous cricketer . . . The doctor said that they hoped a period of rest and seclusion would help her to recover.'

'Three months!' Morton said angrily.

Catherine intervened. 'I can quite understand why you consented to take me in,' she said. 'And, if I was represented to you as being deranged, it was not unreasonable to confine me in my room. Now, give me my clothes, and we will leave you in peace.'

A hangdog expression spread over the matron's face. 'When you discharged yourself . . . yesterday,' she said, 'we got rid of them . . . We gave them to the poor.'

Catherine was furious. But there was nothing she could do. To press further might reveal the actual day of her escape. She fumbled in her mind for some response, then Bragg intervened.

'This guardian who committed Miss Marsden to your care,' he said. 'What was he like?'

The matron thought for a moment. 'He would be about forty-two . . . In his prime, anyway. Dark-haired, clean-shaven . . . oh, and there was a white scar on his forehead, running down to his left eyebrow.'

'God Almighty!' Bragg exclaimed. 'Searle! It has got to be Searle!'

When they got back to the City, the three of them went to a coffee house to mull over what they had learned. Catherine told the others about her conversation with Lady Lanesborough, and the alleged liaison of Searle with Avril Porteus. Then she excused herself. She walked along the streets with a sensation of pure well-being. It was good to see the familiar landmarks again; the trees in the churchyards heavy with leaf. So short a time ago she had despaired of ever seeing them again. This was her milieu, among the restrained certainties at the heart of the empire. This was where she could make her own small contribution to the well-being of the nation. She turned into the offices of the *City Press*, and went up to the editor's room.

Tranter jumped to his feet when he saw her. He opened his

arms as if to hug her, then compromised by taking her hand in both of his.

'I am so very relieved to see you, Miss Marsden,' he said, with evident pleasure in his voice. 'I hope that you are sound in wind and limb!'

'I need to catch up on my sleep somewhat,' Catherine said with a smile. 'Otherwise I am perfectly well.'

'Your fiancé, James Morton, came to see me. He said that you had been abducted from under his very nose! For once in my life I wished that the *City Press* was an ordinary daily. Think of the headlines we could have had. "Woman reporter abducted" or "Carnage in the City"! It would have been sensational.'

'And, fortunately, impossible in so sober a newspaper!'

'Alas, yes! . . . Tompkins, the office boy, suggested "The killing of Poultry", but that somehow lacked bite!'

'I ought to be scandalised at such levity,' Catherine said teasingly. 'It sounds like dancing on my grave!'

'No!' Tranter's face became solemn. 'Everyone here was most distressed and anxious about you, Miss Marsden. And not only we. I have received many letters from our readers, expressing their concern. I shall be able to put a paragraph in tomorrow's edition to tell them of your rescue . . . Yes, I will do that immediately.'

'I owe you a great debt for putting my picture on the front page of Wednesday's edition,' Catherine said soberly. 'I really believe that without it, I would not have regained my freedom.'

'Yes.' Tranter looked a little uncomfortable. 'Your young man was most persuasive . . . but, shall we say, the proprietors were less than wholly pleased.'

Catherine was incredulous. Could they really have preferred her continued incarceration, her possible death, to the breaking of a silly tradition? She opened her mouth to protest; then thought better of it. If the dailies had got hold of the story, it would have gone round the salons and drawing-rooms, endlessly embroidered. That she most certainly would not have wanted. And what did it matter now?

'I am most grateful for what you did,' she said. 'I shall never be able to repay you.'

'Nonsense!' He looked up at the ceiling. 'And will you be returning to us?' he asked in an equivocal tone.

'Indeed I will!' Catherine said firmly. 'Most certainly! I intend to continue for years yet.'

When Bragg and Morton got back to Old Jewry, there was a note from the coroner requiring Bragg's attendance at his chambers.

'When did this come in?' Bragg asked.

The desk sergeant shrugged. 'Just before lunch, I would say.'

'Hmm ... After three o'clock now. I reckon if we just saunter over, he might be out again when we get there.'

But Morton was not in any mood to stroll, he seemed to have acquired boundless energy. In twenty minutes they were at the Temple. Sir Rufus's clerk confirmed that the coroner was still in his chambers. He must have been working on a brief, Bragg thought, for no one went in or came out. Eventually the clerk came over.

'Our lord and master stipulated a quarter to four – stipulated to me, that is. So now is the time for you to beard the lion!'

When they went into Sir Rufus's room they saw him staring into the distance, a pile of documents in front of him. He disregarded them, his brows knitted. Then he narrowed his eyes and nodded to himself. He made a brief note on a pad, then grunted in satisfaction.

'Well, Bragg?' He swung round to the policemen. 'Why are you standing there like delinquent children?' he said amiably.

'You sent for me, sir.'

'Ah, did I? ... Yes, so I did! This Searle case. What progress are you making?'

'The young lady is back with her family, sir!'

'Good ...' Sir Rufus turned to Morton. 'I gather that you are affianced to her!' he said.

Morton smiled. 'I have that honour, sir!'

'You know, Bragg, I have been giving this case some thought ... It strikes me as rather odd that a non-jeweller, a mere thug, should be able to recognise a rough diamond for what it was. Am I not right in thinking that these things are similar to an ordinary piece of glass, until they are polished?'

'That is an interesting point, sir,' Bragg said straight-faced. 'Not many people would pick that up.'

Sir Rufus looked at him suspiciously. 'Well, then?' he asked.

184

'We must assume that he was well coached . . . I expect we shall never know. The word is that he got the first ship to America.'

'And you are prepared to accept that?' The coroner frowned. 'It is my sworn duty to bring the miscreant to justice! And you, as my officer, are the instrument of that justice!'

'Yes, sir. The trouble is that we have no leads. We would not know where to start looking for him. The likelihood is that we would be wasting our time, while we should be looking for the real criminal. The man that paid for the murder to be done; the man who described to the killer what a rough diamond looked like.'

'Hah! You turn my own argument against me! Yet it is not beyond peradventure that some figure lowly in the jewellery business, yet possessing the necessary knowledge, could have filled both roles.'

'You forget that Constable Morton saw the killer, sir. He will confirm that none of the people we have interviewed looks at all like the gunman. But we have an interesting development to report.'

'Well, man. Go on!'

'Miss Marsden, you will recall, was abducted. In fact she was taken to a place called the Greenlands Sanatorium, where she was locked up until she managed to escape yesterday.'

'A sanatorium, eh?'

'Yes, sir. We went there today, with Miss Marsden. The matron described to us the man who had made the arrangements for her committal. There is no conceivable doubt that the man was John Searle!'

'Hah! Well, I doubt if he planned his own death, Bragg. It sounds like what our American cousins refer to, I believe, as a double-cross. I think you should stretch every sinew to arrest the gunman . . . Am I not right in thinking that it is possible to convey a message to America by way of the telegraph system?'

'Indeed it is, sir.'

'Well then, man, discover the name of the ship on which the miscreant sailed; send a suitable telegraph to the American police, and they can be waiting for him on the dockside!'

'But we do not know the man's name, sir.'

'Good God, Bragg! You can describe the man – or at least your constable can. Put it in hand at once!'

185

'Very well, sir. Are you going to pay the cost of this, as the responsible official?'

The coroner's lip curled. 'My stipend does not cover the cost of scribbling pads, Bragg,' he said contemptuously. 'No, this is a police matter . . . under my direction, of course.'

'I see, sir . . . There is one thing you might be interested in. Constable Morton has been preparing a family tree for the Searles.' He took the folded paper from his pocket and passed it to the coroner.

Sir Rufus smoothed it out and scrutinised it. 'Hmm . . . interesting,' he said. 'So John Searle and Wilfred Ibbs were cousins.'

'Who stands to inherit Searle's estate, sir?' Bragg asked. 'Not that there is much to inherit. The business is going down the drain, and his residence will be rented.'

'On the assumption that this document is accurate, then it would certainly be Wilfred Ibbs.'

'Really! Oh well,' Bragg said, 'we might as well go over and break the good news to him . . . After we have sent the telegraph, of course.'

Bragg and Morton strolled out of the Temple in the warm sunshine.

'Are we really going to send that telegraph, sir?' Morton asked.

Bragg chuckled. 'Well, I am in duty bound to obey the instructions of the coroner, since I am his officer. So you can draft it out for us when we get back. Of course, the cost of it will have to be borne by the City police. So, when you have finished it, take it down to the post office and ask them to put a price on it. I reckon the Commissioner will beshit himself!'

They strolled into Poultry and approached Furlonger's shop. It did look rather like a fortress, Morton conceded. Perhaps it was not the ideal setting to appeal to a gently nurtured maiden. He vowed that he would leave the choice of jeweller and jewel entirely to Catherine now . . . There seemed to be no lights in the shop. Yet the gaselier had been burning on the fateful day. And today was no brighter. Bragg went to the door and tried it. It was locked. Then he peered at a small card, wedged in the metal grating.

'"Closed for Mr Searle's funeral",' he read. 'Bugger me! Well,

I'm not for going back to Old Jewry at this time. Why don't we go over to Islington? Ibbs will probably go straight home.'

Morton laughed. 'It is always instructive to be seduced from one's duty by one's superiors,' he said. 'I have the address somewhere.'

He rummaged in his pockets, finally producing a creased bit of paper. 'Twelve, Wenlock Street, Islington.'

'Right, and we will take a cab this time!'

In twenty minutes they were pulling up outside Ibbs's house.

'Do you want me to wait, guv?' the driver asked.

'Might as well,' Bragg said genially. 'I doubt if there are many cab-ranks around here, and it is getting a bit late.'

They strolled over to the door and rang the bell. They could hear children's voices within. Eventually a pretty woman in her thirties opened the door.

'Mrs Ibbs?' Bragg said unctuously.

'Yes?'

'We really wanted a quick word with your husband.'

'Oh, yes?'

'Something to his advantage, as they say.'

A twelve-year-old boy came up behind his mother and gazed at them.

'Well, he has gone to a funeral. I do not expect him back till late.'

'John Searle's funeral?'

'Yes.'

'I thought that would be over by now.'

She smiled. 'He said he would go back to Furlonger's. He said he had things to do.'

A ten-year-old girl squeezed past her mother's skirts and looked inquisitively at the policemen.

'Bloody hell!' Bragg muttered. He doffed his bowler to Mrs Ibbs then swung round and made for the cab.

'Something pressing,' Morton murmured apologetically and ran after him.

'Back to Poultry!' Bragg shouted. 'And quickly!'

The cabby flicked his horse with his whip, and they set off at a rate. But as they neared the City, the streets became ever more congested. Eventually Bragg stopped the cab and marched off, leaving Morton to pay. When Morton caught up with him Bragg was turning into Poultry, muttering fiercely to himself.

'Am I permitted to enquire what has occasioned this unseemly dash?' Morton asked.

'You call yourself a countryman,' he said irritably. 'Have you not got any eyes?'

'Mrs Ibbs seems a comely creature.'

'So you can see! It's just your brain that is addled.'

He stopped at the door of Furlonger & Searle. Through the glass they could see Ibbs moving about in the shop. Bragg grunted in satisfaction, then pushed open the door.

'We have been chasing you all over London,' he remarked cheerfully.

'I was at Mr Searle's funeral,' Ibbs said.

'So I gather. We expected to find you at home; but Mrs Ibbs said you would have come back here.'

'There is a lot to do,' Ibbs said simply.

'Yes ... Do you remember that family tree you helped Constable Morton with?'

'Yes, why?'

'Interesting things ... We did not realise, till then, that you and Searle were cousins.'

'I said as much to the constable.'

'So you did ... Your mother was a Searle.'

'Yes.'

'And, as I think you have said, the Searle broking business was absorbed into Furlonger's. So, when Alfred Searle died, the whole lot went to John Searle ... I can see that must have rankled; even though you were only an honorary Searle, so to speak, by marriage.'

Ibbs shrugged. 'As I said to the constable, you get over these things. There is no point in becoming bitter.'

'That's true. It corrodes the soul, or something like that.'

'Anyway, I got a job here; I was made a partner by Mr Searle. What more could I ask for?'

Bragg allowed a pause to develop. A look of uncertainty spread over Ibbs's face. He licked his lips.

Then: 'I believe you,' Bragg said, 'when you tell us that the business bit didn't rankle. I don't think that money matters all that much to you ... Not compared to some things.'

'Anyway, Mr Searle told me I would benefit under his will,' Ibbs said. 'He was going to make a new one.'

'The trouble was', Bragg went on, disregarding him, 'that Searle was a womaniser. He could not keep his hands off a bit of skirt that was anything like pretty. And your wife is a real beauty.'

Ibbs's face became expressionless, his eyes watchful.

'When he started playing around with her, you must have been anxious because, compared to him, you must have seemed a dull sort of chap . . . Of course, you were stuck in the shop; while he, as senior partner, could go swanning around. Why did he insist on your moving to Islington? So it would take him less time to get to your wife's bed?'

Ibbs looked grimly out towards the street, his hands clenched.

'I expect you came to terms with it in some respects,' Bragg went on. 'You are not a violent man by nature. And you might have realised that Searle was unlikely to marry. You could already have known that you were in line for everything, if Searle died intestate . . . Yes, when he announced that he was going to make a will, it must have been a shock for you. For you knew who would benefit. I have to tell you, Mr Ibbs, that we have seen your daughter Mabel. She has an unmistakable Furlonger nose . . . There is no possible way that his blood-line could have come down to her, unless John Searle was her father. No wonder he gave your wife presents and such.'

Ibbs seemed to crumple. He leaned against the counter, his head down. The silence extended itself, until the very tick of the clock seemed to beat down at them. Then Ibbs spoke, his voice low.

'It is true what the bible says, about those that have not losing even that which they have,' he said. 'Clara is not a bad woman. But her head was turned by that swine. I could have borne anything else . . . A really wicked man! To think that Mabel might be like him . . . He was going to kill me, you know. I could see it in his eyes. His philandering days were over. He wanted to settle down – with my wife! What would you have done?'

'I really do not know, sir,' Bragg said quietly. 'But it is true that he insured your life for two thousand pounds recently. So it all fits in with your suspicions . . . Now, tell us how it came about.'

Ibbs took a deep breath and let it slowly out. 'It was his plot. As you know, the business was not thriving – mainly because he neglected it. He must have been trying to find a pretext. You see, he was planning to get money out of the insurance company.

That was how it started. Then, when he saw the announcement of Mr Morton's engagement in the paper, he was over the moon. Everything was going to come right, he told me. He would get hold of a big rough diamond, invite Mr Morton and his fiancée to come and see it – and arrange to have it stolen while they were there. Impeccable witnesses, he said. Then he would claim on the insurance, and also get the rough diamond back from the thief.'

'In the final plan there were two insurers,' Bragg said quietly.

Ibbs looked up. 'Yes. Just like him; he was greedy.'

'But he did not stick to the plan, it seems,' Bragg prompted him.

'No. I got a whisper that there was going to be a shooting. That Searle had been in touch with the Blackwall gang.'

'Tommy Potts,' Morton remarked.

'Yes. And there was only one person he wanted out of the way; that was me!'

'So, what did you do?' Bragg asked.

'Searle was so big-headed, so full of himself,' Ibbs said scornfully. 'He told me everything that was going to happen, timed down to the minute. He must have thought I was stupid! . . . You were right, sergeant. I had got close to the underworld, and it paid off! I sent a message to Mr Morton, asking that he and his fiancée should come half an hour earlier than the time Searle had set. I employed my own gunman; took over his scheme. When Mr Morton and Miss Marsden came early, Searle's plans were upset. He had to keep yattering on. I was listening from the stairs . . . Till my man came and shot him!'

'And the rough diamond?'

'It is in the safe here.'

'So Tommy Potts came at the time Searle had arranged, and found him dead.'

'Yes.'

'And were you privy to the plans to abduct Miss Marsden?' Morton asked.

'Yes. I even played the part of a doctor when we went to the sanatorium.'

'Could you not have seen that she was released?' Morton asked angrily. 'She was in that hideous institution until yesterday!'

Ibbs shrugged. 'She would have been let go, when the money ran out,' he said.

'Three months in that hell-hole?'

Ibbs did not reply.

'Life is strange,' Bragg said reflectively. 'We came, today, thinking we were going to bring you good news. The coroner, Sir Rufus Stone, told us you were in line to inherit everything John Searle had ... But, of course, you knew that all the time. Didn't you? Wilfred Ibbs, I am arresting you for the wilful murder of John Searle. We will tell your wife what has happened. Who knows, all his money might go to Mabel, if Clara admits her affair with Searle. No court would doubt it, if they saw that nose!'

'I do not understand!' Morton exclaimed.

They were sitting in the drawing-room of Catherine's parents' house. And, in acknowledgement of their engaged status, the door was allowed to be closed.

'Then you must be a simpleton!' Catherine said irritably. 'It is perfectly straightforward. For a year after the death of your brother Edwin, the ladies in your family will be compelled to wear black.'

'Compelled? By whom?'

'By the usages of society – if you wish, by their peers. And society also decrees that they would be unable to come to our wedding in black.'

'Nor would I want them to. Our wedding will be a joyful occasion. I know it will bring optimism and happiness to both our families.'

'Yes. But your mother, particularly, will need time. All your family must have a proper period of mourning. It really is sound sense, James. Society's edicts are not wholly baseless.'

'This is ridiculous!' Morton said. 'Who wants to belong to society anyway?'

'I do,' Catherine said icily. 'You may not realise it, but the esteem of one's peers is valued by women as well as men!'

'And are you seriously saying that if we married within three hundred and sixty-five days of Edwin's death you would be treated with contumely; but a day later everyone would cheer?'

'*Reductio ad absurdum* has no place in this discussion,' Catherine said sharply. 'The usages of society may not be logical, but they are valid nevertheless. And I have no intention of flouting them.'

191

Morton frowned. 'But, good heavens, you will be spending most of your life a world away, in Ashwell! I did not notice my mother pining for the lights of London, avidly reading about society's goings-on.'

'Has it never occurred to you that Edwin's poor health had a bearing on that?' Catherine asked. 'Really, James, you are utterly insensitive!'

Morton looked crestfallen. 'I suppose you could be right,' he said.

'I know I am right! She was the daughter of the American ambassador, after all. Her life till then must have been one long round of parties, balls, receptions.'

'Well, we certainly used to have parties at Christmas ... But, surely you would not sentence us to another year of single life, of celibacy?'

'That is precisely what is going to happen! And, if you doubt the wisdom of that course, then ask your sister Emily. She is not likely to be biased in favour of either of us!'

Morton sighed. 'Well, we appear to have acquired the knack of quarrelling like married people!' he said. 'I suppose that is something.'